Marked by Night

Demi Warrik

Demi Warrik
Marked by Night: Fates Mark #1
Copyright © Demi Warrik 2021
All rights reserved
First published in 2021

No part of this book may be reproduced, stored in a retrieval system, or transmitted in any form or by any means whatsoever without written permission except in the case of brief quotations embodied in reviews or articles. All characters in this publication other than those clearly in the public domain are fictitious, and any resemblance to real persons, living or dead, is purely coincidental. The unauthorized reproduction or distribution of a copyrighted work is illegal. Criminal copyright infringement without monetary gain is investigated by the FBI and is punishable by fines and federal imprisonment.

Editors: Raven Quill Editing, LLC & Proofs By Polly
Cover: Ryn Katryn Digital Art

AUTHOR'S NOTE

Hey there reader, just a heads up. Marked by Night is a full-length paranormal RH and the first book in the Fates Mark series. There are brief flashes of past abuse (not from the harem) violence, and other themes that some readers may find triggering. It contains lots of cursing and does end on a cliffhanger. Thank goodness the series is now complete, right? ;)

Take care, loves.
-Demi

*To all of those who believed in me and all of those who didn't.
Watch me spread my wings and soar.*

1

My fingers sink into the pebbles as I recline on the bank, dipping my toes into the warm water. The lake is relatively calm today, only the occasional wave since it's not windy. The glassy surface is almost hypnotizing to look at, lulling me into a sense of serenity I don't feel.

The trees surrounding me are still and quiet. The occasional bird chirps or a squirrel scurries by, but other than that, it's rather peaceful. Unlike the tumultuous emotions stirring inside of me.

I don't go to the lake often anymore because the memories are painful and it makes me long for my brother to still be alive.

My hand slowly rises to find the silver pendant around my neck, feeling the worn groove that my thumb has imprinted into it from rubbing it so many times. This tiny necklace holds the last of my late brother's ashes. The rest were scattered in the lake where I know he'd want them. This was always his favorite spot—our spot.

Relax, Sadie, my inner voice encourages me.

Yeah, that's a lot easier said than done, inner voice.

I push my sunglasses further up my nose, trying to block out the harsh rays of the sun as they caress my body. Probably should put on sunscreen, but honestly, I can't seem to bring myself to get up—or care.

A little while later, a loud thump and the rumble of an engine startles me, ruining the peace I'm trying to exude. Someone must've run into that humongous pothole on the way in. Amateurs.

I'm sure they're heading back to the main part of the lake, but on the off chance they're not, I reach over and grab my switchblade from my pack. The fork in the road that brings you back to this particular section is so subtle that if you don't know exactly where to turn, you'll miss it. Hopefully, they will.

When I hear the telltale sign of gravel crunching getting louder, instead of further away, my muscles tense.

Who the hell is barreling down my hidden lake road?

And why?

I get my answer a few moments later when a sleek Jeep Wrangler pops into view and is forced to slam on the brakes to avoid crashing into the lake. Clearly, these idiots have never been down here before. If they had, they'd know this path dead-ends straight into the water. It was once part of a road that led into a forgotten, and now completely, submerged town.

Yep, that's right, a town.

The government bought all the houses and forced everyone out, flooding the area when they put the dams in. Or that's the story, anyway. They claim it was for our benefit, but I'm not so sure their intentions were pure. This region's history is steeped in illegal activities.

There are so many miles of nothing but trees and water. No one would ever find you or hear you scream.

CHAPTER 1 | 3

The older folks in town say a lot of the houses are still down there, untouched. As if they were in a hurry to finish the lake. When the water is low, a boat or two have been known to scrape the roofs, but you're not allowed to dive down there to find out for sure. It's conveniently illegal and if you get caught, you will go to jail. Imagine that.

Makes you wonder what vile, evil things the government is trying to cover up down in those dark depths.

Guess we'll never know.

"Moons above, thanks for the warning asshole!" The one behind the wheel seethes as he slings his door open and glares at his friend who is grinning from ear to ear.

"What?" The smirking passenger asks with a laugh as he comes around the vehicle and shoves the driver's arm slightly. Like he thinks it's amusing that they almost ended up in the lake trashing their expensive Jeep. "I couldn't see it until the last second either." He flicks his blond hair out of his eyes in a move that only men seem to be capable of perfecting.

Surprisingly, they haven't seemed to notice me yet. While nothing about them initially sets off my alarm bells, I gently open my center and caress them with my intuition to ease my worry. After a quick examination, they seem to be squeaky clean, but it never hurts to be cautious.

My eyes widen when they start stripping their shirts. I shamelessly watch them from my perch on the bank, telling myself it's to keep an eye on them, but that's a fucking lie.

The blond one has sun-kissed skin, giving him that beachy surfer vibe, while the other is slightly paler and more smoldering. They're talking about something, but I tune out the rest of their words, intending to focus on my sunbathing.

Of course, I'm readjusting my pillow when they notice me. They both stop what they're doing, and their heads snap in my direction. With their full intensity on me, I'm forced to hold back a gasp because holy shit, they're stunning.

Whatever dark Gods created them must have tipped the entire bottle of sexy into their pots with more than a dash of abs and muscles to go along with it. Their looks alone could kill, that's for damn sure.

The one with the pitch-black hair sweeps the area until his dark blue eyes land on my ratty little car, and then they return to mine in a fraction of a second. He's observant, this one, though I'm surprised he didn't notice my car beforehand.

The blond one is laughing again, and his amber eyes are sparkling in quiet amusement as he checks me out while I'm staring at his friend.

With a sigh, I stand up and grab my float before I wade fully into the lake. I'm not in the mood for conversation today. I came out here to escape the world, not deal with two sexy strangers that are likely only here for the music festival in town this weekend, and then they'll be gone again.

"How's the water?" Blondie calls out, abandoning the spot they were about to get in as they start stalking toward me, floats in hand.

"It's comfortable," I shout back, after putting some distance between myself and them. Maybe they'll get the hint.

They don't.

They get in and wade directly toward me.

"What's a pretty girl like you doing out here all alone?" the observant one asks, like that's not creepy at all. Though I don't get those vibes from him. Not one bit. In fact, my lady bits are practically singing his praises already.

He abandons his float in favor of wading in the murky water then looks down and frowns like he's trying to see what's below him, but there's no use. This part of the lake is deep and dark. Like the secrets hiding below us.

I barely manage to hold back my snort. As soon as Skylar and I could swim, our dad was bringing us down here to play. I've been swimming in these waters my whole life, so yeah, I'm not afraid, but that's the thing about fear. Most of the time it's a learned reaction. Irrational, even. Whether it be from experience or someone else's tainted view skewing your own.

Children aren't afraid of shit until someone tells them they should be. I would know, I was one of the unfazed ones. Then my dad died, and Skylar and I had to move in with our uncle. That's when I discovered monsters are real, and that they're hidden inside people.

Snapping out of my thoughts, I realize I forgot to answer his question, "Well, I was trying to relax."

The smirking blond's mouth turns into a full-blown grin as he runs a wet hand through his golden locks. "So, you come here often then?"

"Only when I want to get away from people."

If they can't take the hint, then I mean… fuck, I'll just be blunt about it.

"Feisty, I like it," he says.

"More like bitchy, but I'll take it," I respond and close my eyes, pushing everything out as I try to ignore them. Blondie laughs a deep delicious sound that causes my lower bits to tighten in response.

There's a splash and a yelp before the observant one says, "We're sorry for disturbing your peace. We'll be over here if you need anything."

Still, they don't move very far away from me. No, they stay fairly close. As if they're drawn to me and I'd be lying if I said I didn't feel riveted by them as well.

But fate can suck it. I'm not in the mood today.

Besides, who wouldn't be enraptured by them? They look like they're carved from stone, and trust me, the artist paid attention to every single aspect of their bodies. From their perfect chiseled jaws down to the veins I spotted running down to their nether regions. To the gorgeous dark blue eyes on the observant one, and the fiery amber eyes of the other. Every single detail is accounted for.

My curiosity gets the best of me a few minutes later. "How did you find this spot?" I ask, watching them from my peripheral vision while reclining on my raft.

The observant one pauses, turning around to look at me with his gorgeous blue eyes as he makes his way closer once more. The sun glints off his irises, allowing me to see the lighter flecks in the middle and the dark ring around the outer edge. He shrugs. "I'm not entirely sure. We were driving around looking for a spot to get in and we saw fresh tracks down here. Figured we'd check it out."

Ah, I knew there had to be something that gave me away. Plus, it's valuable information to have. Next time I'll cover my tracks better.

Blondie's amber eyes capture mine and hold. His are a light gold toward the center and fade to a darker copper shade. "It's almost as if we were drawn here," he says, voicing my earlier thoughts aloud. Nice to know they're not the only ones feeling the phantom strings of fate pulling us closer.

The three of us sit in silence for a while, drifting in the water aimlessly. I know I need to be going soon so I can get ready for work tonight, but I can't seem to drag myself out of the lake.

Eventually, a dark cloud blows over, blocking out my rays of the sun, and the next thing I know it starts pouring down rain. The weather in Kentucky is finicky as fuck. I swear Mother Nature likes to pass her beer off to someone else and say, "Here, watch this," while she throws some new fresh hell

CHAPTER 1 | 7

our way. We never know what's going to happen. She likes to keep us guessing.

"Aren't you going to leave?" Blondie asks, gesturing toward the rain like it's bothering him as he hops off his raft and heads to the bank. I suspected they weren't from here, but that confirms it.

"Nah, a little rain won't kill me," I call back.

But then a bolt of lightning strikes, almost as if Mother Nature heard me and said *I'll show her.* Finicky bitch, I tell you. I'm off my float in a millisecond heading toward the shore. Sitting in the lake while it's raining is one thing, it's harmless, but sitting in the lake while it's lightning? That's how you get electrocuted. No thanks.

Blondie chuckles, watching me scramble for the bank while he's on dry land. His eyes glitter playfully as he says, "I thought a little rain wouldn't kill you?"

Asshole.

"It won't, but lightning will," I snap back, which makes him laugh even harder. I reach for my bag as they head for their Jeep, only to realize everything I packed is now soaked. Even my towel.

"Wonderful," I groan. It's going to be a very wet and uncomfortable drive home now.

"Here, we brought extra," Mr. Observant says, jogging the short distance from his Jeep as he hands me a dry one. Blondie follows along behind him.

"Thanks," I say, then turn around to dry myself, using the cover of the large oak tree to help fend off some of the rain.

"I take it you're from this area?" Mr. Observant asks, watching me dry myself with his towel. His gaze travels from head to toe, making me shiver.

"Born and raised... unfortunately," I add under my breath. "I take it you're not?"

The corner of his lip twitches. "How did you guess?"

"Well, firstly the fact that you hit the pothole. The locals know to avoid it, even in a Jeep. Secondly, you almost drove off into the lake." I shrug. "Not to mention you bailed as soon as it started raining."

He nods, watching me appreciatively.

"What are you in town for?" I ask.

His heated gaze traces a path down my body as he says, "The music festival."

Actually, now that I'm paying attention, they're both staring at me. I hide my grin as I slowly slide the towel down my body making their eyes dip to my chest and toned legs. I've never been one to shamelessly flirt, but for some reason, these men make me want to try my hand at it. So here I am, turning over a new leaf in my life.

"I figured as much." That's the only reason that makes sense, but I don't voice that thought aloud. Instead, I drag the towel a little lower. "Maybe I'll see you there?" My voice is breathier than I intended and they both pick up on it.

Mr. Observant opens his mouth to respond, but his phone rings before he can speak. Something dark flashes across his eyes as he pulls it out of his pocket and checks the caller ID.

"Fuck, I have to take this," he says with a sigh. "Catch you later, beautiful." They give my bikini-clad body another long look before they trot back to their Jeep. Mr. Observant answers his phone as they drive away, and I internally smack myself for not getting their numbers. Damn my bad mood.

"You were practically gifted two hot guys and you let them slip from your fingers. What the *hell*, Sadie?"

And now I'm talking to myself.

Yeah, it's definitely time to stop procrastinating and get to work. One more shift before I can immerse myself in the music festival.

Nothing too bad can go wrong in one shift, right?

2

I glance down, checking the time on my watch for the millionth time since leaving home, and let out a deep, relieved sigh when I find I have two minutes to spare.

Unfortunately, I'm cutting it close because my lovely piece-of-shit-car-from-the-90's didn't want to start when I got back home from the lake to change and get ready for work. Which left me without a ride, and I had to run the entire eight miles from my duplex.

Totally winning this whole life thing.

The peeling paint on Harborview's sign greets me as I walk past the entrance. *A fresh taste of the sea; inland.* I snort at the idiocy of that statement. How is seafood that's already prepackaged from a company considered fresh?

Shaking those thoughts away, I yank on the heavy door's brass handle. The hinges give a loud groan of protest and resist my tug.

See? Even the door doesn't want me to work tonight.

As soon as I slip inside, the aroma from the restaurant rushes to greet me, and I'm assaulted with the distinct odor of hot grease and fried food with undertones of stale coffee—

likely still in the pot from this morning. Old saw blades and fishing nets adorn the cedar walls, giving the place a rustic vibe. Complete with a paneled tin roof, which sucks for cell service.

"Sadie! Get a move on. Lillian isn't scheduled tonight and Lauren is going to be late," my boss tells me as I round the corner. I barely hold in my annoyed groan. It's going to be a long night. "I need you out on the floor—" He cuts off mid-sentence when he lifts his widening eyes to mine. "What the hell happened to you?"

"I had to run," I tell him with a shrug. "My car wouldn't start."

"Whatever," he responds exasperatedly. "Get yourself cleaned up and out on the floor."

My lips purse and I nod, holding in my reply. My boss, Cruze, is a stocky guy in his early forties with short greying hair and a growing beer gut. He's one of those people who thinks if you're not fifteen minutes early, then you're late. Which I've never understood. Instead of getting mad when someone shows up at the specified time, why not say you need them fifteen minutes early?

Heading for the back, I snatch my grubby black apron off the rack, cringing at the grease stains, and... is that mashed potatoes? I lift it to my nose, yanking it away in disgust at the stench. I'm not sure what it is, but it's been there a while. I dip my hands into the cleaning bucket, wetting a washrag to wipe off the area. I scrub harshly, but it's not coming out no matter how hard I try.

With a long sigh, I redo my ponytail, pushing my curly locks back into a somewhat presentable fashion. There's nothing that can be done for the sweat and I can't afford to stay back here any longer, so it will have to do for tonight.

The door chimes, signaling the arrival of my first table as I emerge from the storeroom. Talk about good timing.

"Welcome to Harborview!" I call out instinctively. Five years will give you instincts like that. Yep, I've been working here since before I graduated high school.

The giggling teens don't respond as they grab the first open booth in the corner. I reach up and finger my necklace, letting the smooth metal ground me as I paste on my sweetest smile and approach their table.

"Hey, there. My name is Sadie and I'll be taking care of you tonight. Can I start you off with something to drink?"

The teens ignore my greeting once again, opting to stare into one another's eyes in favor of talking to me. I clear my throat twice before they finally look over at me and their eyes widen. Yeah, I'm your server, and this is a restaurant. Eating is the whole point of being here. But I keep those thoughts to myself as I gather what they want.

When I return to the front from inputting their order into our computer system, I can't help side-eyeing the younger boy. One glance and I can tell he's a total hothead and if I had to guess, likely shit in bed too. He's wearing a high school letterman jacket with a football on one sleeve and his last name on the other.

Ah, so this must be the star quarterback I've heard the old crones gossiping about. Supposedly, he's going to the big leagues.

The lanky girl with him is cute with her wide doe eyes and curly brunette locks, but she doesn't seem like his type. Too innocent. She's nervously chewing on her bottom lip while he talks to her.

The front door chimes at the same time Cruze taps the bell signaling their food is ready. The patron darts into a booth before I can get a good look at them.

"Welcome to Harborview. I'll be right with you!" I say, then head to the pickup window to grab the food before it gets cold.

When I approach the young couple, the girl is on the outside facing away from me, but the boy is on the inside staring at me. She startles when I set the plates down and jumps away from him like, well a teenager caught in the act.

Narrowing my eyes, I catch the young guy pulling his hand out of the bottom of her skirt. Nice.

"Uh, can I get you both anything else right now?"

The jock smirks, running his tongue over his bottom lip while he looks me up and down. "Yeah, you can go back to the kitchen and put yourself on a platter. I'll eat you for dessert."

My mouth pops open in shock before I quickly hide my reaction with a cough. Well, isn't this guy a real winner? You can tell he's one of those that hasn't got a clue what the real world is about. I can't wait for the day he's thrown to the sharks.

And this poor girl. I was always taught to watch how a man treats his server because that's how he'll treat you. Obviously, she didn't get the same memo. Such a shame. He reaches over his date and swats my ass, or at least, he tries. I snatch his wrist before he can make contact and grit my teeth.

"Really? This is how you want this to go down?"

"Ouch, what the hell?" he demands, wincing when I apply pressure. Then he starts digging his hole deeper. "You're such a hot piece of ass, that's why you're here, isn't it? To be ogled by men while we eat. What's so wrong with one little touch?"

Outrage flutters through me, making my anger spike. Customer service be damned, this kid needs a reality check and she needs to ditch him. "Take this for what you will, but here's a piece of advice," I say, addressing the girl. "Find someone better than him. Men like this are trash, trust me." I can definitely attest to the douchebags, having broken up with my ex about six months prior.

She sniffles, looking up at me with wide, teary eyes then nods and scurries out of the restaurant. I feel bad, but there's nothing I can do for her. Sometimes you have to learn the hard way.

"Wait!" The jock cries after her. For a moment I think, aww, he's going to chase after her, then he speaks, "I thought you were paying!"

You've got to be kidding me. The fucking audacity.

"If you don't have money, then get the hell out," I tell him coldly.

He looks me up and down, sizing me up. He must decide it's not worth it because he darts for the door, calling out over his shoulder, "You'll be hearing from my dad!" Like that's supposed to mean something to me. News flash; it doesn't.

There's not a single person in this town that I'm afraid of.

Not anymore anyway. I'm still searching for the one person I'm wary of.

I'm busy cleaning up their plates when I remember the door chimed a few minutes ago. My eyes scan the dining room until they land on a man with unruly red hair sitting in a booth on the far side of the room.

I rush over to his table, almost tripping over my feet in my haste. "I'm so sorry about your wait, sir," I say. "It's been a little hectic so far." I smooth my apron down with my hands and my hair too, because damn, he's fine.

The man startles, his vibrant silver eyes lifting from the book in his hands to capture mine making my breath whoosh out of me. They're like two perfect little twinkling stars. I've never seen anything like them. His red hair is cropped on top, and he's also wearing a pair of black-framed glasses. I'm a total sucker for them too. He looks to be a few years older than me, but likely not much.

Most of our customers are regulars, but I've never seen

this man before. Another festival-goer, I'll bet. Three hot strangers in one day, is this luck or something else?

"It's all right," he tells me softly, closing his book. His voice is low, soft, and a little gravely like a smooth exhale. "This was luring me in, anyway."

His response makes me smile. "Nice! I love when books suck you in from the start. What are you reading? I'm always looking for new reads."

To say I'm a giant book nerd would be an understatement. I've been slowly working on my collection over the years and it's getting quite large. Leaning forward, I try to catch a glimpse of the cover, but his large hand shifts, covering the title before I can see anything.

"Uh, nothing," he blurts quickly. Too quickly.

My eyes narrow. Is he… reading a spicy book? Because if he is, fuck yes. More power to him. Although, I take the hint and drop it. Even if I'm dying to know what has his cheeks turning pink.

Brains and *looks? Sign me right the hell up.*

He laughs, and it's a husky sound that goes straight between my thighs.

I lift a hand to my mouth; I didn't realize I'd spoken. "Shit. Did I say that out loud?"

His eyes widen almost imperceptibly, and he coughs looking suddenly uncomfortable. Huh, wonder what that's about.

"Yeah, you sure did. I'm quite flattered."

"Sorry, I have a bad habit of that." I shake my head with a sigh, shrugging off the strange moment and return to the role I'm supposed to be fulfilling. Something about this man distracts me, in a good way, but I can't afford to get fired. "Anyway, what can I get for you?"

"I think I'll take the number seven," he says uncertainly.

"Ahh, the chicken platter. A man after my own heart.

Good choice." I pull out my writing pad and jot down what he wants. "I've never particularly cared for fish myself."

He nods, flashing me a small smile that makes two little indentions poke in.

And he has dimples?

Ah, hell. I'm in trouble.

I'm busy dealing with the last part of the dinner rush when my coworker comes barreling in the door three and a half hours late. According to the clock, we're a little under an hour from closing at this point. Why even bother?

After dropping off the refills on my tray, I glance over to find her leaning against the checkout counter picking at her pretty painted nails.

"Hey, Lauren, if you're going to be here, why don't you go check on table five?" I subtly tick my head in their direction, hoping she'll take the hint.

She huffs, popping her gum at me. "Why don't you? I'm waiting for food to come out."

"Because I can do this nifty thing called multitasking," I snap back.

She ignores me and continues picking at her nails. I open my mouth to speak again when a loud, overbearing whistle echoes through the dining room, followed by a few shorter whistles. My spine stiffens instantly. Whistling is one of my biggest pet peeves. I'm not a dog.

I take a deep breath before searching for the source. When another whistle reverberates through my bones, I find a burly man who barely fits in the chair he's sitting in waving at me. He looks vaguely familiar, but I can't seem to place him.

Lauren looks over and promptly bolts for the back without a word, like she knows something I don't. Perfect.

The dim lights of the diner aren't enough to hide the rough edges of this man. He flashes his expensive-looking watch at me, but it doesn't even look like it's ticking. The suit and tie he's sporting look cheaply made and likely fake. His entire demeanor screams that he's trying too hard.

Take a deep breath and do not let your anger show, Sadie. I coach myself, trying to rein in my facial expressions.

Apparently, it's rude if you look at stupid people like they're stupid.

Who knew?

"I'm sorry, sir, is something the matter?" I ask, my voice dripping with a sugary sweetness that I'm only capable of at work.

Customer service Sadie is a completely different bitch than regular Sadie.

The waves coming off him brush against my intuition, giving me goosebumps. Even sitting down, he's almost as tall as me. Yet I'm not intimidated. Brutes like this are always slow, while I'm quick on my feet. Likely from the training I've been doing lately.

"Yes, ma'am. I need you to take this food back. I simply can't eat it. The taste is horrid," he says, scrunching up his nose. His voice carries across the dining room, making the last few patrons' heads snap in our direction.

Nosey-ass people. I guess that's small-town life for you.

"I'm sorry, sir," I say again. "What's wrong with it?" I eye the piece of fish he's pointing to that's nothing but crumbs.

"It's too fishy!" he exclaims. "Fish. That's all I can taste." He makes another weird, scrunched face.

All I can do is stare at him, too stunned to react.

Did he—did I hear that right? Too fishy. How on earth is *fish* too fishy?

He waves his hand over his plate again when I don't react, and I grit my teeth. If this guy thinks this shit is going to come out of my paycheck, he's got another thing coming. Yes, Cruze makes us pay for orders when something is wrong. Pretty sure it's illegal, but he does it anyway.

"Are you paying attention? I've given you a complaint. I demand an apology and my meal to be taken care of." He watches my reaction carefully. I don't give him anything. "Maybe I should call your boss over if you're only going to stand here."

Dammit, if Cruze comes over my ass is toast.

"That won't be necessary." I reach into my apron pocket to dig out his ticket, and check it over. Looky there, he did order fish. "I'm afraid you did order the fish plate, sir. I'm not quite sure why you're upset." His eyes narrow at my tone. Shoot, I'm losing him, lighten up a bit. "Because if it were me, I'd expect a fishy taste."

Oops. So much for lightening up.

"You little bitch," he hisses, kicking his chair back out of the way.

The loud clang reverberates through the dining room, and the people at the table behind us gasp but don't move to get out of the way. Too engrossed in the show.

"First, you kick my son out without giving him a proper meal and now you're going to treat me like this?"

His son? It sudden clicks.

"Oh, you mean the jock kid from earlier. He didn't have any money. No money equals no service. Or have you forgotten that?"

His face starts to turn red and I sigh. Now I've done it.

"How dare you speak to me that way! Don't you know who I am? My family is on their way to the big leagues," he snaps. If his nose were any further in the air, it'd be in the clouds.

My sugary smile falls as I drop the act, fed up with his attitude. "Not with that crap dye job, fake suit, and watch you're not."

I cannot stand people like this. With their, *I'm better than you attitude.* I've got news for you, buddy. We all end up in the ground someday.

"You're going to pay for this, little girl," he says as the vein in his temple bulges.

Why do men always think the word little is an insult? I may be short, but dynamite comes in small packages, baby.

His large hand snakes out toward my neck, and my training kicks in. I drop, ducking under his meaty hand as I reach up and jab him in the throat with my thumb and pointer finger in the shape of an L with enough force to make him rethink his decision. His ruddy cheeks are so red with rage they're almost purple as he splutters, reaching for my neck again like he wants to wring the life out of me.

Too bad I like my life right where it is, thank you.

Realizing I'm too fast, the man switches gears, snatching his plate of food off the table. My eyes widen as he tosses it at me, and I step out of the way.

But nothing happens.

I look over to find the man with the gorgeous silver eyes and red hair with a tight grip on the man's wrist. He squeezes until the asshole has to drop the porcelain plate. It clatters to the ground, shattering into a million pieces against the concrete floor, making an awful noise in the deathly quiet room. Anyone who isn't already paying attention stops eating to watch the spectacle.

"You think you'll be able to stop me, boy?" the brute spits angrily, rearing back. Red's eyes widen and then narrow in fury. He and I move at the same time, reaching out to block the hit. He beats me by a fraction of a second, looking over to give me a small smirk, gracing me with those dimples. If we weren't in the middle of a fight, I'd give him a high five.

"You think you can pick on a lady on my watch?" Red tsks, turning his attention back to the brute and adjusting the black-framed glasses on his nose with his other hand. Fuck, why does that turn me on?

Red looks at me incredulously and I stare back at him, confused. Then it dawns on me. "Did I say that out loud?"

He nods.

"I've really got to stop doing that."

He chuckles. "I'm going to need you to not distract me like that, Love," he says before refocusing his attention on the matter in front of us. Red drops the man's hand, giving him the benefit of the doubt. Bad idea.

The brute rounds on him, but the younger and more lean man doesn't even blink. Something tells me Red gets underestimated a lot, like I do, but that's how I like it. It's even more rewarding when you hand someone their ass.

Quick as a striking snake, Red snatches his wrist midpunch. A sickening crack reaches my ears before the brute howls in pain, clutching his meaty paw to his chest.

Did he break his wrist?

For me?

Phew, somebody get a fan in here stat.

Red gives the man a scathing look that sends shivers down my spine. If I were a lesser woman, I'd be taking off in the other direction. The brute finally seems to get the picture, because he looks between us, weighing his odds before he takes off, scrambling for the door like his son did. Cowards.

Of course, Cruze chooses this moment to appear. You know—after the confrontation is already over. "What did you do to that poor man, Sadie?"

I gape at him. "But he—he attacked me."

"And I'm sure you did nothing to provoke him," he retorts.

Indignation flares in my chest at his insinuation. "You've got to be kidding me." I note the hard set of his jaw and a rock plummets to the bottom of my stomach. I already know he won't back down from this. I'm going to lose my job and, after the gossip gets around, no one will ever hire me again in this godsforsaken town. Ash—my roommate and best friend—and I will lose the duplex.

Maybe I can sell my car? But even that will only get us through the next month or two.

Red steps forward, interrupting my internal debate. "What she said is true, sir. The man attacked first, and he started the verbal dispute as well."

Cruze's narrowed eyes snap to Red. "I don't care. She knows better than to act like that in my establishment." Then he turns to me. "You cost me a paying customer and that's not to mention the fact you smashed one of my top dollar porcelain plates. Look at all those pieces," he says while looking down at the smashed plate. His expression seems like he cares more for the plate than he does his employee. "Those damn things aren't cheap you know!"

"Cruze, I can't lose this job, please."

It's so silent in the dining room you could hear a pin drop.

"You should've thought about that earlier, huh? If you would've kept your fucking mouth shut, that man wouldn't have done anything to you."

"So it's my fault that the dude has the world's shortest fuse on the planet?" I ask incredulously. "You're going to defend his actions because he merely didn't like what I had to say? Plus his kid was an asshole to me earlier. C'mon Cruze."

He studies me long and hard before he speaks, then of course pisses me off. "Women should be seen and not heard.

All of this is coming out of your last paycheck. Pack your things and leave. Lauren will finish the night out." I gape at him. Now I won't even get to keep the rest of my tips because he's forcing me to leave before my shift is over.

Red gives my shoulder a reassuring squeeze and my skin tingles where his fingers brush across the sensitive skin. "It's not your fault the man got more than he bargained for by picking on you," he says.

Cruze ruins the moment by waggling a finger in my face. I force myself not to bite it off. "You're testing my patience, girl. Get out of my restaurant, both of you, before I make you."

Red's jaw clenches and he stalks off, but not before stopping by his booth to grab his personal items, then he exits without a backward glance. My heart pangs with guilt. Poor guy, taking the heat for my drama.

After gathering my belongings, I square my shoulders, hold my head high, and saunter out of Harborview restaurant for the last time. I already know I'll never come back here.

I'm surprised to find Red waiting for me. Fury rolls off him in palpable waves as he falls into step with me. I'm not exactly sure where we're walking, but I follow his lead. Something about him feels safe and he doesn't set off any of my alarms.

"Hey, thanks for standing up for me back there," I murmur when we're finally far enough away from all the vultures' prying eyes inside. "I didn't mean for you to get kicked out with me."

He shrugs. "Don't worry about it. I wouldn't want to give my business to a prick like that anyway." His lips turn up slightly at the corners and he blushes as he runs his hand through his soft red hair.

"I don't think I've ever seen you before. Are you from

around here?" I inquire, changing the subject to a less depressing one. Despite everything that happened, a part of me wants to get to know this man.

"Nah, I'm only passing through," he responds. "I should be heading home soon. At least, I hope so."

My curiosity peaks and I blurt, "Will you be going to the music festival tomorrow too?" before the thought even fully processes, thinking about the sexy strangers from this morning.

Subtle, Sadie. Nice.

Red's lips turn up slightly. "Sadly, I have other business to attend to, but I'm disappointed I'm missing out. Wicked Unrest is one of my all-time favorite bands."

"Yeah, me too. Their setlist is supposed to be amazing."

He sighs when we round the corner to the parking lot. I didn't even realize we were still walking. He fishes something out of his back pocket—an envelope, if I'm not mistaken—then extends it to me.

"This is for all the trouble they put you through tonight."

It doesn't take a genius to know what's in the envelope. I can see the bank symbol clear as day from here. "Nuh-uh. No way. You helped me tonight, and that's all that I could ask for."

He steps toward me, trying to hand me the cash. "Seriously, you deserve this. Besides, I would've tipped it to you, anyway." I give him a disbelieving look. "I actually had to retrieve it from your table, I was on my way out when that man attacked you."

Oh, so that's what he grabbed.

"Why on earth would you do that? You don't know me." He shrugs, trying to avoid my question, but he's not getting off that easy. "Tell me why, Red." I cringe. I didn't mean to call him that out loud.

He sighs. "Listen, I enjoy helping others. Let me help." He

shoots me a sexy smile that makes his dimples pop out and he sneakily slides the envelope into my pocket while I'm standing there awestruck.

Am I really one to look a gift horse in the mouth?

Pfft, no. I can only hope it will last me long enough to find another job. Preferably a town or two over.

"Thank you, Red."

He gives me a curious look. "Why do you call me Red?"

I cough, reaching up to finger my necklace. "Oh, uh… That may or may not be what I've been calling you in my head because of your hair," I admit.

His grin turns into a full-blown smile. "Is that so?" He flexes his muscles like Superman and the sight makes my lady bits tighten in response. "It's Reed, actually."

Huh. I was close.

His phone vibrates from his hoodie pocket. He shoots me a frown before pulling it out and staring down at it with wide eyes. "I hate to cut this short, but I've got to head out. Have a good night, Love," he says, with a glimmer in his eye before racing off toward his car. Something about those molten silver eyes draws me in completely, wrapping me in their liquid embrace.

"You too," I whisper, but he's already gone.

3

An annoying tinkling sound reaches my ears, yanking me out of my thoughts. I curse myself and jerk my phone out of my bag to turn off the alarm. My heart drops when I see the time. I'm going to be so late for training! Ben is going to kill me. I take off running and I don't stop until I reach the studio.

When I open the door, the familiar sight of the gym greets me, giving a sense of comfort I desperately need. I'll be able to take all my frustrations out on my trainer and maybe even be able to get rid of the three irresistible faces plaguing my thoughts.

"Sorry, I'm late!" I call out, rushing to the back to change without waiting for a response. When I emerge, Ben is standing in the center of the mat, waiting for me to get started. He's a man of few words and doesn't say anything while I get in position.

"Go," he says and then the action begins.

Suddenly, lightning cracks across the sky, basking the training room in an eerie glow as the power snaps out. The shadows come alive in the sudden darkness, dancing as the lights flicker, then wink out completely. The night is where the monsters thrive, of that I am certain. I guess it's a good thing I know how to blend in with them.

The only source of illumination is the harsh brilliance from each flash of lightning, which is messing with my night vision. My eyes narrow, straining to see, but there's no use. I'll have to rely on my other senses to follow his movements.

My fingers flex as I wait for the opportunity to strike, biding my time. A droplet of sweat travels down the side of my face then drips to the floor, soaking into the mat where countless others have come before me.

There! A shift in the air to the left.

As soon as I reach out, his aura is suddenly gone, leaving me momentarily confused. The faint chuckle lets me know he finds it amusing that he's eluding me so easily. My jaw grinds together. I'll make him regret his amusement, as soon as I'm able to get my hands on him.

Instead of reacting to his taunt, I make myself take a deep breath. I focus on keeping my breathing slow and even, despite my racing heart. Seconds later, the air shifts and he goes for my right, forcing me to react quickly. I manage to avoid his fist by dancing to the side and he slinks back to the shadows once more.

Somehow, I can sense him circling me despite the darkness. I suppress a shiver. There's such finality in the dark.

Hopefully, the power comes back on soon.

As if the universe hears my silent thought, the power bursts back to life, briefly blinding me. "I'm Made of Wax, Larry, What Are You Made Of?" by A Day to Remember blares out of the shitty overhead speakers as my playlist resumes, distracting me.

Rookie mistake.

Pain blooms across my abdomen, making it hard to breathe. My hands drop as I pant harshly through the pain.

When I lift my head, my eyes connect with Benjamin's black ones. He smirks, watching me struggle as he goes in for the kill.

There's no mercy in his eyes whatsoever as he takes me down to the hard-unforgiving mat. The force of his shoulder crashing into my side steals the air from my lungs. For a moment, all I can do is lay there.

Ben's chest rumbles as he shakes with uncontrollable laughter. His torso lingers over mine for a moment longer than what I'd consider comfortable, but I've learned to ignore his weird advances.

I clear my throat, trying to shrug his body off but he doesn't make any effort to move which pisses me off. After I tap his shoulder a few times, he finally seems to get the hint, climbing to his feet, and then extending a hand to help me up.

Did I mention he loves taking me down? I think it's his own personal version of flirting, but that's a fact I try my best to ignore. I'm not interested in Ben whatsoever.

"You know better, Sadie. Rule number one—"

"Never lose focus. Yeah. I know, I know. A Day to Remember is my jam though." I fold my arms over my chest in my best fuck-off pose. Unfortunately, it draws his eyes to my cleavage, so I drop them quickly.

He smirks, and it's not an attractive look on him. Usually, when a guy smirks at you, it's at least a little sexy, even if it's a tiny bit condescending. But with Ben? Nope. He looks like he's constipated.

"Your assailant wouldn't give you any mercy and you know that. Focus on your surroundings and nothing else."

Instead of responding I merely nod, gritting my teeth to hold in my snarky response. The asshole treats me like a child sometimes and it pisses me off.

I try to walk away but I'm snatched out of the air and

pulled into a hard chest faster than I can blink. His bare skin makes mine crawl, and the feeling is wrong. I scramble out of his hold and he grabs ahold of my wrist, stopping me in my tracks. "Oh, Sadie…" His gruff voice drips with longing.

"Ouch! What the fuck, Ben?" I yank my wrist out of his revolting hold. There's no doubt in my mind I'll be bruised with his fingerprints tomorrow.

Fan-fucking-tastic.

He looks taken aback for a moment before his face falls and he runs a hand over it. "Shit. I'm so sorry. I get worked up sometimes. You know that, right?"

Don't fucking say anything, Sadie. You need this training. You promised Skylar you'd learn how to become a weapon with your body. Fuck. Even thinking my brother's name is enough to leave a lump in my throat that I'm forced to swallow down. My brother, my perfect older brother. I miss him more than the sun misses the moon.

I don't respond to Ben. Instead, I retreat to the other side of the training room, rubbing my sore appendage. The silence drags on while Ben pretends to be busy tying his shoelace, and I act like I'm not watching him out of the corner of my eye like he's going to pounce any second. Then I realize how silly I'm being and mentally shake myself. I pop the top on my purple water bottle and take a long drag.

Out of nowhere, the stereo cuts out, then switches to the middle of a Bring Me the Horizon song. Oli Sykes' haunting melody pierces the air. Huh. That's strange. Did my playlist not download correctly? I move toward my phone to check when the ominous lyrics of "Shadow Moses" reach my ears making me shudder.

You see, I've always been particularly gifted in the *intuition* department as I call it. I get these feelings that are hard to ignore and this song is bringing all those feelings to the forefront.

Shaking away the strange sensations, I squeeze my palms together while jumping up and down on the balls of my feet a few times to keep my blood pumping. There's nothing better than the anticipation of the next fight.

When I waltz back over to the center of the training mat, I paste on my cockiest smile and drop into the starting position like nothing happened. Even though I don't think I'll ever be able to forget the feeling of Ben's skin against mine. It's not that I have a problem with Ben. It's—well, there's something off about him and I can't seem to put my finger on exactly what it is, but I've never had the warm fuzzy feelings about him.

The guy is my ex-boyfriend's best friend for crying out loud. Tyler and him are two peas in a pod.

Besides, isn't there a bro code about this type of thing? I'm sure if he opens that mysterious book of bro's, there's a commandment in there somewhere that states, "Thou shall not try to fuck your best friend's ex." Seeing as I don't have a dick—a literal one, anyway—I don't know for sure, but men seem to take it pretty fucking seriously from what I've heard. Minus Ben, obviously.

I motion for him to start. "Come on, let's go again."

He strides toward me, making adrenaline flood my veins. I breathe it in, relishing in the rush. "Chin down! Hands up!" he barks, correcting my positioning with a light tap against my fists and chin.

We break apart and he goes on the offensive, making me duck and weave to avoid his fists. I growl, narrowing my eyes on him as he dances from foot to foot. The dick knows I'm still a little frazzled under pressure, and he's going for a quick takedown. Not tonight, buddy.

I push my body to go harder and faster as he throws jabs left and right. We're a flurry of movements as we whirl across the training room floor. A punch to the left, I dodge to the right. A kick to the right, I jump to the left.

When he steps back to recover, he leaves his side open and I take the opportunity, sneakily striking my fist into his ribs. He grunts, giving me a head nod, but I'm sure it didn't faze him. The dude is a freaking tank.

I'll have to do better than one jab if I want to bring Ben to his knees. The man moves with refined grace and precision that only comes from years and years of practice. He's the best in the business for a reason. There are no useless moves in Ben's playbook. And it is exactly why I chose him to be my personal trainer despite everything.

"What the hell is wrong with you tonight? You're off your game," he taunts.

Sadly, he's not wrong. I'm sure it has nothing to do with the sexy strangers who keep appearing in my life—and in my thoughts.

"Don't worry about it." I sidestep a well-aimed fist making him double his efforts to take me down.

Another streak of lightning shoots across the night and the responding clap of thunder shakes the ground so hard I lose my focus. Sheesh, one of the Gods is angry tonight, huh? I don't necessarily know what I believe in, but there has to be more than one God, right? That's the only thing that's ever made sense to me.

The power flicks off, leaving us in total darkness once more. I bite down on my frustration and close my eyes since they're useless anyway. *Feel for him, Sadie. Feel the change in the air.*

There! To the right.

I strike first, calculating where his stomach is based on my memory alone. Unfortunately, he catches my fist with his palm, blocking my hit like he knew it was coming. He's always one step ahead of me, and two steps ahead of everyone else.

Plan B time.

I manage to get my fist out of his hold and since he's still in my range, I feint left then drop under his arm. I shift my weight to the balls of my feet to help with the impact. He grunts as I slam my shoulder into his middle—likely not expecting me to go for a full takedown. I'm smart enough to know not to let him get his hands around me. It's over if he does. I drop like a sack of potatoes and roll out of his reach.

The lights burst to life once more and Ben's sight recovers first. He snarls, furiously stalking toward me. I hop to my feet, barely getting out of the way of his retaliation. When my eyes clear, I suppress a shiver. His grin is vicious.

Somehow, I avoid his next swing by dodging at the literal last second, but I'm not fast enough avoid his knuckles grazing my cheek entirely. That was close. Too close. I don't want to think about what would've happened if he'd stuck that hit. Lights out for Sadie for sure.

He's on me in a blink, not giving me any time to think or recover. I grit my teeth to keep from crying out when he hits me in my ribs for the second time. While I'm stunned, Ben drops, and in a physics-defying move, sweeps my legs right out from under me. Like he's in the damn matrix or something.

My arms fly out to catch myself from face planting as I flail unhelpfully before landing in a heap. A groan escapes my lips and when I glance up, I find Ben hovering above me looking way too smug. That look makes me want to break his freaking nose or wring his freaking neck. Or both. Like he senses his safety is in question, he disappears from my line of sight. Smart man.

I drag myself up off the floor, ignoring the bone-deep exhaustion riding my body. When I turn around, I find Ben with his back to me as he fiddles with the tape on his hands. An idea forms in my twisted little brain because he's committing a cardinal sin, one he preaches to me at least twice during our training sessions.

Rule number two: Never turn your back on your opponent.

Should I take advantage?

On the one side he's going to be pissed, and on the other —eh, screw it. There is no way he'd pass up the opportunity to teach me a lesson if the roles were reversed. And he's always preaching about showing your foes no mercy. Seems like a win-win.

On silent feet, I cross the gym. As soon as I'm directly behind him, I rear back and kick him straight in the fucking balls, putting a little *extra* strength into it but not enough to show that I'm not entirely normal.

Yeah, there's something off about me. Enhanced strength, healing, and intuition. Only my best friend, Ashley, knows about these abilities, and I intend to keep it that way. When you are unusual or unique it tends to cause panic amongst people, and I don't plan on disappearing by *mysterious* circumstances any time soon.

Ben cries out in pain, crashing to his knees. "Fucking hell," he croaks, cupping his balls like they're worth their weight in gold. Gross. "That was a cheap shot."

"I learned from the best," I say, shifting so he can see the wicked grin splayed across my face like the evil bitch I am. So, I'm a little giddy about catching him off guard. Sue me.

Ben stumbles back to his feet, sans my help, and gives me an appreciative head nod while cupping his balls. "Very nice. But you won't find me vulnerable like that again, so enjoy the feeling while it lasts."

"Oh, feeling cocky, are we?"

"It's not cocky if you have the means to back it up. Do you want to keep going?"

I shake my head waving my hand in the direction of the thunderstorm outside. Typical Kentucky weather. "Nah, I think I've had enough for tonight. I better head on home before the storm gets worse."

"All right, I'll drive you home. Let me grab my keys."

Unease slithers up my spine. "No need. Besides, I'd prefer to walk."

He huffs, reaching out for my wrist. "Come on, Sadie. You could get struck by lightning or swept away in the storm." For some reason, his statement makes me snort. I'm more likely to get abducted in this neighborhood, but of course, he's worried about the likelihood of lightning striking me from the sky.

Still, he doesn't look like he's willing to let me go. I sigh. I really don't want to reveal my cards to Ben, but I will if that's what it takes. I'm ninety percent sure my extra strength will at least let me knock him out before he can retaliate.

"It's fine, really. I like the storms."

Which is not a total lie. There's something so calming about the chaos to me.

Yanking my arm from his hold, I quickly cross the gym, making sure to keep him in my line of sight. I snatch my ratty backpack from its cubby and unplug my phone from the speaker, cutting off an I Prevail song.

My eyes catch on Ben's from across the room. His face contorts into a snarl and he looks seconds away from marching over to strangle me where I stand. "Fine. Have it your way," he says.

My instincts are screaming for me to run, but I know better than that. Men like Ben—like my ex—love the thrill of the chase and that will only set him off.

"Have a good night. Call me when you want to train

again, and we'll make it happen." Without another glance, he stalks off.

Sheesh. Whiplash much?

The lights flip off, spurring my stunned ass into action. I bolt for the door. Once outside, I slip my switchblade out of my backpack and run my thumb over the cold metal. The worn grip on it gives me a sense of comfort as I walk. I'm not defenseless. A fact I'm constantly reminding myself of. Bad habits die hard, unfortunately.

My ponytail sways with the wind as I rush through town working up quite the sweat. When I crest the next hill, and my dingy duplex is finally in sight, I can't help but let loose a sigh of relief. Until a clap of thunder startles the crap out of me and I squeal, clutching my chest to stop my heart from leaping out of it. Then, as if the Gods themselves are angry and trying to pour all their frustrations down on me, the rain starts and it pelts me mercilessly.

Seriously, it's like Forrest Gump sideways rain out here.

My eyes snap closed and for one quiet moment. I bask in the pure chaos because it reminds me of my dad. One night, right before he died, I crawled into bed with him and told him I was scared because of the storm. Instead of holding me and stroking my hair like usual, he took me outside and we danced in the rain for hours.

Probably not the brightest idea looking back on it, but my dad was far from a normal parent. That night, he showed me a storm is not always scary if you know how to make the best of it and I've been fine ever since. But now they remind me of him, and of everything I've lost.

A double-edged sword, really.

After jogging the remaining distance, I slam the door behind me with a frustrated groan and lean all my weight on it, replaying today's events in my mind. I can't believe Cruze fired me and acted like it was all my fault. And the way Ben acted tonight was so strange.

But then I smile, remembering my red-haired hero, and the two strangers from the lake. The realization dawns on me that I didn't even remember to grab Red's number to thank him. I truly am an idiot! Even my vagina silently scolds me for being so clueless and careless. I let three totally perfect men slide through my fingers today. One of which handed me an envelope of money.

Well, let's at least find out how much he gave me, I think with a sigh.

As I'm flicking through the cash, my thumb snags on a small piece of paper hung between two of the bills. I unravel it and the sight makes me laugh as relief tumbles through me.

Whirling around, I yank my phone out of my back pocket and dial the number scribbled on the slip of paper in large, looping handwriting. His deep chuckle reaches my ears, making butterflies explode in my stomach. "So, you found it? Took you long enough."

That cheeky fucker.

4

SADIE

"Hurry up! You're going to make us late," Ashley whines from the living room. I swear I can see her pouting through the dang walls.

"I am hurrying!" I yell back.

I don't know why she's complaining. Usually, she's the one making us late because she's a bit of a perfectionist. And when I say perfectionist, I mean she's freaking anal about everything. As for me, I'm more apt to slap on a semi-clean shirt and jeans and call it decent.

Since my car is acting up on me, I've been tinkering on it all morning. I'm fairly certain the starter is going out, but that's beyond my level of expertise and I can't afford a mechanic. I'll take what I can get out of it and make do with the rest. Hopefully, we will make it to the festival in one piece.

As I'm finishing up and putting on a pair of earrings, a new crack in the wall catches my attention. I frown, running my hand over the surface. It's a big one this time. They seem to be getting worse each day. The beige color helps hide the mottled fissures, but I'm not fooled. I'm afraid one of these days it's going to fall in completely, taking us both with it.

And good luck getting our lazy ass landlord to do anything about it either. Believe me, we've tried. Our neighbor even took them to court for negligence, but they're friends with the judge, and nothing ever came of the complaint.

Another plus to small-town life.

I smack my lips together with a pop as I finish applying my bright red lipstick and lean down to tie the laces on my trusty Converse. I hardly go anywhere without them these days. Mainly because I love these shoes more than most people.

Once they're tied, I scuff them across the hardwoods that are scratched, gouged, and in desperate need of repair, but they've been that way since we moved in. The previous tenants were hellions, and it shows.

The band tee I'm wearing is one of Ash's specialties. She cut the sides out and fringed the bottom, leaving the logo intact but with the illusion of a crop top. The tight fishnet stockings pair nicely with it and my ripped jean shorts.

Thankfully, the flowy front covers the bruises from mine and Ben's session last night. They're becoming more and more intense with each lesson. I'm improving but I'm still not where I'd like to be.

Somehow Ash managed to curl my dusty blonde hair into loose beach waves that cascade down my back. I spritz them with one last sprinkle of hairspray but it's likely futile because my hair does what it wants, and it's humid outside. Frizz central, here we come.

"Seriously, Sadie!" Ash bellows, making me chuckle.

My phone buzzes as I'm getting ready to walk out of my bedroom.

"One sec!" I holler, pulling the device out as Ash grumbles something unintelligible at me.

Unlocking the screen I realize it's a text from my mysterious savior last night. I've really got to find a way to thank or repay him.

Red: Have fun tonight, Love. Maybe we can spend some time together before I head back home?

Butterflies erupt in my stomach, making me feel all warm and fuzzy inside. What is it about this guy that makes me so giddy? I know next to nothing about him. Rein it in, Sadie. Sheesh.

Me: You too! Let me know when and I'll be there. :)

Crap, did that sound too eager? Put me in a room with a dude and I can kick his ass but put me in a situation with a hottie and I'm practically clueless. Red sends back a smiley face emoji and that's it. I stare at the screen for a couple more seconds before I decide it's probably a bad idea to keep Ash waiting any longer.

When I spot her leaning against the couch playing on her phone, my eyes widen. I'm not into chicks but she is on fire tonight. She's rocking a crisscrossed black leather shirt with a skin-tight mini skirt. It's just long enough to cover her lady bits with one side trailing down to meet her combat boots—with heels. Oh, yes. Heels. This woman never leaves home without a two-inch lift.

I whistle appreciatively. "You went all out tonight. Are you sure you know we're going to an outdoor festival?"

"Uh, yeah. I'm trying to get that rock star dick tonight," she proudly states, throwing a lock of her burnished caramel tresses over her shoulder.

I shake my head. "I should've known. You always go all out like this when you're hankering for the D. But that's also every day so forgive me for not being able to tell the difference."

Her mouth pops open and she smacks my arm, acting offended. "Bitch," she hisses playfully, mirth dancing in her hazel eyes. "You look hot yourself, you know."

As we're making our way to the door her hesitant voice stops me. "Hey, Sadie. Wait." Her face is downtrodden, and she looks defeated as she studies the ground. Instantly, I know something is wrong. This isn't like her at all. She's bubbly all the time. A bit cynical like me but never... melancholic.

"What's wrong?" I ask, reaching for her hand. Her shiny red nail polish stands out against her tanned skin.

She takes a deep breath and lifts those sad eyes to meet mine. "Have you ever thought about leaving here? Leaving town, I mean. Like after the festival?"

Her words confuse me, leaving me temporarily stunned as I open and close my mouth a few times. None of my thoughts want to leave my brain.

"Of course I've thought about it, Ash—" I pause when her hazel eyes, with soft golden-brown flecks, find mine again and harden.

"Why haven't we done it then?"

"You know why. We have no money, babe. Where's this suddenly coming from?"

She rips her hand from mine and starts pacing the living room. Her heels click against the hardwood flooring as she paces. "There's nothing left for us here, Sadie." She throws her arms up in the air and smacks them against her sides. "Nothing. We're wasting away here! Can't you see that? There has to be more to life than... than this!"

"I didn't realize you felt so strongly about this. I'm sorry—"

"Forget it," she interrupts. "Forget I said anything. Let's go have fun at the festival. We can talk about it later." It's like a flip switches in her demeanor and she smiles, leaving no trace of the sadness behind as she drags me out of the door.

Her words spin repeatedly in my mind as I contemplate what she said. More to life than this. Truest statement I've ever heard in my life, but what can be done about it when you're stuck working your life away?

I sigh, making sure to lock, check, and double-check our front door like I always do before bounding down our rickety porch steps. This may be the south, where everyone leaves their doors unlocked, but not us. Not that we have anything of value, but people can be destructive regardless.

The sound of a flicking lighter catches my attention, and I glance over to find our neighbor, Bedi, sitting outside at her rusty table lighting up a cigarette. She takes a puff, holding it in as she asks, "Where are you young ones heading?" She flicks the ash, watching us with those weary eyes of hers. With her other hand, she moves a strand of grey hair out of her face.

"You're going to kill yourself smoking those, you know," I respond.

She cackles and, as if to prove my point, it turns into a coughing fit. One of those deep hacking type coughs only heavy smokers have. When the coughing subsides, she spears us with a no-bullshit look. "Sure, kiddo. Now I asked you both a question." She takes another long drag off her cigarette, likely to spite me. She's a feisty old bat.

"No need to get touchy, Bedi. We're off to the music festival in town," Ash explains.

Bedi doesn't take her eyes off me, drawing me in with those violet eyes of hers. There's so much age and wisdom there, it's hard to look away. "Ah, well. I imagine it'll be quite life-changing," she says, the corners of her mouth tipping up. "A storm is brewing, and you'll be stuck in the middle, two sides to a coin. If you're careful, you won't have to choose."

The hair on my arms rises with her ominous words. She's always spouting stuff like this, but tonight, it seems more important somehow.

"What do you mean?" I ask in confusion.

She shivers and her eyes clear. "Nothing, dear. You enjoy your festival tonight," then points to Ash with a narrowed gaze. "And you, little missy," she wiggles her finger, "don't get pregnant."

I burst out laughing, forgetting all about her strange words.

"Bedi, I'm on the pill," Ash says, cackling gleefully when Bedi rolls her eyes.

One of the neighbors a couple of doors down gasps and clutches her pearls, which makes all of us giggle even harder. When Ash's chuckles finally subside, Bedi shakes her head at her. "Too much information."

"You started it, old woman," Ash calls over her shoulder.

"I am not old, you little shit!" she shouts after us, making us laugh the whole way to the festival.

5

SADIE

As soon as we step out of the car the humidity smacks me in the face, ruining my carefully curled locks almost instantly. So much for that spritz of hairspray. Extra strength my ass.

It's a short walk to the main part of the park where the stage is set up and the festivities are being held. A sense of rightness fills me as I look around at all the cars surrounding us.

Somehow, I know I'm exactly where I'm supposed to be. But I almost feel underdressed. People are decked out to the nines, with hair accessories and jewelry. Some are less dressed than Ash. As in nothing but loincloths and pasties over their nips.

The wind kicks up a notch, blowing a stray piece of hair into my face. The sky is mottled with rain clouds but thankfully, it seems to be holding off for now.

Ash bats her eyelashes at the security guards, and they let us go through without frisking us, which is nice considering I didn't want to give up my switchblade. A girl can never be too careful.

When we round the corner, my jaw drops. There must be close to five thousand people already here, not including the line of patrons still waiting to get in. I was not expecting such a good turnout. Although, some of the world's greatest bands are here.

"Do you want to check out the merch before the show starts?" Ash asks, eyeing the various tents longingly.

"If by that you mean look at a bunch of overpriced items we can't afford? Then sure, let's go for it!"

She snorts but doesn't correct me.

If I had cash to spare it wouldn't be such a big deal but seeing as I'm recently unemployed and I don't have a hot sugar daddy lined up to pay all my bills, I need my extra money for necessities.

I pick up a rose-colored hoodie and check the price tag for the hell of it. My eyes almost bulge out of my head. Who charges seventy-five bucks for a dang hoodie?

Why is concert merch so expensive? Oh, wait, because people pay these idiotic prices. Not this broke girl though. I'm someone who spends the least amount of money on an item as possible. If there isn't a coupon, I'm not buying it.

Technically, I could afford a shirt or CD with the money Red gave me, but I'm too terrified something will happen, and I'll be fifty bucks short because that's exactly how life tends to go for me.

After glancing at everything and choking at a few more price tags, I decide to stop torturing myself and meet Ash outside when she's done looking. As I'm about to exit, a sparkle catches my eye and my legs practically move of their own accord over to the rack where a small silver chain dangles from one of the display cases, taunting me. I reach out, fingering it gently.

The symbol dangling from the chain is small but unbelievably detailed, displaying a miniature lunar phase chart encased in triangles with a strange symbol in the middle. It feels so out of place with all the band merchandise. Still, it beckons to me like a siren singing an alluring tune. Even my skin prickles with awareness as I finger it slightly.

I'm overwhelmed with an irrational need for this necklace, but I decide not to torture myself and even look for a price tag. I'm willing to bet money it's out of my price range. Instead, I leave the tent.

While I wait for Ash, my thoughts start to wander, spiraling to the dark side but I shove them away. For one night I want to be able to let loose with my best friend at my side. No worrying about work and how I got fired, or how we are going to continue paying our bills and keep a roof over our heads, or the weird conversation we had before we left the duplex.

Nope. We'll find a way to make it work. We always do. Besides, these are problems for tomorrow Sadie—tonight Sadie is going to enjoy the festival without any heavy thoughts weighing her down.

I freeze when a familiar glint catches my eye and I watch from the shadows as a man eyes the exquisite necklace. He lifts the price tag, smirking as he takes it off the rack. Watching him walk toward the cashier gives me the strongest urge to chase after him, snatch it from his hands, and demand that he gives me the necklace. I refrain—barely.

He hands the cashier a bundle of crisp one-hundred-dollar bills and my nose crinkles. Who brings that much cash to a concert? Seems like the best way to get robbed to me, but what do I know?

Before I can analyze it too much, a hand waves in front of my face.

Ash snaps her fingers and the trance fizzles. "Uh, earth to Sadie. Have you even been listening? I've been standing here talking to you for like five minutes." I grimace, turning around to give her a sheepish look. "I'll take that as a no. What were you staring at?"

"Don't worry about it," I grumble. For some reason, I don't tell her and I'm not sure why I'm suddenly so grouchy about the subject. She gives me the side-eye, but I wave her off and she doesn't bring it up again.

Suddenly, the path in front of us parts, revealing a man doing some wicked dance moves, and I walk closer, drawn to the scene. A few of the others in the crowd start rapping a beat to cheer him on. The dancing man seems oddly familiar, but all I can make out is his blond hair bouncing as he spins. His corded muscles contract as his lithe body shifts with each perfectly executed move.

Blondie drops to the ground, using his hands to propel him around, then he flips up on one hand and twists, repeating the motions with his feet in the air. He looks downright wicked as he does all sorts of turns and circles. His shirt slips down, highlighting a set of drool-worthy abs that would turn any girl on. The ladies go wild for him as they chant and cheer him on, Ash and I included.

The dancer notes the crowd's positive reaction to his near shirtless perfection, and he rips it off entirely while continuing to dance. Wonder if he knows any wicked moves in bed?

I've heard dancers are creative lovers.

Is it getting hotter out here or is it me?

We watch, completely captivated by him until the next thing I know, there are six more performers lined up competing in a dance-off. Everyone is cheering them on, but my eyes are on Blondie still.

Eventually, the other competitors drop out but Blondie is going strong. When he realizes he's the last one standing, he does a backflip which makes the crowd roar their approval, before standing and taking a bow. The cheering crowd floods in to congratulate him for winning all at once. Hell, one girl even tosses him her panties.

"Think I should throw mine in for good measure?" Ash asks, admiring the scene with a raised eyebrow.

"Maybe... I'm right there with you." She starts to reach under her dress, presumably for said panties, but I slap her hand away. "I was kidding! Christ, Ash!"

She snorts. "I'm screwing with you, babe. Besides, I'm not wearing any, anyway."

Oh, she did not say that... And judging by the gleam in her eye, she's telling the truth too. I gape at her and do a double-take at her skirt. One wrong move and she really will be flashing her goods to everyone.

"Okaaay," I shake my head, laughing. "On that note, I think it's time we move toward the stage and secure our spot. Looks like the first band is setting up."

Let's get this party started.

6

SADIE

"Hey, watch where you're walking, douchebags," Ash hollers at a couple of wasted guys who happen to stumble into us. The first band hasn't even started playing yet and they're stumbling drunk. What a bunch of noobs.

One of them spills his drink in his stupor and a tiny drop hits one of Ash's boots. Her eyes narrow and she takes a step toward the guy, but I snatch her arm, dragging her away before she gets us into trouble. It doesn't stop the colorful profanities slipping from her mouth, and I don't blame her. But I don't want to get kicked out either.

We squeeze behind another group of teens and—holy shit—a throuple. The girl is in the middle and she's being squished between two guys who are trailing their hands up and down her body. I watch in rapt fascination as the girl kisses one for a minute and then switches to the other. Get it, girl.

Why settle for one dick when you can have two? Am I right?

Ash follows my line of sight. "To answer the unspoken

question in your eyes, yes, it's as amazing as that little brain of yours is imagining."

Her words barely register at first, but when they do, my eyes snap over to hers. "You've had a threesome?"

Honestly, I don't know why I'm surprised. This is Ash we're talking about.

"Um yeah. You could've had one by now too if you weren't such a prude."

"Hey now. I'm not some blushing virgin, you know." That doesn't help my case in the slightest.

She gives a look, like *really bitch?*

Dammit. She knows me too well.

"Timmy from freshman year does not count. Didn't you say you kind of just rubbed against one another until he came?"

I groan, rubbing a hand down my face from the absolutely *delightful* mental image that brings back. She's right though. Poor Timmy. We were like fifteen at the time and he kept fumbling around. Every time I'd offer to help, he'd grab my hand and tell me that he knew what he was doing.

Obviously, he did not and about the fourth time he almost stuck it in my ass, I gave up and lied, pretending when he asked. Then, well, you can imagine the rest.

"Yeah, but that's beside the point. I'm waiting for the right time, you know?"

"No one's first time is perfect, Sadie. At this rate, you'll be eighty before it happens! Hell, my first time I didn't even orgas—oof." She cuts off as I elbow her in the side.

"TMI, babe, TMI." My bestie does not have issues sharing her sex-capades with me. Or anyone else for that matter.

When we finally push past the last of the people in our way, the space opens up to reveal a large stage directly in front of us. I can't help but let out a little whoop of victory as I rest my arms against the flimsy barricade that's supposed to keep fans away from the stage, but the metal looks like it's seen better days. If the crowd gets rowdy enough, I have a feeling it will snap, sending all of us hurtling into the security guards.

Luckily, the stage is low enough that we're not having to crane our necks to see. Or, well, I'm not. Ash is several inches taller than me and doesn't have the same short people issues I do.

"This view is perfect," Ash says and I nod my agreement.

It really is quite the sight.

The anticipation grows as the lights on the stage dim. Everything goes silent, all the murmurs quieting, while everyone waits with bated breath for the performance to start.

The frontman bursts out from backstage, striking a heavy chord on his guitar that resonates within my bones. Everyone explodes into action. We're a sea of waving bodies as we jump to the heavy beat of the song.

"Let me see those fucking hands in the air!" the sexy singer shouts through the microphone between lyrics. Hundreds, if not thousands, of hands shoot up in unison.

My heart rate spikes as fire and sparklers shoot out of a cannon at the back of the stage. The glow banks the whole area in red light, making everything seem much more sinister than it is, but that's a part of the appeal. I lose myself in the heavy thumping as the drop of the bass hits, beating in time to the wild rhythm in my chest.

AFTER THE FIRST BAND FINISHES THEIR SET AND THE SECOND one plays several ass-kicking songs, they announce there's going to be a short intermission before continuing the show.

I reach down to take another sip of my water and frown when I realize it's empty.

"Hey, I'm going to go get some more water, want to tag along?" I holler so Ash can hear me over the noise.

She nods. "Sure, but we need to be back before the intermission is over."

As I'm elbowing my way through the crowd, there's a large commotion in front of us. I'm forced to stand on my toes to be able to see over the man in front of me. I watch in awe, as a large group of people lift a boy in a wheelchair into the air to crowd surf him. The crowd propels him forward as he slowly makes his way to the front. Never mind there's not any music playing, the kid looks like he's on cloud nine. Surprisingly, they don't drop him.

"Holy shit." I don't realize I'm still walking until I smack into a wall of solid steel, bouncing right off. I land flat on my ass and know I'm going to have a bruised tailbone tomorrow.

Perfect. It'll go nicely with the fingerprints around my wrist from Ben.

I groan. "Who the hell decided it would be smart to put a wall right out in the open?"

Ash bursts out laughing, and I shoot her a murderous glare over my shoulder as I use the wall to climb back to my feet. Huh, why does this wall have a belt buckle—*oh, shit.*

Well, this is awkward.

Turns out the wall isn't a wall at all, but a man. One whose dick I used to climb like a ladder. Fuck me. Awkward Sadie wins again.

Time to face the music, I guess. My eyes dart up, connecting with dark blue orbs that capture me whole. My wall—I mean the man—peers at me curiously under dark lashes that I'm instantly jealous of. I watch transfixed as his eyes travel down the length of my entire body and up again.

My skin buzzes under his scrutiny like there are tiny little fires all over my flesh from his eyes alone. He visibly swallows and it highlights his chiseled jaw, sporting a bit of stubble and I wonder what it would feel like to run my tongue down it and feel the harsh scrape against my lips as I nibble—Nope. Down girl. Bad ovaries. I somehow manage to hold back the groan that wants to escape my throat.

"I—I'm so sorry." Apparently, my lady balls have also left the building.

"That's quite all right. Besides, I should be the one apologizing to you." His statement catches me off guard. I used his dick as a pull-up bar… and he thinks he is the one who should be apologizing to me?

Steel—as I'm dubbing him—grins and it lights up his whole face. His presence demands my attention and like a moth to a flame, I'm powerless to take my eyes off of him. Something about him niggles at the back of my thoughts, but my brain is thoroughly fried from our casual eye fucking.

My gaze snags on his t-shirt and I realize he's wearing the same one as me, then dips lower. The jeans he's wearing are perfectly tight in all the right areas if you know what I mean. Steel clears his throat, snapping me out of my inspection. I've been standing here checking him out for way longer than what a normal person would consider polite and I still can't seem to place where I know him from.

Talk to him, Sadie.

"Twin-sies!" I blurt and then clamp a hand over my mouth.

Nice. Nailed it.

Ash cackles behind me and leans forward to whisper, "Real smooth, babe."

I shoot her another death glare without any real heat behind it. It's not her fault I'm a dunce when it comes to men. Like I said, I suck with the opposite sex. Throw me in a training room with them and I'll hand them their ass, but knowing how to flirt? Not my area of expertise.

"Yes, I see that." Steel's deep voice rumbles over my skin, and it makes me wish I could bottle it up and save it for later. If his voice were an audiobook I'd listen to it daily. Speaking of which, I wonder if he could make me come while reading some lady porn out loud... I'm fairly certain I'd have a mini orgasm from his raspy voice alone.

"You—uh, you're hot." I complete my awkwardness with a two-finger salute. I did not say that. I did not give him the two-finger salute. Oh, but I did.

Why does he look so damn familiar?

Another solid wall of muscle comes barreling through the crowd knocking into my side. I fall flat on my ass for the second time in less than five minutes.

"Whoa. Falling for me already, Angel? That has to be a new record," A second voice says, but his voice is much lighter and way more amused, like everything in life is a joke. It can be, I guess. I'm more of a glass half-empty gal.

As I rise to my feet, my eyes ping-pong between the two men, mesmerized by their magazine-worthy looks. Suddenly, I'm itching to reach out, to touch them, and know exactly what their skin would feel like against mine. I quickly snatch my hands back—who have a mind of their own and are already halfway there—before I can follow through with that last thought.

Bad hands. It's not polite to touch strangers.

I level my gaze on the one who knocked into me. "Is that supposed to be a corny pick-up line about me falling from heaven? Because you're going to have to do better than that."

His amber eyes meet mine as he runs a hand through his sandy locks that seem so damn familiar. The first guy has black hair and observant blue eyes. The second one has blond hair and a smirk fixated on his kissable lips.

Wait a damn minute.

I gasp as everything clicks into place. "You're the guys from the lake!" Then another thought registers and I motion toward Blondie. "And you're the one who won the dance-off." I blame the dark and excitement of the concert for not realizing sooner.

Blondie's smirk turns downright naughty. "I was wondering how long it would take for you to catch on, Angel. We could never forget a face like yours."

"Yes, it's quite a pleasant surprise finding you again," Steel adds with a warm smile, making my insides all tingly again. "My name is Kaos King, and this is—"

"Dante," Blondie cuts in before he can finish. "Dante King." His eyelids are half-closed when he says it and I find myself imagining what those would look like in the bedroom while I'm riding his... Jesus, my libido has skyrocketed in the past five minutes.

Ash coughs, snapping me back to reality.

"Oh, and I'm Sadie. Sadie Sinclair."

Ash steps forward. "Hey there, boys. I hate to break up the lovefest but, I'm Ashley. Sadie's best friend. Figured I'd get that out of the way while everyone is being introduced." She looks between us with clear interest. "Although, you three already seem to know each other somehow."

Kaos and Dante's eyes dart toward her, seeming to notice her for the first time. They both give her a quick once over before their gazes settle back on me. I lap up their attention like the thirsty bitch I am.

"Yeah, these are the guys I ran into at the lake yesterday morning."

Dante's eyes twinkle and he opens his mouth to say something but doesn't get the chance.

"Mercedes!"

I curse silently, turning my eyes skyward to question why

the universe hates me so much. Because I'd recognize that voice anywhere. The question is, why is he here? And more importantly, what does he want from me?

"Mercedes!" The voice shouts, louder this time.

I keep my focus on Kaos, Dante, and Ash. Maybe he's like a T-Rex and he can't see me if I don't move or acknowledge him. But that's not how my luck works. Besides, I'm not one to cower from anyone, but I'm so not ready to deal with this right now.

My ex-boyfriend and my trainer make a beeline straight for me, shoving unsuspecting people out of their way. My ex smiles like the cat that killed the canary while he does. And it's a vicious sort of smile. One that instantly puts me on edge. I discreetly pull my switchblade out of my pocket.

Kaos, ever the attentive one, narrows in on the action. He gives me a questioning look but doesn't get a chance to ask because the two stooges are upon us, and they don't look happy.

"It's Sadie, but you already know that," I say through clenched teeth before he can speak. The jackass knows I hate my given name and yet he still uses it. Probably to get this reaction out of me.

My ex-boyfriend, Tyler, shrugs. He leans in, smacking a kiss on my cheek that burns like acid. He slings an arm around my shoulder, but I shrug him off, scrubbing at my cheek furiously, trying to get rid of the feeling of his lips on my skin, but it's no use. "What the fuck are you doing here, Tyler?"

"I came to keep an eye on my girl," he responds with a devious glimmer in his eye. "Is that so bad?"

Yes, it is bad. Ugh, I should've known this twat would pull something tonight. I've only been talking about this night since they announced the tour a year ago and we only broke up six months ago. You know, when I came home after work one night to find him balls deep in Harley Addison.

Harley fucking Addison.

What kind of name is that?

Of course, Tyler tried to blame him screwing Harley on me and the fact that I wouldn't have sex with him. *"But Sadie, a man has needs,"* he told me.

Yeah, well, fuck your needs, Tyler.

Although, I got the last laugh when I went all Carrie Underwood and took a Louisville Slugger to the headlights and body of his brand-spankin' new Ford Raptor. Now that I think about it though, I really should've gone all Miranda Lambert in her music video for Kerosene and burned his house down while I was at it. With him in it. Am I a little psycho? Probably. But eh, semantics.

"If you put your hands on me again, you'll lose one. You lost your privileges the moment I came home to find you with your dick in someone else. I am not your girl, Tyler."

His fists clench by his side but he otherwise looks calm. "Sure, and the sky ain't blue, darlin'." He laughs, a caustic sort of laugh. "Besides, Harley meant nothing to me. Not like you do."

Indignation flares through me. We haven't been dating for six months and he thinks he can waltz back into my life the first time a guy—well guys—show interest in me? Who does he think he is?

The way he stares at me reminds me of a predator watching their prey. He even makes sure to keep Dante and Kaos in his line of sight while he does. In this case, Dante and Kaos are the bigger threat.

Ben folds his arms over his chest, and the movement reminds me that he's still here. I'd totally forgotten. That's the thing about him, he's awfully good at blending in with his surroundings and although he doesn't say anything, he watches me with those penetrating black eyes of his.

"You know what, both of you can back right the hell off. Now." Ash rushes forward in my defense. "Sadie has already moved on to much greener pastures than your ass, Tyler." She levels her glare on Ben next. "As for you, why are you even here? You can't actually enjoy letting Tyler drag you around by the balls."

Ben's face contorts in rage and he steps forward.

Kaos surprises the hell out of me by stepping in between us. "You heard the ladies. I'm inclined to agree with them. Why don't you head on back to wherever you came from." Not a question, a statement.

Swoon. I mean, uhh... I don't swoon. Nope, all badassery over here.

Tyler's eyes flick toward Kaos and then Dante, dripping with disdain. "Who the fuck are you?" He puffs out his chest like he's about to have a brawl in the middle of a metal festival. Bad idea, bud. Knowing this crowd, they'd think it's the start of a mosh-pit and join in. Then we'd have chaos on our hands. Heh, literally.

A dark chuckle brushes along my spine, setting my nerve endings alight. But not in a bad way. Quite the opposite really. "No one you need to concern yourself with, prick. I'd suggest you run along and leave Sadie alone before we really decide to get involved," Kaos says, his voice reminding me of the sharp edge of a knife.

Tyler's face morphs from mad to murderous. His cheeks and neck turn red as his anger level rises. I know that look and it's not one I want to be on the receiving end of ever again. I flick the blade down on my switchblade as inconspicuously as possible. If he wants to come at me right now, it'll be one hell of a fight, but at least I'll be able to maim him or screw up that pretty little face of his.

I'll never understand what I saw in him. He may have never sexually assaulted me, but he sure didn't mind getting physical. There's a monster lurking under that tanned skin and perfect baby blue eyes of his and he hides it well.

Now I know better.

And nobody messes with Tyler Maynard and walks away unscathed.

The air shifts and I feel a fist coming my way before I see it. Dante snatches Tyler's wrist out of the air before I can blink. When his fiery amber eyes meet mine, they're hard as ice. His jaw is clenched, and he stands there holding the appendage like it's a personal affront to him and not me. What is it with strangers saving me this week? Step it up, Sadie.

Tyler tries to pull his fist away and Dante's fingers tighten around it like he can strangle the life out of him through his hand. Tyler grunts trying to yank his wrist back, but it doesn't budge.

My ex levels those dangerous baby blues on me, and I already know I'm in trouble now. "You cheating bitch," he snaps, eyeing me like I'm a butterfly he wants to squash under his boot. Kind of ironic really, considering the position he's in right now. At the mercy of two strangers that feel the need to jump in at my defense.

"Pot meet kettle, asshole."

Ben charges forward to back up his buddy but he doesn't stand a chance. Kaos flips him over his shoulder and onto the ground like he's nothing and hasn't been trained in hand to hand his entire life.

Kaos sneers down at him, keeping his large boot in the center of his chest. You know what they say about big feet.

Yep, big socks.

Tyler's nostrils flare when he sees his friend on the ground, then his eyes dart between all of us like he's sizing us up before they land on me again. "You wouldn't fuck me, but you'll fuck these two dicks you don't even know?" His lip curls in disgust like the idea of my having a threesome repulses him, even though I've seen his porn history.

If men don't have shit else, they have the Godsdamn audacity.

"What is it with men and their toxic mindset when it comes to sex?" I grumble. "Why can you screw whoever you want, and it's no big deal, but a chick does the same thing and it's suddenly such a sin? Fuck that, and fuck you, Tyler."

He chuckles. "I always knew you were a secret slut, Mercedes, but this is a new low. Even for you."

"She already told you to call her Sadie," Dante interjects, shaking Tyler's wrist until he groans again. "And that's no way to speak to a lady, is it?"

"This isn't over. Mark my words, Mercedes," Tyler whispers ominously, clearly realizing he won't get anywhere with me with my two unexpected bodyguards around.

"Yes. It is," Kaos responds, a hint of finality in his tone. "Come near her again and you won't like the ramifications."

Before anyone else has a chance to speak, Ash darts forward, grinning like a maniac as she kicks Tyler straight in the balls with her combat boots. Fairly sure she flashes her hoo-hah while she's at it, but she doesn't look like she cares.

"Dammit! Why didn't I think of that?" I pout as Tyler howls in pain, dropping to his knees. Dante still has a hold of his wrist, so he doesn't go far. His arm makes a strange popping sound, making him bellow in pain and hop back up.

She smiles. "I've been wanting to do that for so long. Ever since you brought that jackass home." I have to admit it's nice to see him finally getting a taste of his own medicine.

I watch Dante whisper something in Tyler's ear before he finally releases his wrist and Tyler stalks off, blending into the crowd without a backward glance. Kaos removes his boot from Ben and he's up in a flash. Watching them disappear I realize that somehow the silence seems more deadly than Tyler's outright threats.

His words echo through my mind, tainting my thoughts. *"This isn't over."*

Something tells me he's right.

7

KAOS

The more I learn of Sadie, the more she intrigues me. I can't take my eyes off of her. I literally can't keep my eyes off this enigmatic girl. It was the same way at the lake. Dante and I both felt drawn there as if the fates were leading us to her location. And when I physically saw her, I was a goner right there on the shore.

She looks as stunning as she did yesterday morning with her lovely blonde hair curled down her back and those tight-ass shorts with the fishnet leggings—or whatever they're called.

The way her hip juts out when she places her small hand on it makes me smile. Her eyes narrow and her cheeks burn as she confronts this man she apparently knows, who has a damn death wish. It fuels the bloodlust inside of me.

Nobody fucks with a woman—any woman—around the Kings unless they want to die. And these two seedy pricks aren't getting the memo fast enough for my liking. Even with one of them under my boot.

It makes me want to castrate them. Women are meant to be treated with respect, as equals. Not toys.

And the way these two are staring at her? They think she's a toy to be played with. Not on my watch. Though, she seems quite capable of defending herself. No one else noticed when she slipped her knife out of her pocket, but I did. Something tells me there's more to uncover under the surface of this girl.

Sadie flicks a lock of her hair over her shoulder and straightens her spine. The dim light reflecting off the stage illuminates her face, basking her in a glow that highlights her slender nose and bright full lips as she stares everyone down. She's spunky, for sure.

A few moments later, her friend kicks the mouthy one in the balls. I hold back my wince because he doesn't deserve my sympathy. Although, I appreciate her sassy attitude. She gives us all a wide smile while readjusting her tight outfit.

Normally I'd be appreciative of the view, but her looks do nothing for me compared to Sadie. I'm used to the pretty girls fawning over me, and I long for things to go deeper than the surface level. I want to make connections and find a bond that's beyond any scale of comprehension.

The shithead, Tyler, I think, says something hateful to Sadie again, but I don't quite catch it. Whatever he says makes her hands clench around the handle of her blade and my blood boils. I've never felt this possessive over a girl before—let alone a total stranger—but it feels right with her. Easy even. She draws me in like no one else ever has. It's absolutely riveting.

I'll be the first to admit I find something so intriguing about Sadie, even at the lake, and I could've kicked myself for forgetting to grab her number. If it weren't for the call from the Elders distracting me, I would have. Then maybe we could've arrived together and I would've had more time to get to know her, to analyze her moves.

Speaking of the phone call, the Elders informed me we

have a month to pick a mate or find our Link. Total bullshit, but there's nothing we can do about it. A match be forced upon us whether we like it or not. All in the name of bettering society.

I cast a glance over at Dante and judging by the way his eyes soften as he gazes at Sadie, I'd say he's as much of a goner as I am.

Do you think it's possible? I project my thoughts into his mind.

What? he asks.

For her to be our Link.

The signs are there, from what I've heard at least. We're not given any information on mates anymore because the Elders don't want us to learn the fake bonds they force upon us are wrong but my mother taught us better.

I don't know, but is it bad that I kind of hope she is?

Yeah, me too. Me fucking too.

Too bad it's impossible.

Although, I'm starting to doubt that.

8

SADIE

"Listen," I blow out a breath. "Thanks for the towel yesterday morning and defending me with my ex back there, but you don't have to stick around. I know that I'm a lot and…" I trail off with a shrug, figuring it's better to give them an out now. I always do this. Bail before the going gets rough.

Kaos observes me like a puzzle he wants to figure out. Ha. Good luck with that. Many have tried and failed.

He looks to Dante and nods. If I didn't know any better, I'd say they were having a mental conversation. "I think I speak for both of us when I say we like being around you. Let's see where this night takes us, if you'll have us?"

My stomach flutters and I find myself agreeing. A part of me doesn't want to let these men slip through my fingers. "Sure, let's have some fun, shall we?"

Dante grins as he waltzes over to stand beside me, offering his arm. "We should go enjoy the rest of the show. I think the intermission is almost over," he says and none of his earlier ire shows on his face. I can't decide if the humor is a mask or if it's a part of who he is.

CHAPTER 8 | 63

When Kaos shoulder checks Dante out of the way before I can place my arm in his, I burst out laughing. Then they both shrug and move to either side of me in sync. A woman could get used to this.

"I'm so jealous right now," Ash says with a pout which makes my heart pang for a moment. She's not used to all the attention being elsewhere, but she doesn't seem upset. Still, no need to rub it in her face. I extract myself from between the hotties. Barely. I mean I do have some self-control. Sometimes.

"I'm sorry, Ash. Tonight is supposed to be about us. I'll tell them to get lost." I am not going to be that friend, the one who bails on their bestie for a guy. Or two guys in this case. No way.

She gives me an incredulous look and leans in closer. "Absolutely not. Have you seen those bodies? Phew, and I bet they're packing too."

"We are," Dante says without missing a beat.

"See? I told ya, babe. I'm not letting you miss out on that."

Did my best friend help set me up with two of the hottest guys I've ever laid eyes on in my life? Fuck yeah she did. I knew I kept her around for a reason.

"After you, ladies."

Not even a minute after we regain our spot at the front of the crowd, the next band starts playing their setlist. And they're who we came here for. Wicked Unrest. The hottest metal band around right now. They've been in the top five on the charts for weeks now.

I sigh, letting the song flow through me. Nothing can wash away the pain, the anxiety, and the bullshit life likes to throw my way quite like music can. It's like a balm to my battered and torn soul. Always has been.

It doesn't matter that there's sweat dripping down my spine, and my hair is a frizzy mess. It doesn't matter that we're standing out in the open, or that there are two dreamy guys watching me as I dance. There are thousands of us out here and it allows me to blend in, giving me a sense of anonymity to let my feelings bleed as I move and let all of the negative feelings Tyler stirred drift away.

The tempo picks up toward the end and I belt out my favorite part of the song.

"The silence grows as the music fades... A tortured soul you left in your wake; you still haunt me... Shadows spin and weave a scene, leaving a broken-hearted melody. You still haunt me..."

Dante gives me an approving nod and the heat in his eyes is strong enough to light a damn bonfire. He leans in close to whisper against the shell of my ear, "Color me surprised, Angel. Not many know this song." The huskiness of his voice startles me out of my trance, but I don't have a chance to respond.

"All right, you crazy motherfuckers!" The lead singer, Brandon Luck, shouts before he takes a long drink out of his water bottle. "I want to experiment with something for this next song. If you're here with a girl, whether it be a casual fuck or a committed relationship, I want you to grab her and put her on your shoulders!"

A pair of muscular arms lift me into the air so fast I can't track the movement. My breath whooshes out of me until I'm upright again. When I look down, I find a glorious head of blond hair, and before I can stop myself, I grip a handful of it. Which in turn makes Dante groan. I quickly drop it making Dante's shoulders shake with laughter.

Nice, Sadie. Real nice.

Trying to distract myself from the mental image of me riding Dante's face into oblivion with my hands tangled in his hair, I look over to find Kaos sulking for not getting a hold of me fast enough.

"Why don't you lift Ash?" I suggest, not wanting my bestie

to feel left out even if it makes me growly for some damn reason.

They're strangers, I remind myself. Little good it does for my vagina though. That bitch has a mind of her own and she's panting like a dog in heat all over Dante's neck.

When the song ends, Brandon chuckles evilly through the microphone. The sound echoes all around us, bouncing off the trees. "If your girl is still on your shoulders, congratu-fucking-lations." He smirks, placing his foot on one of the box speakers. "Now, when you get back to wherever it is you're going, I want you to do this again."

He pauses for dramatic effect, making sure everyone is hanging on his every word before he continues. "But I want you to shift her to the front and then throw her against a fucking wall. I want you to bury your heads between your girl's thighs until she's screaming your goddamn name."

A chorus of groans meets my ears at the naughty-ness of his words.

"You're fucking welcome ladies!"

And now I can't shake that image from my brain.

Half the crowd disperses after his erotic announcement is over. Likely trying to find places to have a quickie. I bet some of them are heading back to the campground to screw in tents, while the others will probably find a nice tree to bang against.

As for us, we continue to enjoy the show, but I find myself enjoying the view of *them* more.

9

SADIE

The next few songs go off without a hitch. That is until Brandon Luck spots Ashley dancing in the crowd and trips over the lyrics he's singing. He recovers quickly, but his eyes never leave hers. He's been known to choose one girl from each show to bring back to his tour bus, but I never dreamed it'd be one of us. And it's usually after the show, not during the middle of it.

When the song ends, he hops down from the stage—much to the security guards' chagrin—and jumps over the rail. The crowd rushes toward him, reaching out to touch him. One chick even fondles his long black hair, but he barely notices. Like a man possessed, Brandon Luck ignores the crowd, shrugging off the advances as he makes his way through them. Ash's chest rises and falls rapidly as she watches him.

What is happening right now?

I'm not the only one wondering if the looks his fellow bandmates are giving him are any sign. They're staring down at him with raised eyebrows and open mouths. Hell, their drummer even has his hands poised above the drums waiting for Brandon to resume singing.

When he finally makes it through the crowd, he stops in front of us and holds his hand out for Ash to take and she does with a breathy sigh. I've never understood the thought behind treating celebrities like they're anything more than regular people, but Ash is enthralled.

"Hello there, gorgeous," he says, his voice low and husky. He wraps a sweaty arm around her, like they're old friends and not strangers from completely different worlds. "I saw you shining down here like the brightest star in the night, like a beacon beckoning me forth and I couldn't resist the urge to come down and speak with you. You're the inspiration love songs are made from, my dear."

This man. Always speaking in terms of song lyrics. Seriously, you should hear his interviews.

"Is that so?" Ash smiles, batting her eyelashes at him playfully.

He nods, running a black painted fingernail down the side of her face. "Would you care to join me on stage?"

Her eyes almost bug out of her head. "Yes, absolutely, yes! But uh, only if my bestie doesn't mind?" She takes a step back from him and gives me the puppy dog face which she knows I can't resist. Not that I would anyway. This is a once in a lifetime opportunity and after she just set me up, it would be wrong.

"Of course I don't mind. You told me to shoot my shot with these two. The same goes for you. You're insane if you think I'd let you pass this up."

"You mean more to me than getting some hot rock star dick, Sades."

Wow, way to be discreet about it, Ash.

I smirk. "You do love me after all."

"Duh," she says as she shrugs Brandon's arm off and pulls

me into a bear hug. "But I'm worried about you. With Tyler here and..." She trails off but doesn't have to finish her sentence. I know where she's going with it.

"I'll be fine. Don't worry about him. Besides, I can take care of myself, and I have two hot bodyguards if all else fails."

She watches me for a moment before responding. Her eyes travel to where Brandon is waiting patiently, and she waltzes over to him with a little more pep in her step than I've seen lately. I can't believe I haven't noticed sooner how sad she seems.

"I hate to break up the moment," Brandon says, "but if you're coming, we need to go. I'm holding up the show." He holds his arm out for Ash to take and then they're off.

She glances over her shoulder one last time, giving me a thumbs-up before they climb the steps to the stage and disappear behind the curtain. They reappear a moment later and the joy on Ash's face gives me chills. I watch her lip-syncs their hottest song on stage and party with one of the most famous rock stars in the world to boot. He's practically a king, and she's his queen, if only for a night.

I pinch the toned flesh of Dante's arm. "Ouch! What was that for?"

"Making sure I'm not dreaming," I murmur.

What? Why would I use mine when I could use his?

Mirth dances in those amber eyes of his. "And you had to pinch me for that? Pretty sure that's not how it works, Angel."

"Eh, it seemed like a good idea at the time."

"Who's ready to rock out with my lovely lady here? Let's get those devil horns up!" Brandon calls out.

I throw my hand up and the charm on my bracelet snags in my long curls, burrowing itself in there. A pained yelp escapes my lips as I try to pull it out, grimacing as it tugs on my scalp. Kaos reacts instantly, whipping a knife out of his

CHAPTER 9 | 69

crotch somewhere. Or at least I think that's where it came from. Is there a hidden pocket next to his balls? No. That's an accident waiting to happen. What if it pops open and then bam, severed dick?

"Uh... Sadie? My eyes are up here," he says, while he gently cuts my wrist free from my hair.

I quickly snap my attention back to his face, but not before I see a bulge starting to form, and not in the form of a crotch knife. All coherent thought leaves me as I struggle to formulate sentences. "I... Um... Yeah." I can't seem to help myself as my eyes travel back down to see the outline poking through his faded blue jeans as he subtly adjusts himself.

"I know. It's impressive, isn't it?"

Dante watches the spectacle with a raised eyebrow. "Fucking hell. I'll show you mine if you'll stare at it that intently."

Don't look down, Sadie.

Do. Not. Look. Down.

I totally look down.

I glance back up at their faces, thinking maybe they didn't notice. No such luck. "Fuck, I like dicks, okay?"

Am I going through an awakening period in my life or something? Because holy hell. I mean, I've always had quite the appetite. Considering I have at least ten different vibrators at home, but this is different. These men are flesh and blood and they're lighting me up from the inside out like no one else ever has.

Dante straight up loses it. I'm talking full-on bent over while hyperventilating, slap your knee kind of losing it. Kaos smacks him upside the head, but he can't stop the little peals escaping his lips too.

That's it. I'm hanging up the hat and becoming a nun.

In desperate need of a distraction, I turn around to watch the show but it's no use. I can't get the image of their two huge outlines out of my mind. All I want to do is find somewhere quiet and say to hell with everything.

As I let go and let the song control my movements, feather-light touches caress my hips, burning into my skin. Technically, it's not the best music to dance to, but who cares? Dante moves like he's communicating with his body instead of words. Like he's made to move like this. The girl from the throuple earlier pops into my mind as I wrap my arm around each of their necks and bring them in closer.

Maybe I'll get my own threesome after all.

10

ELIAN

My pocket watch clicks as I close it and tuck it back into the front of my leather jacket with a sigh. Those fucking assholes are late again.

Dante would lose his head if it wasn't attached, and Kaos follows along with his little schemes too easily. Therefore, I'm not surprised they got sidetracked. I only hope they're not out trying to find some blonde bimbo to fuck. That's the last thing we need right now with the goddamn Elders breathing down our necks to choose a mate.

What a fucking sham. There hasn't been a true Link in so long and these little fake pairings that the Elders like to force upon us are a fraud and a disgrace to the Night Goddess.

But Weavers can't reproduce without their true mate, and female Weavers are scarce as it is. Before the pairings stopped, the males outnumbered the females five to one. Now people are desperate and we're slowly dying off. Though, the Elders claim they've had a breakthrough on the fake pairings they produce.

This is partly why I considered having our Circle choose that awful red-haired snake so badly, even though she's not our mate. She's powerful, and at least we'd have one, which is more than some of the others could ever hope for, but I've never cared for her.

Our Circle happens to be the product of some of the last true pairs. The decline in mates started with the generation before our parents. Only a handful would meet their Link until they stopped finding them altogether.

There's also the issue of the Elites stalking the woods outside of the festival. Another one of the Elders' ploys they think we can't see through, but I know that it's no accident they're here tonight. Their presence taints the scene and permeates the air with their dark metallic energy and hatred. It ruins the vibe of the show completely. Though they're not stupid enough to step out of the shadows. So, I'll hunt them down myself, because the night, the shadows, and the darkness are all my playground. I crack my inked knuckles in delight. Yes, blood will be spilled tonight. That's for certain.

Now, where did those fuckers head off to? My eyelids flutter closed as I begin to picture the silvery threads that connect us as a Circle until they're bright enough to lead me straight to them. The crowd parts for me with ease, like the humans can sense there's something strange about me and they need to steer clear. It comes in handy. *There they are. Against the fence line.*

The last of the patrons step out of the way and I almost call out to them, but the sight before me makes my frozen heart seize, then crack, threatening to shatter the ice I've carefully been building around it for so long. Goddess, no. This can't be. Her aura is so strong and vibrant she might as well be the fucking sun.

And she's my mate.

The girl stands out while she dances, shining more brilliantly than the most beautiful galaxy. Her aura is equal parts darkness and light with a mixture of grey in between. It beckons me to her like a siren's song lures a sailor to his death.

Moons above, she's even blonde. But this girl is no ordinary blonde bimbo that the others are looking to play around with and fuck for a night. No. Those assholes are smitten with her. I can tell by the star-struck looks in their eyes as they gaze down at her like she's the last woman on earth.

My jaw clenches in icy fury. This girl will be a distraction we don't need—one we can't afford. My plans are so carefully concocted, even the slightest deviation will throw the entire thing off balance. I can't afford to let it happen because I value our lives.

As much as it pains me to do so, I must save our own asses to protect every single one of the people we know and care about. Or that's what I tell myself, anyway. Because Links only amplify powers and the Elders already have us on their radar. Keep your friends close and your enemies closer is practically their motto.

I can't afford to bond with her.

Our sacred Link.

Our one true mate.

And I hate myself for it.

Goddess, please forgive me.

11

SADIE

Everything is going smoothly with Dante and Kaos. We're enjoying the show and chatting it up. Basically, having a good time. Then, tingles explode up my spine, lighting me up like one of those people's houses who love Christmas entirely too much. Something big is coming.

One glance at my surroundings doesn't initially reveal anything, but on my second sweep of the area, my gaze snags on a wickedly handsome man storming our way. He's not even looking at me and yet I can feel my heart stutter in my chest from the vehemence wafting off him.

He reminds me of a thunderstorm rolling in, ready to drench and destroy everything in its path. A part of me wants to look for cover, but the other is anticipating the ride.

"Where the fuck have you two been?" His hands clench into fists at his side as he looks Dante and Kaos up and down. "We were supposed to meet under the veranda ages ago." Gods, that voice. It's thick and smoky and it matches his smoldering eyes to perfection.

Kaos and Dante look a little dumbfounded like they're

struggling to find a reason, so I clear my throat and step forward. "Uh, hey there, I'm Sadie."

The newcomer's jaw ticks before he finally lifts those cold eyes to mine. The intensity completely takes my breath away—and all my thoughts. I fumble for words, trying to grasp onto anything, but it's not working and I'm standing there dumbfounded.

Speak, Sadie, it's not hard.

"Yeah, I kind of stole their attention when I ran into Kaos—"

"Literally," Dante interrupts, a grin tugging up the corners of his mouth. "Then she ran into me. As you can see, it snowballed from there."

"Yeah, and we happen to like her pretty little ass," Kaos says.

Dante scoffs. "Dude, that ass is anything but little," he says which does not help my position with the new guy one bit, judging by the vein pulsing on his forehead

The stranger's gaze flicks down my body, leaving my skin tingling like a blast of icy air. Which should be impossible considering it's late summer. When he looks back up, his eyes meet mine and stay there.

Now that he's focused on me, I notice his irises are a darker green near his pupil, and it stretches into the light as if it's trying to take over. There's not a single brownish blond lock out of place on his head and his clothes are immaculate. His designer jeans are ripped near the knees and trail down to a pair of black combat boots.

Honestly, I don't understand how he manages to look so put together at a rock concert, but hey, more power to him. He's definitely dressed for the right audience.

His inked fingers reach up and curl against the zipper of his leather jacket as he straightens it. Which boggles my mind.

"It's hotter than Hades' nut sack out here and you're wearing leather? Do you have a death wish?" I ask, then add, "Because that is most definitely how you have a heat stroke."

Helpful. Real helpful, Sadie.

Seriously though, a leather jacket and tattoos. Is there a cupid in the void fucking with me or something? Because bad boys are exactly my type.

For one tiny second, humor dances in his emerald eyes, then he quickly douses it with ice. "No, but apparently you do," he says and if his disdainful expression is any indication, he finds me severely lacking. I reach up to smooth my hair down, cringing when my fingers land on the frizzled strands. I also notice the grass and dirt stains on my Converse from the muddy ground for the first time.

Fuck. I can't imagine what I must look like to them. Yet I never felt self-conscious with Dante and Kaos. They made me feel like I was the only girl around and while it's a possibility that they do this to every girl they hook up with, I did feel a tiny bit special for a moment.

Kaos watches my face fall and he turns to his friend. "Come on, don't be an ass, Elian. We're only joking with you."

Oh, his name is Elian. *El-e-an. Why do I kind of like it?*

Elian ignores him, reaching into his jacket to pull out a pocket watch. He checks the time before slamming it closed and shoving it back inside. He dismisses me with a flick of his eyes and pulls Dante and Kaos to the side to have a chat with them, turning his back on me.

So, he doesn't consider me a threat, but that's all right. I'm used to it. Men like Elian always underestimate me until they're lying flat on their backs with my Converse crushing their airway.

I blow out a nervous breath, trying to fight the tingles dancing across my skin now that the four of us are standing so close. Despite the fact Elian is a total fuckboy, something about him has my skin desperate for his touch.

Elian's chest rumbles; it's a deep, dangerous warning sound. "Don't say I didn't warn you," he says. His eyes flicker to me and his lips curl like I'm the gum he suddenly discovers on the bottom of his shoe. "Come find me when you assholes get bored with your new *toy*." Then he stalks away without so much as a backward glance.

New toy? Oh, hell no.

But, sadly by the time I take a step forward to confront him, he's already gone and I refuse to chase after any man. I guess it's a good thing I know how to bide my time.

Instead, I spin around and spear Dante and Kaos with an inquisitive glance. "What crawled up his ass and died?"

"I don't know. He's not normally such an asshole," Dante says.

I scoff. People always say that about the assholes in their lives. They're not always like that. Yeah, and I'm not always short.

"Whatever. I've dealt with worse."

"I gathered that," Kaos adds dryly.

My phone vibrates in my back pocket, distracting me from the snarky reply wanting to burst from my lips. I unlock the screen with my thumbprint and smile when I see the text.

Red: How's the concert going, Love?

A brief pang of guilt smacks me in the chest when I think about my company for the night, but I shove it away. I'm not obligated to anyone.

Single pringle right here.

Me: It's amazing! Hope you're having a great night also! :)

Red: I'd much rather be there enjoying the music and your company.

I don't know what else to say, so I send back a frowny face and slip my phone into my back pocket. Or I try to, but someone yanks it away from me.

"Oh, juicy. Who's Red?" Dante rumbles right next to my ear.

"Fuck, when did you get so close? You almost gave me a heart attack!" I smack his side. Little good that does, probably hurts my hand more than it does him.

He chuckles, booping my nose. I'm not sure if it's cute or if it annoys me. "You didn't answer my question."

"He's just a friend. Don't worry about it."

"A friend, eh? So, friends call friends Love now?" He reads the messages back to me then shrugs. "Don't worry, I agree with Red. Does that make us friends as well?"

I roll my eyes. "Sure. Now give it back." I lunge for my device hoping to catch him off guard, but it doesn't work. He holds it out of my reach with a devious grin.

"Well, in that case, here's my number." He quickly types it into my contacts and I hear his phone ring for a split second. I give him a questioning look. "That way I'll have your number too," he says while slipping it back into my pocket.

I open my mouth to give him a snarky retort when a familiar face catches my attention. My muscles tense and I freeze. "You've got to be kidding me. Again?"

Both Ben and Tyler stand a few feet from us, watching me like a cougar might watch a wild hare it's stalking. Unfortunately for them, this girl has teeth and claws and she's not afraid to use them either.

"What's wrong?" Dante and Kaos ask in unison. Their hands hover above their crotches while their eyes scan our surroundings simultaneously. It's kind of freaky how in sync they are. But those fucking crotch-knives. Why are they so sexy?

Kaos' nostrils flare when he spots them and Dante loses

his carefree smirk, reaching over to give my shoulder a squeeze. My skin lights up under his touch and I bite back the groan that wants to tumble from my lips.

"Come on, let's see if we can lose them," he says.

Begrudgingly, I agree. Usually, I'm not one to back down from a fight, but there's no winning with men like Tyler Maynard and Benjamin Crawley.

What's that saying about not poking the bear? Oh, yeah. Simple, don't poke it.

12

DANTE

I force my anger down as I lead Sadie through the crowd and away from those motherfuckers. I don't know the whole story between them, but I don't have to because I saw the way they looked at her, and the possessiveness in their eyes when they saw us with her.

My fingers run through my hair as I exhale. I may look like the happy-go-lucky guy of the group, but I'll wring their necks as swiftly as the others. And if those dicks think I'm going to let them treat a woman like that, they've got another thing coming.

"You guys are some crazy motherfuckers here in Kentucky!" Brandon pants through the microphone. "This will be the last song of ours—" The crowd roars their disapproval, interrupting his speech. Brandon sticks his hands up in surrender. "—I know, but take it up with the schedulers, not me. We've enjoyed playing for you tonight! Now let's get rowdy to help welcome the next band!"

Sadie's eyes light up in excitement, diminishing the wariness there previously. The sight of her smile is fucking distracting. For all her bravado though, I sense more underneath the surface of her. She looks tough and she acts even tougher, but there's also a reserved quality about her. Quite like me, I guess.

Then again, humor is my crutch, my second skin, my armor. If you don't show you're bothered, then they can't continue to rile you up. Make a joke, take a jab, it doesn't matter. Let it roll off your back until one day it truly doesn't faze you anymore. Or it's buried so deep, it no longer matters.

Maybe it's why she resonates so well with me because I recognize the same behaviors I use to deflect. The way she wraps herself in snarky quips and comebacks like me. Goddess, what is this woman doing to me?

I know Kaos seems to think she might be our Link—even Elian acted weird when he found us with her—but I'm not getting my hopes up. There hasn't been a true Link in years. Why would this girl be any different?

On the other hand, there *is* something different about her, but I haven't been able to put my finger on what yet. She has a sort of silent power in the way she carries herself, the way she smiles, the way she laughs. The potent energy rolls off her in waves. Though, she seems none the wiser to the magical presence circling all around her.

Could it be true?

Could she truly not know?

She grins, tucking a lock of her gorgeous blonde hair behind her ear and turning her face toward mine. Our eyes lock and she looks down at my lips. We're so close it'd be easy to kiss her, but I don't. I pull away because I'm not ready yet. If Kaos is right, she'll be ours.

Our perfect mate.

Our true Link.

And that's a lot to process, especially for someone who sucks with emotions.

Real emotions.

13

SADIE

Dante leans in close, whispering against the shell of my ear, sending a shiver of lust down my spine. I turn to catch those amber eyes of his sparkling mischievously.

A puff of air tickles my lips and I glance down at his plump ones. He watches me closely, leaning in until our lips are a hair's breadth away. His eyes flash and he turns away suddenly, leaving me disappointed. That's silly, right? I barely know the guy.

My phone vibrates three times in a row, which never happens. No one ever texts me and I don't think it's from Red since we just talked. I yank it out of my pocket and hit the unlock button thinking, please, whichever God is listening, don't let it be an emergency.

Bestie: Holy fucking shit!
Bestie: That show was incredible.
Bestie: Brandon is so hot.

Ash's rapid texts make me chuckle and I blow out a relieved breath that it's not serious. A fourth text comes through before I can even type out a response.

Bestie: Oh shit. He's inviting me back to their bus. *wiggles eyebrows* Will you be all right with the two hotties by yourself?

Me: You know I can handle myself. Get that rock star D!

She sends back a series of eggplant and peach emojis making me burst out laughing. Dante looks over at me with his signature smirk in place but he doesn't comment.

While the next band is setting up, Dante and Kaos lead me toward the VIP section. I figure we'll head around it any second now, opting for the bleachers in the field, but no, it seems like Kaos is heading straight for it. As much as I'd love to have bought a VIP ticket, Ash and I couldn't afford it. They were triple the regular admission. A burst of giddiness flutters through me. Are we about to hop the entrance? Because I am so down. I don't voice my thoughts though and go with the flow.

Much to my disappointment, nothing nefarious happens. We literally walk right past the bouncer who takes one look at Kaos and Dante and doesn't even bat an eyelash at me. Where were they when Skylar and I tried to sneak into a concert and got caught? We ended up sitting outside the building and listening to the heavy music anyway.

We hop into the seats at one of the tall tables, giving me an unobstructed view of the stage.

A server comes rushing over. He's a squirrely looking guy, with long hair tied back into a bun at the nape of his neck. He barely looks old enough to serve. Kaos takes the liberty to order for everyone, but I stop the server before he can leave.

"A water for me instead, please."

His attention flickers over to Kaos who nods and then the server scurries off. What the heck? "Can I not order for myself?"

Dante chuckles. "Of course, you can, Angel. I think he was just nervous."

"Do you not drink?" Kaos inquires.

I shake my head no, not elaborating further.

Talk about a sore subject. My uncle was a raging alcoholic in addition to being a shitty human being all around. His beatings were always worse when he was three sheets to the wind.

Not to mention, it tastes horrendous and the feeling it gives you is only temporary, anyway. When the high is gone, you still have to face the music.

One of his eyebrows raises, but he doesn't question it further, likely sensing my reluctance to talk about the situation. "I'll be sure to ask before ordering next time."

Next time, eh?

The three of us sit in companionable silence, savoring the music until the server comes bustling back a few minutes later with one of those huge round serving trays—the ones you carry on your shoulder. He stumbles and I'm a hundred percent certain all that delicious-looking food is going to end up on the ground, but he manages to right himself at the last second.

"Nice catch," I say as he sits the mound of food on the table. "There's a lot of people that say serving isn't a real job, but don't listen to them." He doesn't make eye contact with me and scurries off before anything else can be said. I frown. What a strange kid.

Dante glances over at me. "I take it you're a server, then?"

"Well, I was until I got fired yesterday."

Kaos picks up a giant smoked turkey leg off a plate, watching me with those sharp eyes of his. "What will you do now?" he ask, but I'm too busy scoping out the food to really hear him.

The platter of cheese fries sitting in front of me makes my

mouth water as the delicious scent of gooey goodness wafts into my nostrils. My stomach rumbles loudly, reminding me that I haven't eaten yet today. Hopefully, they don't mind me digging in. There are the usual fair-type foods, but my eyes keep going back to the fries. Is that chili?

Sold.

I unravel one of the metal forks from a biodegradable paper napkin which makes me happy. At least someone is doing something to help save the turtles.

Immediately, I dive into the cheese fries, groaning when the saltiness hits my taste buds then I remember Kaos asked me a question. "Um..." I pause around a mouthful of food. What *will* I do now?

A friend from high school called me this morning wanting to confirm the rumors. Apparently, the man I upset has been spreading the word around town that I'm a menace to society. Exactly what I need.

"I have no idea. I haven't really thought that far ahead," I respond, but that's a lie. I've stressed about it all day. However, there's no need to spill all my burdens on them, considering I've known them all of a few hours.

As I shovel another fork full into my mouth I ask myself why haven't I eaten today? Oh, right. Too busy working on my car and getting ready for the concert. Not to mention there's barely any food left in our refrigerator. This week's paycheck was going to pay for groceries. When the silence drags on, I glance up and find Dante staring at me so intently —or my mouth, rather—with wide eyes.

I grimace. "What? Do I have something on my face?" I didn't think I was being that messy but maybe I was. I wipe my face with my napkin to be sure.

"There's nothing on your face, Angel. But those noises you were making sure were heavenly," Dante murmurs, his voice low.

"In my defense, I haven't eaten today."

He waves me off. "Don't be embarrassed. We like a girl that can eat."

"Good, because I could definitely eat my weight in chili cheese fries."

Kaos motions toward me with his fork. "What were you doing at the lake?"

I shrug. "That's my spot, and it's peaceful there. Sometimes I need to clear my head from all the clutter. It's been a rough couple of days."

He nods. "I can see that. We were only there for a few hours and it was quite serene."

"What about you? Why venture into the woods?"

"We heard it was the only fun thing to do around here," he says.

"Yeah, and whoever said that right. This town is a freaking bore."

"True, but we enjoy the outdoors," Kaos continues.

Men after my own heart. When you grow up poor and in the country, the outdoors become your best friend. The possibilities are endless if you have an imagination. I'd rather spend a day in a cabin in the woods over the beach any day.

Dante reaches over to snatch one of my fries from my red-checkered boat and I smack his hand away, making him accidentally drop the fry on the table.

"Are you trying to lose a hand?" I snap, incredulity tingeing my tone. Nobody touches my food. Nobody. "And look, you wasted a perfectly good french fry!"

He extends a hand to snag another one but promptly snatches his hand back when I almost stab him with my fork. He dares to chuckle at me. I make sure to give him my best stabby eye.

"Easy now, Angel. I only want a taste." Something about his tone implies he doesn't mean the fries.

I open my mouth to reply when suddenly my left shoulder blade twinges, sending a sharp pain shooting through me that slowly crawls toward my spine. When a quick survey of the area doesn't reveal anything out of the ordinary, I almost turn around and dismiss the feeling as a fluke, but my intuition is never wrong. I may ignore it sometimes, but that always results in something biting me in the ass. That's when I spot a familiar face behind my left shoulder.

Elian. His emerald green eyes seem to glow brighter when they connect with mine, spearing me from across the expanse of tables. He's not alone either. A beautiful girl with long auburn hair and model-worthy legs wraps her tiny arms around his neck and kisses his cheek. A hot pang of possessiveness shoots straight through my heart. *Get a grip, Sadie.* I scold, shoring up my defenses. Who cares if you feel the same tingles around him as you do Kaos and Dante?

Two dicks are enough.

Elian's tattooed fingers grip her chin, as if to remind her who's in charge.

Holy hell, if only that was me. Wait, no. Bad libido! Haven't you learned your lesson with assholes yet?

Elian surprises me by shoving the girl backward. She trips, arms flailing in the air. Her heels get caught in the grass and she falls to the ground, flat on her ass. She recovers surprisingly fast, clambering to her feet then dusting her gorgeous mini dress off. Her heels are worse for wear though, and she takes them off, grimacing when her dainty foot touches the bare ground.

He says something to her that makes her lip curl and her gaze lands on mine, zeroing in like a shark does a fish it's about to devour. Then her eyes flick between the three of us, and understanding dawns on me.

It's not only Elian she's after.

I turn my back on them before I do something stupid, like go over there and gouge her eyes out with my fork. Or lick him. I've heard that if you lick something, it becomes yours. Maybe I should go ahead and lick Dante and Kaos. For good measure, of course.

The little fires dancing across my back clue me in that Elian's eyes are on me once again, but I can't find it in me to care. Kaos shoots me an indecipherable look before searching the crowd with those sharp eyes of his. When he sees them, his hands curl into fists and he crushes his drink cup, spilling the alcohol down his fingers.

Trying to expel the tension that's riding the air, I clear my throat but it's pointless. Neither Dante nor Kaos are paying attention. They're too busy glaring at their buddy and the hot chick.

Eventually, Dante's attention returns to the present and he places his hand on my knee under the table. Kaos' eyes narrow before laying his own on my other side. My skin crackles from the intensity of both of them at once and I suck in a gasp.

Dante smiles deviously. "Tell me something, Angel."

I shiver from their combined closeness. If only we were alone...

"Hmm? What is it that you would like to know?" I ask, taking a sip of water to help hide my pure want.

"Everything. I want to know everything about you," he murmurs, twirling a strand of my blonde hair around his finger. He leans in until all I can see are his smokey amber eyes.

Oh hell, this is going to be interesting.

KAOS

. . .

THE MERE SIGHT OF SAVANNAH IS ENOUGH TO MAKE MY HANDS clench around my drink, squashing the flimsy plastic cup, yet I barely feel the liquid gushing over the side. She's a slimy one, that girl, and it will be a frigid day in the Night Goddesses' realm before I ever allow our Circle to bond to her.

We never wanted to be one of the Circles who were forced to bond with someone and I could strangle Elian for even entertaining the notion of her becoming our Link. It's a slap in the Night Goddesses' face, but the Elders have set their sights on us and won't be satisfied until we choose. I've never liked choosing things. I've always been quite the sharer.

Then there's Sadie. I know next to nothing about her. Yet, I can't seem to stop myself from wanting to get closer. To know exactly what makes her tick. I even want to know the mundane things too, like how she likes her coffee, or if she even likes coffee at all. Or if she likes pineapple on her pizza —let's hope not, but for her, I'd consider suffering it.

The instant connection makes me suspicious but in a genuine way. I have a hard time believing it's merely instant attraction—it feels like so much more than that—yet the likelihood of her being our Link is low. I've been itching to connect our palms all night and find out for myself, but that wouldn't be right. She doesn't seem to know who or what she is.

Besides, I'd rather her be the one to initiate contact. My gut is telling me she's the real deal though. I can feel the power rolling off her. Hell, I could sense her energy at the lake. It was weak there, but seems to have grown from yesterday. Excitement flutters through me. I never thought this day would come. None of us did.

Most of the knowledge the Weavers possess on mates and Links is likely in a vault somewhere in the Elders' mansion and that place is locked up tighter than Fort Knox. They hoard knowledge worse than a dragon hoards treasure, and they execute anyone willing to share insight. Greedy pricks.

Dante grins like the devil himself, twirling a piece of her gorgeous blonde hair around his finger. He leans in, and she follows him, entranced. "Tell me something, Angel," he says.

"Hmm. What is it that you would like to know?" she murmurs, looking pensive. She hasn't quite figured out our antics yet, but she will. Though even she can't hide the curiosity behind her eyes as she takes a sip of water.

He lifts a piece of her hair, twirling it around his finger as he says, "Everything. I want to know everything about you."

"Go on then. Ask your questions," she responds, watching him carefully.

"What's your favorite sex position?" he asks, making her eyes widen. "Mine's doggy." The fucker wiggles his eyebrows, acting like he's thrusting his hips into an imaginary ass.

Moons above, this asshole. Something tells me he and Sadie's friend, Ashley, would get along.

Sadie chokes, spluttering on the french fry she shoved into her mouth. Dante reaches over and pats her roughly on the back a few times all the while grinning like the cat that got the canary.

"You okay over there, Angel?"

"No, you asshole," she says between gulping her water down and coughing. "You can't spring a question like that on a girl when she's got her mouth full."

Dante's lips twitch and he fails to hold in his laugh. She swats his arm, but even I admit that she walked right into that one.

So much fire in such a small woman. I'm fucking here for it too. I can't wait to see what that fire does in the bedroom—

and if I have my way, that's where she will end up before the night is over. Now all I can picture is one of us in her ass and the other in her pussy as we tag team her into oblivion. My cock jumps at the thought.

"Well? I'm waiting," Dante says between chuckles.

"Oh, fuck off, Blondie. I wouldn't know," she snaps.

She's a virgin?

Fucking hell. I barely rein in my groan before it escapes my lips.

"Though something tells me I'll find out soon." Her cheeks turn slightly pink before she straightens her spine and levels a glare on both of us. "Before you dickwads get any ideas in your heads, I'm no prude, I've just never done the big she-bang."

"I, for one, am not bothered in the slightest," I say to help ease her ire.

Hell, the mere thought of being the first to claim her has my already hard cock turning into solid steel. At this point, I'm going to need to go yank one out in the bathroom to keep my head on straight.

Dante takes the opportunity while she's distracted to steal one of her fries and when she notices, she looks pissed instead of amused. Uh-oh. He's in trouble.

"Soon, huh? Right now would be perfect," he says.

She cocks one of those perfect blonde brows at him. "And what makes you think I'd fuck you?" She takes her fork and stabs it in between his fingers resting on the table. The metal sinks into the wood.

Yeah, there's no doubt. She's definitely a Weaver.

Dante jolts then gives her a feral smile. He reaches over to grab a fist full of her hair, tilting her head to the side to expose her neck while I stroke a finger down the inside of her thigh, making her shiver with desire. Her face and neck flush beautifully, tingeing that creamy skin perfectly as her pupils dilate and she sucks in a sharp breath.

"That right there, Angel. That right there."

She gulps. "Well, that backfired."

In the best possible way. She looks between us like she's sizing us up. Something tells me she still hasn't worked out that Dante and I like to share. A thrill shoots straight through me.

This will be so much fun.

14

SADIE

We're making our way over to finish the show when my bladder hits me full force, and I decide I need to make a detour to the large concrete structure that houses the restrooms.

"I'll meet you guys back out here in a sec," I call over my shoulder before heading down the path to the women's bathroom. Kaos smiles and Dante winks playfully back at me. Those two, I swear.

When I'm far enough away I blow out a breath between my teeth. I did not expect the night to go like this. I figured Ash and I would rock out to some badass music, she'd meet a guy, have a quickie in his car, and then we'd go home. I never expected these two intriguing men to hit me out of nowhere, but a small part of me hoped to see them again after meeting them at the lake.

Reaching the door to the bathroom, I frown in confusion. Seems there's no one around. Strange considering the line for the women's side is usually a mile long. Something feels *off* but I can't seem to put my finger on what, though my intuition is crawling with unease.

Shaking my nerves off because I really need to go, I step inside, cautiously avoiding a suspicious-looking wad of toilet paper with an eye roll. My nose crinkles as I side-eye the three empty condom wrappers on the floor. Gods, I hate my fellow humans sometimes. They're disgusting.

Maybe I made a mistake, I think, stepping outside to double-check the sign on the door. I usually triple-check the sign before I ever step foot inside. To my surprise, *Ladies* is indeed written on the sticker slapped across the grungy door. There's so much graffiti on it I'm not sure what the original paint color is.

I debate my options for a moment, but there's no choice. I hastily dash into the first empty stall and do that thing where you straddle the toilet and not actually touch it. You know what I mean, the public restroom squat.

Squattle?

Straddle?

Squat—Whatever. The emptiness is starting to give me the heebie-jeebies.

When I finish and wash my hands, I realize the paper towel dispenser is empty and there's not a single hand dryer in sight. Ugh. There's nothing worse than walking out of a bathroom with wet hands. Guess my shorts will have to do.

I suck in a sharp gasp as chills suddenly explode up my spine, alerting me danger is nearby. The intensity almost brings me to my knees.

A pair of hands wrap around me from behind, and Ben's rules pop into my head. *Rule number three: Never let them get their arms around you. If you do, you're toast.* I thrust my elbow into their sternum, satisfied when I hear a grunt.

Unfortunately, their hold doesn't ease even as I wriggle and writhe, straining to break free. It's like there are two iron bars around me, trapping me against them. When my attacker speaks, shock ripples through me. "How nice of you to join us tonight, Mercedes."

Gods, I'm so stupid. Of course, they're going to try something tonight. I should've known Kaos' warning wouldn't be enough.

"So unaware of what lurks around you. And such power. Where did it come from? You've been a non until today. Hell, you were a non a few days ago."

Confusion ripples through me and my brow furrows. What the hell is a non? I raise my eyes to meet his through the mirror, staring unflinchingly into his black bottomless eyes which confirms what I already know.

This isn't a random attacker. Nor is it a random attack.

"Now, you're going to be a good little thing for us, aren't you?" he asks, voice dripping with cocky arrogance.

Absolutely fucking not.

"Fuck you, Ben." My fingernails rake down his arm, likely drawing blood, but I don't care. He grunts but still doesn't let me go.

I'm so going to make him regret this, that much is certain, because when I'm able to get my hands on him, I'm going to strangle the life out of him. For now, I need to get myself out of this corner.

I make the split-second decision to kick my leg up toward his groin, hoping to catch him off guard. He expects it, catching my leg in between his thighs. I throw my elbow back into his face, but he's too fast, inhumanly fast. Although, this time he needs to let go of me to dodge and I make a run for it.

Ben is little more than a blur of movement as he slams me into the wall with enough force to steal the air from my lungs. My head smacks against the concrete hard enough I see stars.

His fingers wrap around my throat, cutting off my air

supply. After a minute, my vision starts to go dark and he must sense it too. He drops his hand from my neck to grab my wrists, pinning them above my head. I cough and wheeze, desperately trying to pull air back into my lungs, but it's painful and ragged.

"Oh no, baby, there will be no passing out on us." A different voice, one that makes my blood turn to ice in my veins. I stare into a pair of perfect blue eyes. So it wasn't Ben who slammed me into the wall. Fuck, this is so much worse.

"I want you awake while I bond you to this Circle," Tyler says before he cracks me across the cheek so sharply my mouth fills with blood.

"What the hell is a Circle?" I demand, then add, "Why are you doing this?" Maybe I can keep the idiot talking long enough to get a handle on my switchblade. The problem is both of my wrists are bound by his hands.

Tyler smirks at me, so I spit in his face, watching with sick satisfaction as it drips down his nose and onto his shirt. He stares at me incredulously before he cracks me across the cheek again. It hurts, it hurts so fucking bad, yet I bear the pain without a sound. There's no way I'm giving him anything to get off on. He thrives on others' pain.

He leans in and his foul breath assaults my nostrils. "You'll pay for that." But I'm no longer listening because all I can smell is whiskey— my one weakness—the scent wrapping around me in a dark embrace.

"Ben, grab the dagger. We're doing this now. She's too feisty," he calls out when I manage to get a knee up and kick him in the shin. "Such a fighter, aren't you? I bet you didn't expect this." He continues talking, but I can't focus.

My mind sways, jerking me back to the past as my current reality mixes with the memories of my childhood.

The air is thick with Mickey's tainted alcoholic breath. The scent of Jack Daniels seems to leak straight from his pores. Some-

98 | MARKED BY NIGHT

how, the man always seems to have an endless supply, despite the fact we're dirt poor.

Mickey paces across the tiny trailer while he takes another swig straight from the bottle. He never comes home before dark, but of course, this particular night he chooses to come back early. The night Skylar went to pinch some food from the grocery store, leaving me alone with him. My brother is going to be furious when he returns.

"You are fucking useless!" he screams, spittle flying out of his mouth.

With malice in his eyes, he throws the empty whiskey bottle at the wall inches above my head. The glass shatters into a million pieces and the shards rain down on me, slicing open my skin. I barely register the pain. I know better than to react. A tiny drop of whiskey hits my cheek, mingling with the silent tears streaming down my face. He throws something else, but I also know better than to move. It'll only get worse if I do.

Mickey stumbles over to the liquor cabinet and rips a new bottle off the shelf. He unscrews the cap and takes a long gulp before returning his attention to me. Then he lights up a cigarette with his other hand, and the smoke mingles in the air. "I should've killed you when I had the chance." He blows out a breath in my face before staggering into his room and finally leaving me alone for the night. His words no longer faze me. Sometimes I wish he would've, too.

Why? Why me? I cry out to the universe, the Gods, anyone who will listen.

Unsurprisingly, no one answers my cries. Or cares.

The glint of a dagger coming my way is enough to snap me out of my wretched thoughts. This isn't my uncle. This is Tyler and Ben, and I'm going to make them pay.

Something inside of me snaps as I watch Ben pull a leather-bound book from a backpack and stalk toward me. Somehow, I know if I let them finish this, whatever this is, I'll never be the same and that's not going to happen. I let the rage simmering in my bones flow through me, let it fill the cracks within my soul.

While Tyler is busy watching Ben, I react, thrusting my knee up to catch him in his junk. He yelps, letting go of me to nurse his balls but I don't stop there. I punch him square in the nose, making sure to tuck my thumb in as I follow through. The cartilage breaks under my knuckles with a sickening crack.

Tyler curses, forgetting about his crotch as the fresh pain of his broken nose registers. Blood floods down it freely. He sniffles a few times before looking back at me with all the hatred one can muster in his baby blue eyes. So deceiving. Those eyes should belong to an angel, not a devil. It only amps up the hatred stirring inside of me.

A force hits me from the side as I'm stalking toward him again, throwing me off balance. Before we hit the ground, I shift my weight to make sure I end up on top and I land on Ben's chest. He bucks, but I lock my thighs around his torso and hold on for dear life as I wrap my hands around his neck and squeeze until his face starts to turn purple.

Tyler grabs a hold of my left arm and jerks me from the ground, yanking my hand behind my back. A loud pop reaches my ears as my shoulder pops out of the socket and I barely hold in my anguished scream. Luckily, the adrenaline pumping through my veins is enough to keep the pain at bay for now, but I know I'll be hurting later.

What did I ever do to warrant this? I want to scream, but I hold it in because I already know the answer. Nothing. Men like this will always want what they can't have, and even resent you for not giving in to their sick demands.

Well, fuck them. If I'm going down, I'm taking Ben and Tyler with me.

As discreetly as possible, I slip my switchblade from my

pocket with my only working hand, and flick out the blade, making sure to keep it hidden while Tyler is distracted by his friend.

Ben coughs as he draws in air to his empty lungs and rises off the ground, rubbing his throat. "You fucking bitch. I'm going to make sure you regret that," he snarls.

I smile ferally at him, making his brow dip in confusion. Blood drips from my mouth and onto my chin, but I don't care. "You're going to be the one regretting this. You'll rue the day you ever decided to fuck with Sadie Sinclair. Today is your reckoning, Benjamin." I launch my switchblade at him and it sails end over end in the air, gliding straight toward my target. I've practiced this move more than once.

His eyes widen, but it's too late, and it sinks into his chest. He freezes, making a gurgling choking sound as his fingers reach for his heart. Blood blooms across his shirt and drips to the concrete. One drop after the other until it turns into a steady stream that I know there's no stopping. He crashes to his knees and promptly falls over. He doesn't move anymore after that.

Tyler lets loose a pained grunt and the pressure on my shoulder blade eases as he's forced to let go of me. Bewildered, my eyes meet downright murderous ones. I suppress a shiver at their fiery intensity. *Dante.*

Gone is the easy-going man from earlier. There is no trace of humor left in his eyes—now the fires of hell dance within them, ready to burn the entire fucking world down for me.

He looks like a Godsdamn avenging angel of death, complete with a halo of dusty blond hair as a flame appears in his hand. Distantly, I know that this should be impossible. Yet, my eyes aren't playing tricks on me which means they're different. Like me.

Relief surges through me. I've never been so happy to see someone in all my life. Their darkness calls to mine after all.

"We'll take it from here, Angel," Dante says, flicking his wrist making a huge burst of fire fly toward Tyler. Dante flicks his hand again and the fire splits, encasing Tyler's torso in a perfect ring which prevents him from moving unless he wants to get burnt to a crisp. The asshole is smart enough not to move, much to my disappointment. What a shame.

Tyler mouths something and throws his hand up at Dante, which makes Dante's hair blow slightly. Tyler's eyes widen in shock before quickly morphing into fear when nothing else happens. Their silent standoff fizzles and crackles throughout the air.

Dante smiles and as soon as he lets the ring of fire drop, Tyler takes off down the hall. He doesn't get far before Dante is on him. Dante seems to morph with the air as he crosses the length between them in a split second, flinging Tyler like a rag doll down the hallway. Tyler's face skids across the floor before smacking into the wall with a sickening crunch.

If Dante is an avenging angel of death, then Kaos is the raging storm, seconds before it destroys everything in its wake. In two long strides, he's at my side and he folds me into his arms. Which does nothing to help my injured shoulder.

I flinch, drawing Kaos' attention to my injuries. He takes in the damage and without a second thought, snaps my shoulder back into place. This time there's no stopping the cry that bursts from my lips, but instantly it feels a lot better than before.

"You're fucking amazing, Sadie. I'm so proud of you for taking Ben down on your own," he tells me.

"I don't need you to fucking baby me," I snap, but feel guilty. I shouldn't take this out on them. "I'm sorry, but

Dante did totally ruin my moment to shine," I quip, trying to lighten the moment again.

He chuckles. "We've got you. Let us take care of you, Little Flame."

His words melt my heart a little and I step back into his embrace. "Fine, but for the record, I don't need anyone to take care of me. I'm allowing it."

After Dante's finished tying Tyler's arms and feet together, he's at my side seconds later, whispering sweet nothings in my ear. I let his smoky scent and Kaos' leathery one wrap around me until it's all that's left.

It's in this exact moment I realize I don't want to let these strangers go.

15

DANTE

Savannah saunters toward us outside the women's restroom with an exaggerated sway to her hips that does absolutely nothing for me. If anything, my dick shrivels at the sight. She looks like a demon with the blood-red dress she's wearing. All she's missing are the horns.

Do you think she's here to start trouble? Kaos projects into my mind.

Why else would she be here? I reply sarcastically.

The snake herself splays her palm across my chest, leaning in to whisper about how dreamy I look tonight or something, but I can't focus on her. Sadie should be returning any minute. She's been in there for quite a while now.

Speaking of Sadie, I wish I could read auras like Elian. I'm sure it would prove she's our Link and we'd know for certain if she's going to be sticking around.

Apparently, my lack of attention makes Savannah angry because she screams—like full-on toddler temper tantrum screams—complete with stomping her foot like one too. The penetrating sound makes my teeth grind together. People always say nails on a chalkboard is the worst sound imaginable, but this is so much worse. She sounds like a banshee had a baby with a bobcat. Not to mention, it draws everyone in the vicinity's attention.

"What the fuck are you doing, Savannah?"

The screaming instantly stops when my eyes meet her murky brown ones. "Much better," she says, in a voice I'm sure is supposed to be sultry but only puts me on edge. "Now that I have your full attention, I'd like to discuss some Weaver business."

My patience with her is practically nonexistent. "What about it?"

She attempts to rub her tiny tits against my chest but I back away. Her smile falters as she clears her throat. "The Elders want us to proceed with the bonding as soon as possible if I'm to become your Circle's Link."

Her words shock the hell out of me. Of course, they do. The meddling bastards. The thought alone is enough to make my heart drop to the pit of my stomach and turn my mouth dry. But it's no surprise they lied about giving us the option to choose. I'm sure they've had Savannah lined up from the very beginning.

"Absolutely not," I say, venom dripping from every syllable. "We still have a month."

"You realize I'm the most powerful female Weaver around, right? I literally have six other Circle's lined up ready to go, but I chose yours."

I roll my eyes. Like that's supposed to convince us.

"The little whore who's been sniffing around you all night will no longer be of consequence soon."

I study the glee reflected in her eyes. She's done something, but I'm not sure what.

My spine stiffens, but I make sure not to display any outward signs. She's a shark and they can sniff blood in the water from miles away. There is no way I'm giving her any ammo to use against us, or Sadie.

Calm down, Dante. Don't let the anger consume you.

"What have you done?" Kaos demands, tension riding his body, and every word he speaks.

"Oh, nothing." Savannah's eyes flash dangerously before she suppresses it, pasting a brilliant smile across her face, but I'm no fool. I caught the darkness lurking beneath.

When we don't speak, she folds her arms over her chest and sighs. "Why are we even still talking about her? You should be worried about your Link instead of some lowly bitch who doesn't matter in the slightest. Her power is nothing compared to mine."

"You'll never be our Link as long as I have a say, Savannah."

"Watch yourself, Dante," she says, leaning in close to whisper against the shell of my ear. "I hold the power to destroy your pretty new toy in my hands. We don't want that, now do we?" She kisses my cheek before sauntering off without another word. Her kiss leaves my skin crawling with unease and I want to erase it, and her from memory.

"Do you think she's bluffing?" I rub my hand across my cheek to wipe away the feeling, but sadly, it does nothing.

"No," he responds simply. "But we will deal with her when the time comes."

A trickle of fear slides under my skin, burrowing inside my chest like a warning—an omen.

Kaos starts rubbing at his chest in the same spot as mine. "Do you feel that?"

The fear hits me full force before he can even finish, like a train slamming into the side of a vehicle left on its tracks. A familiar presence niggles the edges of my mind and I know something is wrong with Sadie. Dammit! We let Savannah distract us enough to let our guard down. Knowing her, that was the point. Savannah is nothing if not conniving, and I will kill her my damn self if something happens to Sadie.

Wait… her energy is in my head and that can only mean one thing.

She's my mate!

Our mate.

There's no denying it now and it would explain Elian's weird behavior earlier. The self-destructive moron already knows. Elation fills me, chipping away at the rotten layers around my heart. I'm so excited that I'm almost giddy, until I round the corner, and then all I can see is red. So much fucking red it bleeds into my vision, fueling the fire within my soul. Fucking hell, this girl is something else.

No one touches our mate without losing a body part. Or their life.

I reach inside myself, feeling for the place in the center of my chest that I know my magic rests. Flames burst to life in my palms as I fling a ball of my fire magic at the man holding Sadie. At the last second, I flick my wrist and it breaks apart, only to come back together, encasing him in a perfect circle. I leave barely an inch of space between him and the flames, likely singeing him, but I don't care. That slimy motherfucker was stupid enough to put his hands on my mate.

A vicious snarl breaks free from my chest. He's a dead man walking. Consequences be damned. He's smart enough to freeze, recognizing if he moves that my magic will incinerate him.

I stalk toward him, flames blazing, and murder on my mind. He sends a gust of air at my flames, but nothing happens. Unfortunately for him, I'm one of the strongest fire Weavers out there, if not *the* strongest. It'll take more than a weak-ass blast to extinguish my magic. Our eyes connect and his widen as mine harden.

Ahh, there it is. Fear.

How? he mouths and tries to run away, but it's futile.

One second, I'm at the end of the hallway and the next I'm using my extra speed to latch on to his arm, tossing him away from Sadie. He sails down the hall, gliding across the pavement before landing in a boneless heap.

The asshole was such a weakling that his power didn't register on my radar until now. Still, I should've known. I'll need to be more careful in the future because our kind has the lowest morals. Thanks to our good-for-nothing Elders reinforcing the sick and twisted behaviors.

We all have our issues—especially me and Elian—but the Elders? They're some of the most corrupt, vile monsters I've ever met in my life. I'm ashamed to be a part of the same society they run. Thank the Goddess Kaos' family was our Circle household. They raised us to believe in the old ways even though they were ridiculed for it.

After we hold Sadie for a while, reassuring ourselves more than her that she's okay, I give Kaos a meaningful look over her head. *I'll have Vinson come to collect them. We'll take them back to the mansion for questioning.*

He scoffs. *If the first one isn't already dead, he'll never make it to the mansion. Look at the puddle.*

One glance at the blood surrounding him shows Kaos is right. Ben is dead, and I feel absolutely no remorse over it. Because the marks and bruises marring Sadie's perfect skin threaten to make my rage spill over and I don't know if I'll ever be able to staunch the flow if that happens.

I'll cast an Illusion to hide the blood and bodies until Vinson comes to clean up.

Kaos nods, nuzzling the side of Sadie's head.

I take a deep breath, inhaling her tangy aroma. I know we need to clean this up, but Sadie is addicting. She smells like a mixture of fire and rain, which shouldn't be possible, but it's not. I'm starting to wonder if anything is truly impossible with her. She has a burning passion within her, yet she's also the sunshine peeking through the trees after a storm has passed.

"There's nothing to worry about, Angel," I tell her. "You're one of us now."

16

SADIE

Dante stays behind to clean up the scene and *take care* of Tyler and Ben. His words, not mine, but I'm silently grateful to him. Kaos even retrieved my switchblade from Ben's body for me, wiped the blood off, and stuck it back into my pocket without a word.

If it weren't for them, there's no telling what Tyler would've done in retaliation. I shudder thinking about it. What if…

No, don't go spiraling down the what if rabbit hole, Sadie. It's not worth it. Yet my brain still wants to replay the event over and over. Like the dagger in Ben's chest and all the blood surrounding him. So much blood. I force all the trauma down in a box like I always do, locking it down tight and throw away the key.

But my thoughts still wander. What about the mysterious fire that encased Tyler's body before Dante threw him across the room.

What the hell was that?

Magic?

I scoff. Impossible. But what other explanation is there?

None. Not any plausible ones anyway. I watched Dante control it, wield it, and dissipate it all with a flick of his wrist.

"What are you guys?" I ask softly.

Kaos' muscles tense. "You truly don't know?"

"Uh, know what?"

His eyes flicker to the crowd then back to me. "We'll explain everything, but not here. There are too many eyes and ears. Can you trust us for the time being?"

Can I truly trust them? My gut says yes—and my gut is never wrong—so, I decide to go with it for now. "As soon as we're out of the public eye, I want answers."

"Fair enough," he says.

One more mystery to add to the ever growing list that is becoming my life. I mean, I've always known I was different, and now I'm that much closer to finding out, it seems like I'm still so far away.

Though, I understand his hesitation. Talking about sensitive things out in the open isn't a smart choice. My brain knows that, but it doesn't stop the itch of curiosity from riding me hard.

Kaos resumes walking, leading me a safe distance away from the crowd. The warmth of his arm around me is the only thing helping keep me tethered to reality. Every few seconds he glances in my direction, a silent apology in his eyes. I know he's refraining from asking if I'm okay again, and I'm glad he doesn't because I am. At least as much as I can be after what happened. I meant what I said.

Then again, a small part of me expected Tyler to try something like this. I ignored everyone's warnings because he was the perfect gentleman when we first started dating, but the monster was always there. Lurking. Tyler is all valiant words and pretty promises that mean absolutely nothing. Some of the things Dante and Kaos have said to me already have meant more than our entire relationship.

Sadly, I remember the day his switch flipped, how his whole persona changed from nice to evil, like it was yesterday. My shift at Harborview ran over and I was late for our anniversary dinner. I knew as soon as I walked into his apartment that something was wrong. The air was stifling and suffocating, but I didn't run.

I should've.

Especially when I saw him sitting at the table set for two staring blankly at the then cold dinner he cooked, with a knife propped up in his hand like he was waiting to dig in. He carefully set it down and the minuscule noise from the metal hitting the table made me flinch. I'll never forget the look on his face.

"You're late," he whispers with barely controlled rage. His voice was like blood, so dark it could be misconstrued as black, tainted, overflowing with malice. The coppery metallic tang coated the air, banking his apartment in violence.

That moment was the metaphorical nail in the coffin of our relationship because that was the first time he allowed me to see the monster lurking beneath that perfect boy-next-door exterior and those deceiving eyes.

Dammit all to hell. I kick the ground, splashing more mud and dirt onto my Chucks, but I don't care. I'm so angry with myself for letting the stench of whiskey on Tyler's breath distract me from kicking his ass sooner. For even dating him in the first place. I should've killed him like I should've killed Mickey Sinclair. My uncle hasn't been in my life for over five years now and yet he still finds ways to haunt me from wherever he is. Whiskey is a weakness I cannot afford moving forward. A fear I need to face someday.

Today is not that day.

A lone bench appears in my line of sight and Kaos leads

me over to it. It's at the perfect angle to watch the festival, but far enough away that we have a sliver of privacy.

"Thank you," I tell him, trying to convey my gratitude for him through words.

Kaos' face softens and he puts an arm around me, pulling me into his chest. It's extremely hard for me not to get choked up again. I'm forced to suck in several sharp breaths to keep the tears from rolling down my cheeks.

I don't cry.

"Tears are a sign of weakness," Mickey used to say. Ugh. I've got to stop letting his words control me, but some behaviors are harder to break than others. A fact I'm acutely aware of.

"I'm sorry we weren't there sooner," Kaos rumbles, guilt swirling in his dark blue eyes as he looks down and pushes a piece of hair out of my eyes as I look up at him. He caresses my cheek with calloused fingers.

"You couldn't have known."

His eyes flash and he looks away, dropping his hand.

"But, I suspected," he says. "We were approached by a woman named Savannah outside the bathroom while you were inside. She has been vying for our attention lately and I think she was sent here to distract us..." He trails off, rubbing a hand over his chin.

My gut churns. "Really?"

Kaos proceeds to explain what happened beforehand. What the fuck? Why can't women uplift other women? It's hard enough in this world as it is without adding petty chick drama.

"Sounds like this Savannah chick has it out for me." I conclude after he's finished, "and she has Elian in her pocket. Pants too, more than likely," I mutter under my breath. Not good. Not good at all. Something tells me I'll have to deal with her sooner or later.

My eyelids flutter closed as I hum along to the music,

letting the beat enter my soul and erode all the bullshit trapped there. My eyes pop open when Kaos joins in with me and then we sing our hearts out. Never mind the lyrics or what they say, it doesn't matter. There's only me and Kaos.

Another piece of hair falls into my eyes and he reaches over to tuck it behind my ear. The warmth that blooms across my face makes me shiver and gooseflesh rises on my arms. My eyes pop open and lift to his.

"Aren't you two cute as fuck. Is there room for one more?" Dante's arms flex as he sticks them in his pocket and rocks on his toes like he's shy, giving me a sideways look with his abs on full display. I don't know him too well yet, but something tells me he doesn't have a shy bone in his body.

Kaos tosses a shirt—seemingly from nowhere—at Dante and it smacks him in the face, catching him totally off guard. Somehow he manages to recover and catches the shirt before it hits the muddy ground, giving Kaos a lazy smirk. He's back to his usual goofy self once more.

A laugh bursts from my lips unbidden, but not unwelcome, which makes Dante's amber eyes swing to mine and his signature smirk turns into a megawatt smile that takes my breath away.

"Put the fucking shirt on, asshole," Kaos barks but his words hold no real heat.

Dante rolls his eyes and turns around, slipping the cotton tee over his head.

Did I mention he has back dimples? Because he does and they look downright lickable. I shake that thought from my brain. For God's sake, I was attacked by my ex-boyfriend and my self-defense trainer not even an hour ago, and here I am lusting after two men I met yesterday.

"Don't do that to yourself," Kaos tells me, pulling my attention to his.

"Huh?"

"I saw your smile fall and your whole demeanor change. I don't have to be a mind reader to know what you've got going on inside that beautiful head of yours. You wear your emotions across your face, my Little Flame," he says, cupping my cheek and pulling my eyes to his. "There's no timeline for grief."

I mull that around in my brain for a moment. My mind is at war with my body. "But isn't it a little crazy or even wrong?"

The corner of his lip turns up into a small sad smile and he shakes his head. "Your mind may be tripping over the fact you've known us no more than a day, but your body recognizes us."

Oh, so they feel it too. This undeniable connection between us. Everything seems to be driving us together. To prove his point, he trails a finger down the side of my jaw. Heat breaks across my skin, pulling a small moan from my lips.

"You need to trust yourself, and your instincts, Sadie." He punctuates his words with a poke to my heart. He's right though. My instincts have never steered me wrong and I need to let them guide me.

Our eyes connect and subconsciously, I know that I'm inching closer to him and that Dante is still standing beside us, but I can't seem to focus on anything other than his plush inviting lips as his gaze dips to my own. Every part of me longs to close the distance, so I do.

Apparently, he has the same idea as me. My breath hitches as my lips meet Kaos' halfway and he instinctively lifts me into his lap. My fingers thread through his dark hair, making him let out a gruff moan that drives me wild, spurring our kiss deeper, into more intimate levels that I'm not ready for. Yet. I pull back slightly, his swirling blues meet mine and I realize I'm so fucking gone.

Without thinking, I reach down with my other hand to link our fingers together, pulling his hand up to his chest to rest it between our bodies. Our lips crash into each other's again as I try to meld his body into mine. The little distance between us is too much. I need him closer.

Somehow, he reads what I need without me having to say anything out loud. He coaxes my mouth open with his skillful tongue and I part with ease, allowing him entry with a soft sigh. It's like we're two star-crossed lovers and not two practical strangers. His tongue brushes against mine as we languidly explore each other's mouths like we have all the time in the world. That's the funny thing about time; you always feel like you have more than you do, but you're never guaranteed tomorrow.

"Grab today by the balls," Skylar always used to say. That's the funny thing about grief too, it hits you out of nowhere. Sometimes years after the fact. I know that I'll never fully be over my brother's death and the only thing that brings me a small amount of comfort is knowing that when I run into Mickey Sinclair the next time, I'm going to kill him.

The thought jolts me from our kiss and I lean back to take a deep breath, trying to come back to earth from kissing the living daylights out of Kaos. That's when our still connected hands start to vibrate. I glance down at them in confusion.

What the hell?

The odd feeling continues to intensify, sending spirals up my arm. My head whips up, eyes locking onto Kaos' and his expression takes my breath away. The look in his eye is awe. He's in awe over me. It's absolutely the most transfixing thing I've ever experienced.

Dante's sharp intake of breath startles me. "Holy shit, it's happening. It's really fucking happening."

My entire body starts to become heavy as little needles poke and prod me all over. All the muscles in my body simultaneously lock, rendering my defenses useless. I try to fight the sensations, but nothing happens. I strain and strain, but my lips don't even move.

Kaos' eyes widen at the same time a flare of black smoke surrounds us, stopping a knife inches from the side of my skull. I catch the tip of the blade in my peripheral before it clatters to the ground, leaving me unharmed.

You're okay, my Little Flame. I've got you, he tells me, yet his mouth doesn't move. So many questions want to tumble out of my mouth, but I'm frozen to the spot, paralyzed.

"Shit. Fuck. Shit!" Dante curses, springing into action. Every muscle in his body tenses as he shifts into action mode. It's kind of freaky how easily his switch flips from carefree dancer to badass fighter.

I watch from my spot on Kaos' lap as he dispatches two men with similar daggers in their hands stalking toward us. Unfortunately, he left our rears open and I sense a shift in the air as someone else rushes toward my exposed back. Before he can strike, the same black energy flares to life, saving us for a second time. Though if I'm guessing, I'd say the shield is coming from Kaos. His eyes are screwed shut in concentration.

Dante manages to end his fight, flicking his fingers to send a bright orange-blue flame over our heads at our attacker. The unsuspecting man grunts and falls to the ground. Dead.

Again I ask, what the hell?

I strain against the sensation plaguing my body, tugging and jerking against the invisible bonds until my jaw finally unlocks. Sadly, it's the only part I'm able to unfreeze. I don't like feeling so helpless.

"What the actual fuck is happening?" I demand, voicing

my thoughts aloud. "And why is no one helping?" I shoot a glare at all the unassuming patrons passing us by, blissfully unaware. "There's a fucking dead guy on the ground for shit's sake."

Kaos' eyes swing to mine. His body doesn't seem to be cooperating either. "It's called an Illusion. They can't see us right now, or else it would cause a panic," he responds distractedly. I can tell from the strain in his eyes that he's wrestling as hard as I am against the paralyzing effects. His leg twitches underneath me and somehow, he manages to stand, but his movements are sluggish.

"We've got to get her out of here!" he calls out to Dante.

Dante nods, rushing over to take me from Kaos who is still struggling to stand. "Let's move. We're surrounded and they're only going to keep coming. We can't keep dropping bodies," he says.

Kaos nods. "Don't worry about me. Get her to the limo."

Dante obliges, carrying me out of the park, whispering words of encouragement into my ears, but it doesn't settle my frayed nerves. If I were smart, I'd run away from them, but I'm too curious for my own good. They know what I am and what's happening to me. I'm dying to know too, and it might *actually* kill me to find out.

17

SADIE

Kaos and Dante work like a well-oiled machine to get me out of the crowd, despite Kaos still being halfway frozen. They take me to a limo that's waiting for us outside of the front gates. Dante slides me in first, arranging me inside before piling in behind me. Kaos climbs in after and slams the door shut.

After a few minutes, I'm able to move my neck and take in my surroundings. There's a freaking crystal chandelier dangling from the ceiling, a fully stocked bar on the left, and it's complete with a super hot Dante and Kaos sitting across from me. Wow, this is fancy.

The rest of the feeling slowly starts to return to my body. The experience is like when your leg falls asleep and you get pins and needles until they finally go away. It's uncomfortable, to say the least. When the tingles finally subside, I rub my aching temples, groaning as I stretch out my tight limbs.

"I think we lost them for now," Kaos says, moving his gaze from the window to mine. "We have a few minutes, at the very least, anyway."

"Lost who? What the hell happened back there? Why do

you have a limo? I thought you drove a Jeep. Why did Kaos and I freeze?" The rapid-fire questions burst from my mouth like a too curious toddler learning about something new for the first time.

Dante shrugs absentmindedly, his knee bouncing a mile a minute as he stares at me in wonder. "To answer your first question, we drive this to events. As for why you froze, well, you and Kaos bonded to each other."

Questions. So many fucking questions.

"Bonded to each other? Say what now?" I pause, rethinking my line of questioning. "You know what, never mind. The first thing I want to know is why the hell those guys were attacking us. I almost took a dagger to the side of my skull, you know!"

Kaos' jaw clenches. "Those were the Elders' Elites, a seasoned group of hunters banded together to act as enforcers. They were watching us. Waiting for the perfect moment to strike."

"Elite? Elders? What are you talking about?" I ask, running my fingers through my thick blonde hair as I try to smooth out the knots to no avail. I'm sure I look like a drowned rat. "Tell me everything. Starting with who the hell you guys are. Moreover, *what* you are."

They share a loaded look and my overworking brain threatens to send me spiraling. At the moment, I can only think of the worst possibilities. Are they in a gang? Is this like... mafia-related? But with magic? Ash and I read a vampire mafia book once, and it was hot as fuck. I don't think I'd be upset if that's the direction this is going in.

Dante smirks at Kaos and places his index finger on his nose. Kaos opens his mouth to protest but it's too late. Dante, I-shit-you-not, shouts, "Nose goes!"

Oh, he did not just 'nose goes' this because he doesn't want to be the one to explain to me what the hell is happening. My nostrils flare. "You two have three seconds to start talking before I—"

Kaos interrupts me with a wave of his hand, expending a long, suffering sigh, as he places his fingers at the bridge of his nose at Dante's antics. Guess this means he's going to be the one to tell me and I'm glad. My mind is spinning and I need answers. Stat.

"We are a race of magic users called Weavers," he starts, pausing to take another breath. "The Elders are our leaders and the Elite are their enforcers. We broke the rules tonight by using our magic out in the open. Although, how they found out so soon, I still don't understand. I'm also assuming they didn't realize you're a Link. You're too precious to kill."

His words shake me to the core, and I startle, almost flying out of my seat. If Dante's strong arms hadn't bounded around my middle and tugged me onto his lap, I probably would've sailed straight out of the limo.

Magic actually exists? I almost scoff, but a little voice in the back of my mind whispers that I have a few unexplained attributes myself. Like advanced healing, strength, and my strange ability to sense danger nearby. Plus Dante's ability to control fire. I saw that with my own eyes. Wait, he said we.

"We? As in you and Kaos are Weavers?" I ask.

"Elian as well," he pauses, seemingly searching for the right words. "You are too, Sadie," he tells me softly like he's ripping a band-aid off the proverbial wound. His expression is guarded, but hopeful.

My heart stutters and I laugh to mask the feeling. "You're saying I'm a magic user too? What, like a witch?"

Dante's lips twitch. "No, Angel. We're Night Weavers. There's no such thing as a witch or wizard. The silly humans are the ones who named us that. And they were wrong about our powers too. Everyone has different skills," he explains. "Our powers are derived from the night and as such, we worship the Night Goddess, the God of Dawn, and the God of Dusk." Ha! I was right about there being more than one God. "Then there are the Light Weavers. They're our total opposites," he continues. "Their powers derive from daylight and they worship the Sun God."

"Weavers," I say it slowly, testing the word on my tongue. Nope, still seems insane. "All right. I'm going to need a second to process that. You still haven't explained why we were paralyzed."

"That's easy," Kaos responds. "Our powers transfer through our palms, so when you held my hand our powers transferred. That's how the bond forms. Sometimes the transfer of magic can render you unable to move. This only happens in the case of true mates."

True mates? I snort. Did I suddenly fall into a shifter book or something?

"Shouldn't this require… I dunno, like sex or something? I mean, in all the books I've ever read, it requires sex!" My voice rises a few octaves. Can you blame me though? This is a lot to throw at a girl.

Dante can't smother the grin that overtakes his face. "Not in this case, I'm afraid." I glare at him. "Though, I wouldn't be opposed."

I roll my eyes. "Fine. I'll entertain the idea for a moment. You said, 'true mates,'" I air quote him. "But that means nothing to me. Are you trying to say you are shifters, too? Like wolves or something?"

Kaos interrupts, cutting off what I'm sure would've been a snarky retort from Dante. "No, Little Flame. Only magic users, but we have mates similarly to the shifters." Mates similarly to the shifters…

"Wait, you mean there really are shifters? I was joking!"

Kaos inclines his head, trying to hold back a smile, but he fails miserably. Asshole.

I let loose a breath. "Well, this night keeps getting better with every revelation." I'm typically rather good at rolling with the punches because life has thrown me a lot over the years, but damn. This is wild. The real question is do I believe them?

A part of me says yes, because I've always felt different. But another part of me rebels against the idea. I narrow my eyes in suspicion and start searching around the limo, expecting Ashton Kutcher to pop out any second and tell me I'm on a new season of *Punk'd!* but nothing happens.

Dante—whose lap I'm currently in—turns my head with his thumb on my chin, forcing me to look at him. He caresses my cheek with his finger, and I lean into his touch. I turn slightly so I can catch Kaos' face too. His eyes—the color of a roaring ocean—lock onto mine as he eyes me and Dante affectionately.

A small part of my brain recognizes that I'm supposed to be Kaos' mate and I'm sitting in his friends' lap with a rapidly hardening outline poking my ass. And it's definitely not one of his crotch knives poking me either.

This is truly insane.

Maybe I really am still stuck in a dream and this is all a figment of my imagination. I pinch my leg since I pinched Dante's earlier instead. The sharp sting confirms that this is indeed real life. Is that a drum I'm hearing or is that my heart beating too fast?

I force myself to start taking deep breaths to keep the panic under control. Inhale. Count to ten. Exhale. I repeat the process over and over until the thundering pulse in my ears even out. This is not the time to get flustered.

When I look up, I find both Kaos and Dante staring at me with such sincerity and vulnerability that it makes my stomach flip-flop. Then the logical part of my brain catches up and I shake my head. "I need proof. I can't…" I take a deep breath. "You can't expect me to take all this at face value."

Kaos nods as if he expected as much and he slips his hand into mine. His calloused fingers rub small circles on my wrist, and the sensation sends tingles down my spine. Suddenly, the limo feels hotter and more closed in, like a sauna, and not an air-conditioned box. I barely resist the urge to fan myself, despite the cool breeze flowing through the vents.

"Don't worry, I'll show you. Are you ready?"

My eyebrows dip in confusion, but I nod. Even though I'm kind of scared of what all this means, I'm more curious than anything. I'd rather know than be left in the dark.

Kaos slowly turns my hand over and I gasp, staring at the inky design in wonder. A black crescent moon now adorns my wrist, next to a large 'K' which I'm assuming stands for Kaos. The curve of the moon rests to the right of the letter and small lines connect them together.

With shaky fingers, I run them over the pattern, sucking in a breath as the black morphs into a glittery silver. "Whoa. It's beautiful," I whisper in awe.

Kaos turns over his arm, showing me a matching design, only my initial is next to his moon instead. Tears spring to my eyes unbidden and I close them, actively holding them back so they don't run down my cheeks.

"What are they? Tattoos?" I ask.

He nods. "The marks only appear like this when the bond is real."

"When a bond is real? Can a bond form without being real?"

He shudders, suddenly looking uncomfortable. "Unfortunately, but I've heard it's excruciating as hell, and the bond never fully settles, always clawing at you underneath the surface."

"That sounds awful," I respond. "Why would you want that? Do people really do it? Form a fake bond, I mean?"

"Sometimes. Some Night Weavers have gotten desperate in the last few years…" He trails off, his gaze seeming far away. I run my fingers over his mark, and it lights up again.

"You keep saying *our* Link. Who does that consist of, exactly?"

Surely, they don't mean *both* of them, right?

A girl can dream though.

"My brothers and I are called your Sworn. Our Circle consists of myself, Kaos, and Elian," Dante replies casually like it's not a big deal.

To him, maybe it's not, but for me? Well, the idea is as terrifying as it is intriguing. I suck with men. Ashley is the one who knows how to deal with them. I lack the same amount of finesse.

"None of us would pressure you into anything you didn't want," Kaos assures me and Dante murmurs his agreement.

"Though something tells me you wouldn't mind, would you?" Dante thrusts his hips into my ass, making me gasp. He's right, I totally wouldn't mind. Holy crap.

Kaos smacks him upside the head. "You can take your time, make up your mind about us at your own pace. Okay?"

I nod my head yes, readjusting myself on Dante's lap, and for extra measure, I wiggle my ass. He groans, but I don't give him time to speak. "My gut says to trust you so I will, but one wrong move from any of you, and I'm gone. Got it?"

"Deal," they say at the same time. Freaky. They're so in sync even though they're almost the total opposite of each other in looks and in personalities.

Pop. Pop. Pop.

My heart leaps to my throat as the loud cracks surprise me. Dante and Kaos shove me down to the floor, cushioning my head to protect me. "What the fuck? Are we getting shot at?"

"Yep," Dante says, making my eyes swing to his. I give him a questioning look, but it's Kaos who answers.

"They're bullets of the magical variety," he explains. "They're likely set to stun instead of kill." Like that makes me feel any better.

"Thankfully, the windows are bulletproof," Dante adds.

Bulletproof? Gods, I've done it this time. Why couldn't I have run into a couple of sexy lawyers? Oh no, in true Sadie fashion I had to run into *Weavers* and uncover a secret world that I'm a part of.

Perfect.

Kaos pulls a gun from his waistband—a Glock if I'm not mistaken—and Dante's hands light up in a blueish orange glow which I now recognize as his magic. I wonder when mine will appear or if it'll even manifest like his.

Dante lifts his head, scoping out the enemies. Bullets pelt the window in rapid succession in the spot where his head appears.

"Fuck. Stay down!" he curses, jerking his head down.

"Yeah, like I'm going to stand up while someone is fucking shooting at us!"

"How did they find us so damn fast again?" Kaos growls, quickly typing out a message on his phone before tucking it away.

Pop. Bang. Crack.

"We have to go. The windows won't last forever," Kaos says, reaching for the button to roll down the partition between us and the driver. "Step on it."

"Wait! We can't leave Ash," I say, fear crawling up my spine. I can't leave her. She's the only family I have left. Kaos hollers to the driver not to stop until we lose them. "No! We have to get her!"

My heart seizes painfully in my chest when they ignore my protests. The limo lurches forward and I panic, scrambling for the door handle opposite where the bullets are coming from. Kaos and Dante finally seem to hear me because both heads whip in my direction and their eyes widen. Dante reaches out to stop me, but it's too late.

The door opens and I tumble out, tucking my body to roll so I'm a harder target. My ribs and neck ache, but I don't let it slow me down. Pain is temporary.

As soon as I slow down enough, I launch off the ground, heading in the direction of the festival. I make sure to step left and right, dodging the trajectory of the bullets. There can't be more than a few shooters, but they're on me in a flash.

I glance over my shoulder to see Dante and Kaos clamber out after me with muttered curses, only they don't roll like me. Instead they land easily on their feet. Assholes.

"Your first instinct is to run *into* the danger when people start shooting at you?" Kaos asks incredulously, catching up to me in a few long strides.

"I told you. I fucking like this one," Dante quips, joining Kaos and I.

For some reason, I expect them to scold me for being an idiot, but they don't. It makes me a tiny bit less mad at them. A ghost of a smile crosses my lips as determination settles in my bones. I dip and weave, avoiding the mayhem as best as I can until we reach the cover of the trees. I'm so thankful that I put on my trusty Converse instead of letting Ash talk me into heels like she wanted.

"Shadows take us," Kaos calls out and suddenly, the night itself seems to overtake us, casting us in a haze of darkness to give us more cover. Now we're not running targets because of my stupid ass.

Hmph. Neat trick.

Balls of light start to join the bullets in all shapes and sizes and it's ten times harder to dodge. My intuition gives me a leg up, alerting me to their presence before they hit me.

The closer we get, the louder the music gets. It's practically deafening at this point. Almost as if something or *someone* is projecting it louder to cover the gunshots. I spot one or two shadows trailing beside in my peripheral with their hands out, ready to attack. *Faster, Sadie.*

"Grab her!" one of the men shouts. "We need her alive."

The spike of adrenaline his words cause help to propel my body onward. I force my feet to go faster and harder than ever, despite the twinges of pain plaguing my body. I refuse to be anybody's prisoner. Hell no.

The finale of the show must be happening soon because little fireworks and balls of fire shoot into the sky, radiating the park in a fiery sheen. The pyrotechnics are astounding, but they're for show. The ones the Weavers are tossing our way are life-threatening. The guests probably think it's a part of the show. Either that or Dante and Kaos are casting another Illusion.

The entrance to the park looms before us, but unfortunately, we lose the cover of the trees as we break into the clearing. Kaos gives me a small, determined smile before pivoting to return fire, covering our tails as we make a mad dash for the gateway where all of the security guards are. Dante's face is scrunched in concentration as he throws ball after ball of orange-blue flames at our assailants, protecting Kaos as he reloads his handgun that looks so out of place next to all the magic flying around us.

A giant black sphere appears in my peripheral and I have mere seconds to react, ducking out of the way. It grazes my cheek as I barely avoid the blow.

Shit. That was close.

Dante howls in pain as an orb of blue magic nicks him on

the calf. The sound of his cry tugs on my heartstrings, but I can't afford to stop and check on him, so I grit my teeth and push forward.

My sole focus is getting to Ash as quickly as possible and then getting the hell out of dodge. She's the only family I have left, and I refuse to leave without her. If something happened to her, I don't think I'd survive. *You can't think like that. Ash is going to be fine. We'll get to her in time.*

"Keep going! I'll be all right." Dante pushes on, albeit with a bit of a limp.

Finally, we cross the threshold of the park, pushing past the protesting security guards, and hop over the turnstiles, narrowly escaping our pursuers. Still, I can't help but peek over my shoulder before we delve into the crowd. The sight of eyes sends shivers down my spine as they watch our movements through the trees. More gunshots ring out and more magic flies as they seem to turn on each other.

Interesting.

"Looks like the Elites only play nice when it benefits them. It's going to be a bloodbath out there with the Light Weavers involved," Kaos says, noting the same thing I did. He discreetly tucks his gun away at the same time Dante shakes his hands out, making their glow disappear as we pass some unsuspecting festival goers and we silently blend into the crowd.

"The blow that hit me wasn't meant to kill, only to maim. Thankfully there wasn't enough juice behind it to take me down which means they want all of us alive," Dante explains and his words send chills through me despite the sweat rolling down my spine from exertion.

People are after us, and I don't even know *why*, but I intend to find out, even if it's the last thing I do. I protect the people I care about.

18

SADIE

Kaos overtakes the lead as we sprint toward the backstage area that's so well hidden, I'd likely never have found it on my own. The bouncer guarding the gate doesn't even spare us a second glance as he lifts the latch, holding his arm out to allow us entry.

The workers scurry around backstage carrying props and checking wires as they frantically try to keep the show running. One crew member even has two guitars strapped to his back as he heads up the stairs leading to the stage. Another lady checks her clipboard feverishly every few seconds, like a nervous tick. I bet she's the scheduler everyone is now mad at.

We search everywhere for the tour bus but it's nowhere to be found, and I'm starting to get super frustrated. We've asked several workers, but they keep walking, muttering vague directions that make no sense, even to Dante and Kaos.

Trust me, the urge to start knocking heads is strong. I finally decide that's the best course of action until I spot a familiar head of blond hair, standing out amongst the sea of black-clad workers. The guitarist for Brandon's band, Wicked Unrest rushes past us like a man on a mission.

"Hey, Danny, wait up!" I call out. He turns, sees me and my entourage, and stops, shooting a confused look over my head.

"I'm looking for my sister, Ashley," I say between breaths. Running for my life has made me realize I need to work on my cardio. "She has brown hair, and she's wearing a short black skirt with a—"

"Oh, you mean that hot groupie chick Brandon's obsessed with for some stupid reason?" he interrupts with a sneer. I nod, biting my tongue to keep from giving him an attitude adjustment. "Yeah, they got on the bus about fifteen minutes ago, but I wouldn't disturb them if I were you."

I shake my head. "Will you take me there? It's an emergency."

He eyes me dubiously like he's expecting me to be some obsessed groupie chick with some sob story about meeting Brandon Luck. One warning rumble from Kaos has him scurrying off.

"Your fucking funeral," he mutters under his breath.

We walk in silence as he leads us through the maze of the backstage area until we reach a large tour bus with their logo printed on the outside. The band's smiling faces stare down at me. It's kind of creepy.

I open my mouth to thank the guitarist when he interrupts me. "Don't say I didn't warn you, baby doll." My mouth snaps closed. What a dick.

Spinning away from him, I wrench open the tour bus door and a loud cry of pleasure reaches my ears, a couple of grunts, and a lot of smacking sounds. I sigh heavily. There are some things you should never have to know about your best friend, and their sex noises are one of them. Top of the list too.

Dante snickers, and I shoot him a look that makes him cover his ears as Ash screams over and over in ecstasy, getting louder with every passing second.

"La, la, la. I hear nothing," he says.

"Smartass," I mutter as the ugly green monster in me threatens to rear her nasty head, but I shove her back down. I'm not ready to lie down and accept this mate thing yet, anyway. I want to get to know them before I go in blind. Life has taught me to be cautious. Fate and I tend to not get along because I make my own damn decisions. "Stay here while I go get her."

The bus itself is super swanky, but I pay it no mind. There's no time. I head toward the direction the sounds are coming from and jerk the master bedroom door open.

Damn, I really should have taken Danny's advice.

Brandon's bare bum is the first sight to greet me as he thrusts into my bestie like a screen door bangs against the frame in a windstorm. Then there's Ash, who is laying on the bed, totally spread eagle under him, her head thrown back with a look of pure bliss across her features. He's slamming into her like his life depends on it until he finishes with a guttural grunt. Gross. I quickly cover my eyes with my hand, but I can't help to peek through my fingers like I'm watching a cheesy horror movie.

I must make a noise though because Brandon turns around. "Is there something I can do for you, darling? As you can see, we're about to start round two."

My eyes bulge, probably making me look like one of those freaky toys you squeeze, and their little googly eyes pop out as his already re-hardening length jumps at me. I kind of feel bad for interrupting their moment, but then I remember I'm being hunted by powerful magical beings and that snaps me out of my guilt.

"Hey, Ash. I hate to cut this short, but shit hit the fan and we need to go. Like *now*," I add for emphasis when she makes no effort to move.

Her hazel eyes flash. "Come on Mer, don't be jealous. This is a once in a lifetime opportunity. You said so yourself!" Uh-oh. She knows I hate that nickname and she only uses it when she's upset with me.

"Ash. I'm freaking serious. I'll explain as soon as we get out of here, but we're sitting ducks right now. We need to go. This is a code *purple*." I use the code name we came up with as kids for an SOS situation.

She startles, finally seeming to realize how serious I am, and shoves Brandon off her. "Shit, did those hotties from earlier hurt you? Do we need to kill them or hide some bodies?" She pauses while pulling her pants up then looks me dead in the eye and says, "Because I know a guy."

"How the fuck do you 'know a guy'?" I air quote, eyeing her warily.

"I mean it's no Benny's pig farm but…" She shrugs, referencing a reverse harem romance by Tate James we both read and loved. Everyone needs someone they can share their favorite book recs with, and Ash is my person. We're firmly team why choose.

"No, Dante and Kaos didn't hurt me."

Her eyes narrow in on my neck where I'm sure I'm already bruised. All the injuries I've sustained tonight are starting to catch up to me, but there's no time to stop now. Besides, I'm no stranger to pain.

"What the hell is going on, Sadie?" Then the lightbulb goes off. "They didn't hurt you, but someone else did?"

"Yeah, Tyler. Ben was in on it too. Now we're being hunted by some big bads and—"

"Oh, hell no, say no more babe," she says, gathering her clothes and hastily throwing them on. "Those bastards are dead men. Where are they?" She whips her cellphone out. "I'll call my guy right fucking now."

"You'll have to get in line, babe. Dante and Kaos went all macho alphahole on them already." I blow out a breath and shoot her a grin. "It was hot as fuck."

Her lip pokes out in a pout. "But I wanted to use my guy."

"Uh, I'm sorry? I think?"

Brandon steps forward, drawing my attention to his totally naked and toned six-pack perfect for ogling. That's going in the spank bank for later. "You're really going to leave?" he asks her.

Ash lets out a breathy moan as she stares at him. "Best lay I've had in a long time," she says.

Hello, bucket of ice cold water, meet my face.

Yep, that's our cue to skedaddle. Ash practically makes me drag her off the bus. "Finally get dicked down by my rock star and there has to be an emergency," she whines as I drag her away from her latest conquest. "Why does the universe hate me?"

We're the same, she and I.

"My number is in your phone, Ashley. Feel free to call me if you ever want to hook up again!" Brandon shouts. I've never seen someone of his stature so enthralled with a normal girl before. It's cute honestly.

Then again, Ash is no normal girl.

As soon as we exit the rolling den of sin, Kaos and Dante's eyes find mine. Both of them have their crotch knives out again and their bodies are tense. Their eyes scan our surroundings every few seconds. It's hot as hell. They're my version of Brandon Luck.

Ash takes one look at them with their knives out and turns toward me with her eyes wide. "What kind of trouble are you in exactly? My guy can help with that too."

"How do you freaking know a guy?" I ask, rubbing my aching temples. Then change my mind on knowing the answer. "You know what. I don't want to know. Yes, as I said, there are people after me. Dante and Kaos have kept me safe from them so far."

"We're going to continue to protect you, Little Flame," Kaos says, his blue eyes intense as he stares me down.

"I can protect myself," I declare, locking eyes with him until he's prowling straight toward me. My mouth goes dry as my core simultaneously clenches. Sadly, Dante sideswipes him, breaking our trance before he can back me into the tour bus and have his way with me because that's exactly the impression I was getting.

Cockblocked by my other mate—my fucking happy go lucky mate at that. What kind of shit is that?

You're being hunted, Sadie. There will be time for hanky panky later, the rational part of my brain reminds me. Now I'm being cockblocked by my own brain.

Seriously, what kind of shit is that?

19

SADIE

Dante and Kaos decide the best course of action is to drive separately and try to throw the Elite and the Light Weavers off. Dante leads us to a well-hidden hole in the fence, but if he knew about it, then I'm sure many people have slipped in and out of here tonight. This little entrance sure would've been nice to know about beforehand. Could've saved myself a lot of money and time.

Is this my life now? I ask myself as we walk through the parking lot. My life has always been a little messed up, but I never expected this level of insanity. This was supposed to be my and Ash's weekend. Our stress-free weekend. We see how well that turned out—*oh shit.* Tingles explode up my spine as my senses come alive letting me know danger is nearby, but where?

There!

The man is nothing but a black blur of motion as he steps out from behind a car, leaping toward Dante. I barely catch the flash of his knife glinting off the moonlight as he reaches for Dante's exposed neck.

"Watch out!" I scream but my shout only makes the whole

situation worse. Dante's head whips in my direction instead of toward the threat aiming at his neck. Luckily, Kaos is on it and deflects the blow before the asshole can reach Dante.

In a blink, Dante regains his focus and is blocking a blow from a second attacker I didn't even sense coming because I'm too focused on protecting them. *Get your head in the game, Sadie. Let's try not to die tonight.*

While my Sworn are busy fighting their cloaked assailants, a third slips from the cars with his gaze trained on me. His emotionless pits-for-eyes make me shiver and I reach into my pocket to pull out my switchblade, flicking out the razor. I'm glad Kaos thought to retrieve it for me because it's deadly sharp, easy to handle and I would've been mad at myself for losing my favorite blade.

"Wow, you weren't kidding about the emergency," Ash stammers, as she watches Dante wield his knife and fire equally. I blink, glancing at my terrified bestie. She's taking this better than I thought she would.

From my peripheral I see another step from the shadows, stepping toward Ash. Hell no. Nobody threatens my family.

"Stay behind me!" I call out, as the third man rushes toward us. I swiftly dispatch him with a quick jab to his jugular from my switchblade.

What the heck? That was way too easy.

His lifeless body slumps to the ground, but I don't have time to make sure he stays there because the second guy is barreling toward Ash.

"Where do they keep coming from?" I dodge the incoming blade of yet another man that slips in from the side, aiming to slit my throat. His moves are sloppy and jerky as if he's a puppet with strings someone is pulling. Whoever these men are, they most certainly aren't trained.

I get a better look at him when he raises his arm and his hood falls. My attacker has no defining features whatsoever.

Same build, height, and clothes as the other three. Actually, now that I'm paying attention, all the men are exact copies from their weapons down to their blank, almost void, facial expressions. Strange.

"Dispatch them quickly. We've got to get a move on!" Kaos says while blocking his own blows from his assailant.

Out of the corner of my eye, I watch as Dante strikes, using that lean dancer's body of his to stab the man directly in the throat. I almost gag, expecting blood to start rushing out but nothing happens. He doesn't even cry out in pain as he poofs out of existence.

"What in the Buffy the Vampire Slayer kind of shit is this?" I exclaim, watching Kaos stab his attacker in the chest and he also poofs into thin air.

No blood. No pain-filled cry. Nothing. If I were a betting woman, which I am, I'd say the one I stabbed earlier is gone as well. Taking a glance behind me, I find that I'm right. Well, that's fucking handy.

Dante and Kaos race over to where I'm holding my own with my attacker, but three against one aren't good odds and he soon disappears like the others.

"They aren't real people," Kaos explains, noting my confusion. "They're projections, but that also means someone powerful is trying to kill us. The level of magic needed for a spell like that alone is astronomical."

"We need to hurry," Dante agrees, ushering me onwards.

I don't have to be told twice. Neither does Ash, and we double our pace to the parking lot. There's no way I'm dying tonight. Nope. Eventually, these bastards will pay for messing with me.

When I point to the location of where my car is, Kaos scrubs a hand down his face. "That's literally right out in the open."

"Excuse me for not realizing I would need to park in a better area."

"It's okay," he says, gentler this time. "We're going to get you to your car. Dante is going to take the limo and Elian and I are going to take our backup vehicle to try and throw them off."

The air around us crackles and someone unexpectedly pops out of a cloud of black smoke in front of me. I jump and let out a little screech until Dante wraps his hand around my mouth and shushes me. His warm breath fans my neck.

"Shh, it's Elian," he says with a chuckle.

"Ugh, give a girl a warning next time! I thought you were another bad guy." Then a thought occurs to me and I point my switchblade at him, flicking the blade down with my finger. "Actually, how do I know you're not?"

Dante snorts at my question, giving me a placating look. "Don't worry about him right now, Angel. We'll protect you from him."

"Trust me, it's not me you'll have to protect."

"That I'd love to see," Elian responds, delight sparking in his eyes at the challenge which sends a zing straight to my clit. Oh, boy. How I'm looking forward to the day I finally kick his ass.

Now that I'm paying attention, I don't know how I didn't recognize his aura sooner. Elian oozes heartache and destruction. Quite the potent poison if you ask me.

When we reach my car, I see Elian's lip curl as he eyes my car in disgust like he's never seen such an atrocity before. "This is what you drive?" He glares at me when I nod like it's my fault I have a minimum wage job and can't afford a better vehicle.

"Not everyone is dealt the wealth card, asshole."

He ignores me. "This is a terrible idea. That bucket of rust is likely to break down before she makes it a mile down the road."

I shush him before my car overhears. "He's a little beat up, but he still runs," I defend, patting my car reassuringly, as if I can protect it from Elian's judgmental stare. "Most of the time," I add under my breath.

He scoffs. "It should have stayed in the nineties where it belongs."

Kaos, Gods love his perceptiveness, readily intervenes before I can give Elian a piece of my freaking mind. "Dante will follow behind you in the limo. You're going to go home and get your essentials while Elian and I grab the other vehicles."

"Wait, shouldn't you come with me too?"

"No, they're going to be on the lookout for the limo and won't be expecting your car. Dante is the one who needs to do it because he's not bonded with you yet."

I want to ask *why* that's the case but there's no time. Kaos is kissing me on the cheek and racing off into the night as the shadows surround him protectively. For some reason, my gut trusts him.

I hear Skylar's voice in my head. *Trust your instincts. Because if you can't trust those, you'll never make it in this world.* He's right. I've got to start trusting myself more or I'll never survive. There's no time like the present, right?

After I rattle off our address to Dante and hop inside my car, I take a moment to collect myself as Ash gets in the passenger seat. When my moment is over, I grit my teeth and turn the key in the ignition, praying it starts. The engine takes a second to turn over, but when it does, I slam on the gas and fly out of the park like a bat out of hell.

"Are you finally going to explain what the hell is going on?" Ash asks, her voice rising toward the end.

I repeat everything that's happened. I tell her about the

Elite and the Weavers. I tell her about Tyler and Ben. I even explain what happened with Kaos and she only nods, letting me get it all out. When I finish and she doesn't instantly respond, my thoughts start to wander.

Won't they be able to find me as easily at our duplex?

Are we being followed now?

My hands clench on the steering wheel as I try to keep my breathing even. *Focus on something else.* I start to make a mental checklist, so I know exactly where to look when we get home. My go-bag is under my bed, packed and ready for a moment's notice. The money Reed gave me—shit, don't think about him right now—is in the coffee can in the kitchen. *You're prepared for incidents like this, Sadie.*

Well, not exactly like this, because *bonding* to a smoking hot stranger who has *magic* and getting sucked into their *magical world*, was definitely not on my freaking bingo card this year. Apocalypse was though, so my emergency bag is locked and loaded.

Yeah, yeah, I know. Preppers are crazy, but hey? Who is kind of prepared right now? Me. That's who.

"That's a heavy load," Ash eventually says after mulling it over, pulling me from my thoughts.

"You're telling me," I say.

She quirks a brown brow in my direction, telling me she's as skeptical as I am. "Do you believe them?"

With a sigh, I hold out my wrist to show her the design now adorning the smooth skin there. I've always wanted tattoos, but never could afford them.

She gasps. "Shit, babe. That's like... *permanent?*"

"Yeah, it is," I say.

"At least it's gorgeous," she responds and I give a noncommittal shrug even though she's right. Kaos' mark is stunning. I'm too stubborn to admit it right now.

"Oh, I skipped the best part," I say with mock cheer. "They're all my mates. Plural. *All of them.*"

Her mouth pops open and she sits there gaping like a fish for a moment before recovering. "You lucky bitch!" she says, smacking my shoulder. "I totally would have gone with them instead if it meant I got to be in their sinfully salacious sandwich!"

"Sandwich? More like Big Mac, babe."

If her eyes get any bigger, they're going to pop out of her head. "You mean all three of them? Including Mr. Tall, Dark, and Leather Jacket that showed up at the end?"

I snort at her accurate description of Elian, then nod.

"Jesus, Sadie! That's one for each hole!"

Now it's my turn to gape at her. "You did not say that."

Oh, but she did. Her maniacal giggles confirm it. Have I also mentioned my bestie is a little crude?

"What? It's true," she says simply, like that explains everything.

Now all I can picture is the three of them in bed with me. Elian would take my ass because he's an asshole, therefore it fits. Dante would take my pussy because he's greedy and Kaos would take my mouth since he's the nice guy of the bunch. Well, nice-ish guy. Something tells me there's some steel underneath that watchful exterior.

"I still don't believe it. I mean, they can't mean all of them, right?" I scoff. "That's like reverse harem book-worthy shit and my life is far from a fairy tale."

She snorts. "Babe, I hate to break it to you, but you found out magic is real. You got the validation you've been searching for years about your extra abilities. Your life is most definitely turning into a fantasy novel."

She's not wrong though.

20

DANTE

Sadie rattles off her address and I commit it to memory as I race over to the limo that Vinson pulled around for me. The windows look a little worse for wear but hopefully it holds until we can get back to the Estate, and behind Elian's safety wards.

"C'mon man. We need to catch up with Sadie," I tell my driver, encouraging him to go faster. Vinson is the best driver we have, and he's an okay dude for a shifter.

The guys and I don't hold the same prejudice against them as most of the Weavers, but we still need to keep up appearances lest we find ourselves missing a limb or two for disobeying the Elders. Although, with what we pulled to get out of the concert safely... and with their Elites after us, we may lose a limb after all.

Vinson complies, effortlessly sliding the huge limo onto the freeway. We get strange looks from other cars as we pass by them, but I don't exactly care what they think. I can't afford to spend the energy to cast an Illusion in case I need it for something else.

For a moment, I think we might get off scot-free, but

that doesn't happen. Fate is a fickle bitch sometimes. An SUV comes flying up behind us. Vinson is forced to slam on the gas pedal to avoid being rear-ended. The limo lurches, barely evading the bull bar adorning the front bumper. I curse, smacking the dash in my frustration.

Taking a deep breath to extinguish my ire, I use that frustration and channel it into magic. My hands heat as the fire rushes to them and I exhale. There's nothing better, nothing more addicting than using my fire magic.

I roll down the window, tossing a few orbs out the side, casting an Illusion at the same time to disguise them as trash. I'd rather the humans think I'm littering than expose the entire magical community. That would most definitely get us killed.

Unfortunately, the SUV evades my fire, doubling down on their efforts to hit us. The one behind suddenly veers around the first and then they spread out. One swerves into the far lane and the other onto the shoulder. It doesn't take a genius to figure out their plan.

"They're going to run us off the road," I warn.

Vinson slams on the breaks and the SUVs go sailing past us.

"Nice thinking," I tell him, nodding my approval. He glances over at me and I flash him a daring smile.

Vinson hits the gas again and we race down the highway at breakneck speeds, giving me an adrenaline high. The Blazers make a U-turn in the median and make their way back toward us, spraying bullets and magic across the front windshield. When they reach us again, they go rocketing past us.

At least they didn't hit us head-on.

I watch as they make another U-turn and start gaining on us again.

"They're doubling back," I say, trying to help be Vinson's eyes.

This damn limo is one of the worst ideas I've ever had. Yes, it was my idea. I thought if we arrived in a limo it would make us look important and help us pick up chicks. I snort at the idiocy of that. Little did I know I'd meet my mate tonight and none of that would matter.

Although, the fact that both the Elites and the Light Weavers were able to find us so quickly and efficiently proves what Kaos and I have been guessing for months. We're being watched.

Sadie doesn't know it yet, but she just threw a bomb into our community and people are going to be gunning for her on all sides, and she doesn't know a single thing about us or who she is. Keeping her safe is going to be hell.

And Goddess, that temper she has. All I can imagine is that hot mouth wrapped around my cock as I thread my fingers through her blonde hair and slide into her over and over.

My dick stirs inside my jeans. Really? Now is not the time. For shadow's sake, we're in the middle of a high-speed chase and all I can think about is her flushed cheeks when I whispered in her ear that I'd fuck her earlier. I subtly adjust myself away from my zipper. Boners in jeans are not fun.

Fortunately—or unfortunately, depending on how you look at it—one of the Blazers rams into us again, snapping me out of my lust-filled thoughts.

"Sir! We're about to pass the exit for her duplex. Do you want me to keep going?"

I scrub a hand through my hair, debating my options. We have no choice, but to keep going. We can't exactly lead them straight to her, but it'll be difficult to get back to her now. Hopefully, she can hold her own until I get there.

"Yeah, keep going!"

He slams his foot down on the gas again, shaking the one tailing us. The other one beside us is forced to change lanes to avoid a slow-moving car, giving Vinson time to sail out ahead of both, but it doesn't last long. Two SUVs against this long ass limo are terrible odds.

"We have to do something, sir. They're gaining on us again."

I check the mirror and sure enough, they're both right on our asses again. With another string of curses, I let the Blazer on my side get to the passenger door before I roll my window down and throw a bright blue orb of fire at their tire. This time, my magic sails true, hitting its target. I whoop with my small victory, watching as the driver jerks the wheel and starts spinning out of control.

My plan also backfires.

The rotating vehicle clips our tail end, threatening to send us spinning alongside him. Vinson curses, his hands wrangling the wheel in the direction of our spin as he desperately tries to keep us from flipping.

I send up a silent prayer to the Night Goddess. I can't die before getting to mark my mate, dammit. My entire life, I've looked forward to the moment I'm finally able to meet her. Even if I'd given up hope the last few years. Not to mention Sadie seems perfect for us. I can see her clicking into place, fulfilling a part of our team that's desperately needed.

Thank you, Goddess, I think as Vinson manages to right the limo. When I check the rearview mirror, I'm relieved to find the SUV upside down in the ditch.

One down, one to go.

"We need to end this," I say, my voice hard. Vinson nods and flexes his hands on the steering wheel.

Suddenly, I feel Kaos' presence in my mind. *Dante! Where the fuck are you?* he growls through our mental channel.

Ran into some trouble on the freeway, I respond. *Did you and Elian get there first?*

Please say no.

Yes, and we have bigger problems now.

Fuck.

On my way, I tell him.

Goddess, this night keeps getting worse.

We'll talk about your tardiness in the training room later. Our mate could've got hurt in your absence, Kaos says.

He's right, but I don't have time to argue because the other SUV is pelting us with bullets and magic. He can kick my ass in the training room later. I cut the connection off and refocus on my surroundings. The bullets are rapid-fire in succession. Ah, pulling out the big guns, are they? Oh well, time to wrap this up.

Get ready to meet the Night Goddess, fuckers.

Closing my eyes, I reach inside myself, running my mental fingers across the silver threads of my magic. I follow those threads until I find the big ball at the center and tap into it, letting my magic loose. It starts as one giant orange-blue ball then breaks off into hundreds of small fires.

The second driver opens the door and bails, rolling across the pavement as the SUV explodes, sending shrapnel in every direction. Luckily, no humans are around to get hurt. This stretch of highway is relatively deserted. Still, I disguise the Blazer into the surroundings in case any drive by.

"Hell yeah!" I whoop, patting Vinson on the back. "You did well. I'll talk to the others about increasing your pay." The man deserves a raise after this.

"Thank you, sir. I'd appreciate that."

I clear my throat, trying to make my voice sound businesslike. "I trust you'll dispose of the body in the trunk and bring the live one back to base for questioning after you get rid of the limo?"

"Yes, sir. Go. I've got this," he assures me while not taking his eyes off the road. I don't need to be told twice.

Closing my eyes, I imagine the silvery cords of my magic once more, but this time I picture the threads that connect me to my Circle. When I find the silver thread that connects me to Elian, I tug on his string, borrowing his ability to walk through the shadows. Elian can, and will, yell at me for it afterward, but I don't care. I need get to Sadie and make sure she's okay.

Sadly, it weakens the borrower when we use our other Circle members' magic, but this is an emergency. We only use it in dire situations and I think this classifies as dire.

When I pop back into existence, it's right beside Sadie. She jumps, clutching her chest with one hand and her switchblade with the other. Smart girl. She's always prepared.

"Feeling stabby, are we, Angel?"

"For the love of fuck, you guys have got to stop doing that! I'm going to have to put bells on you or else you might actually get stabbed!"

And I don't doubt she would for a second.

This girl. She's going to give us a run for our money, I already know it. I'm one hundred percent looking forward to it. The Kings take care of our own and, even if she's still fighting it, she's one of us now.

21

SADIE

Something is off. The feeling hits me as soon as I pull off onto the little suburban street that leads to our duplex and all the hair on my body stands on end. My spine stings with a thousand little pinpricks confirming there's trouble nearby.

While I wait for Dante, I circle our block twice and scope out the scene, but nothing out of the ordinary jumps out at me as I make another loop. Yet my internal alarm continues to make my neck and spine ache with dread.

Where the hell is he?

On one hand, I want to take a stand and make sure these jerks know that no one messes with Sadie Sinclair. But on the other, they have magical abilities beyond my comprehension, and I'd be an idiot to fly into this blind.

"I figured he would have pulled in right behind us," Ash says, voicing my thoughts aloud.

Time feels like it's ticking in an invisible hourglass and I can't afford to wait any longer. My intuition is driving me to make a move and every nerve ending in my body feels like a live wire getting ready to snap. Wrenching my car into our assigned space, I sigh. "I want you to stay here. I'm going to run in and grab our stuff. Do you still have your go-bag packed?"

"Forget it. Let's leave. Or wait for Dante to get here, but don't go in alone, babe."

With a sigh, I take my phone out of my pocket and go back to my recent calls. The last call went out to Dante and hopefully, he'll answer. The contact name for himself makes me smirk. *Blondie.*

It rings and rings, and the noise sounds deafening in my ears, rivaling my racing heart. *Come on, come on. Pick up.* The line clicks and the voicemail lady starts talking. Stupid robotic bitch. Then of course my phone beeps signaling it's dead.

I curse. "I have to, Ash. We can't wait any longer and he's not responding. Where is your bag?"

"Under my bed," she pauses, grabbing my hand. "Look, I was going to tell you tomorrow, but I have a thousand dollars saved inside it."

I gape at her. "You have *how* much? Why the hell did you need me to cover your half of rent last month? I had to pull a bunch of doubles! You know how much I hate putting up with that place."

She shrugs like it's no big deal. "I've been working two jobs, plus I wanted that new eyeshadow pallet that came out last month."

My eye twitches, but a flash of light reminds me why we're here.

"We'll circle back to this conversation when we're not in danger from unseen magical forces, missy," I grumble, wagging my finger at her. Taking a deep breath, I look out the window again. "If I'm not out in ten minutes, I want you to get in the driver's seat and get out of here as fast as possible." She starts to protest, but I hold my finger up to stop her. "Don't worry about me, I'll be all right until Dante gets here."

Before she can protest further, I yank open my door and rush toward our duplex. When I reach the front door, I find it slightly ajar. The sight makes my stomach sink to my toes. I know I locked it before we left because I *always* lock it. Which means someone has been here already or is currently in here. Great. Frustration surges through me. How do these people already know who I am, when I didn't even know until a few hours ago?

I don't dwell on it though, instead, I flick open my switchblade and take a moment to calm my nerves by running my fingers over Skylar's necklace. Then I discreetly make my way inside with something unseen urging me onwards like the phantom hands of fate.

Pausing in the doorway, I listen for anything out of the ordinary. There's no sound other than my slightly heavy breathing and the soft pad of my footsteps against the hardwood. Which is odd. Usually, our duplex is filled with noise. Whether it's the coffee machine in the kitchen beeping for water, or the neighbor's yappy little dog barking a few houses down. It's never silent.

Well, guess I'll be using the training Ben taught me after all. How to clear rooms. Thinking about that bastard makes my blood surge, threatening to send the rage I locked down back to the surface. I don't allow it to though, I need to be clearheaded. Pushing that fiasco out of my mind, I quickly scan the entrance and yank open the coat closet door to find it completely empty. Phew.

Now, where should I search first, the kitchen or the bedrooms?

My answer comes a few seconds later when I hear a faint noise from the kitchen. That's exactly my luck, considering in the movies there always seems to be a knife-wielding psycho in the kitchen. Plus, I'm blonde and everyone knows the slashers always prefer the hot blondes. Wonderful.

Good thing you can take on slashers, huh?

With my switchblade poised to strike, I stealthily dash around the entrance, but to my disappointment—I mean relief—there's no one waiting for me to stab them. No masked man wielding a butcher's knife. The noise is the drip coming from our sink. It's leaky and has never been fixed.

I waltz over to open the cabinet above the stove, pushing the half-empty boxes of cereal and crackers out of the way. I'm too short and I'm forced to stand on my tiptoes to reach the old coffee can where I stashed the money from Reed. I pop the top and shove the wad of cash down my bra with a grimace. I hate sweaty boob money as much as the next person, but the stack won't fit in these shorts and I'm not taking any chances.

If things go sideways with my—er, mates... Ash and I will need money to survive. If there's one thing life has taught me, it's to always have a contingency plan.

With meticulous movements, I make my way back to the living room and turn down the hall that leads to the bedrooms. I have every inch of this duplex committed to memory and I know each of the boards that squeak or make noise when you step on them. I dutifully avoid those until I reach the bathroom and grab the handle, nudging it open.

I'm relieved to find there's no one out in the open, but I toss open the shower curtain just in case. I let out a deep breath when there's no scary monster in my shower.

Yes, I have a somewhat irrational fear of someone hiding behind the shower curtain. Can you imagine being midstream and someone pops out of that bad boy?

Yeah, you'd end up with pee everywhere.

Screw that. Check the curtain before you squat. My life motto right there.

Ashley's room is next, and her door is already open. There's nothing out of the ordinary, but I open her closet to be safe. Nothing.

Her go-bag is exactly where she said it was, underneath her bed. Hopefully, she packed enough essentials because who knows what we're doing or where we'll be going from here. As I'm pulling it out from under the bed, the zipper breaks and all her stuff tumbles out, scattering across the floor. I groan and start shoveling it back into her backpack.

Sheesh, she has a lot of stuff packed.

Her words from earlier pop into my head. *"Have you ever thought of leaving here? Leaving town, I mean. Like after the festival?"*

My stomach sinks as I finish putting the last of her stuff away. Was she planning on running away with or without me? A conversation for another day.

I make my way into my room, which is also the last hiding place. A switchblade to the chest will kill anybody though, right? Just need to get to them before they can get to me.

My door springs open, revealing a giant freaking mess. My room is trashed, and all the pages of my precious book collection are ripped to shreds and are scattered everywhere. My clothes are strewn across the room alongside every item in my closet. Guess there's no way I'll be grabbing extra clothes now.

Whoever did it even upended my bed, cutting it open so that the springs are falling out. It looks like a war zone, but unfortunately, that's not the worst part.

Someone strapped our neighbor to a metal chair in the center of the room. They tied her arms behind her back and both of her feet to the chair legs with a rope. Judging by the faint glow surrounding it, I'd say it's not a normal rope either. That thought gives me pause. Is our sweet little neighbor not human?

When she sees me, she starts struggling against her bindings, and her wide ancient eyes meet mine. "Bedi! Are you okay? Who did this to you?"

"Mmergh."

Right she's gagged. Duh.

The first thing I do is cut the gag out of her mouth, but as soon as I do, all the sound rushes back into the house. The onslaught of noise makes me jump and I almost nick Bedi with my switchblade. What the actual hell?

"This isn't supposed to happen," Bedi says, looking around the room frantically. Like something will jump right back out of the shadows and gag her again.

"I'm so sorry, Bedi! I don't know who would do this to you or why."

After I cut both her arms free, she grabs mine with surprising strength for someone her age and rises from her chair. She stares at me so intently I can't look away and a small gasp escapes me when her lavender eyes turn black. Even the whites.

"I do." She lifts the gag off the floor, pointing to a silver symbol in the center of a scrap of cloth, like it's supposed to mean something to me but it doesn't. No, not a scrap—a handkerchief.

"They may want you alive, but they don't care what condition. I need you to leave and never return here." A lead weight settles in my stomach with the finality in her words.

"But I don't understand—"

"Stay with your men," she tells me while shoving the handkerchief into my hands. "Show them this and know they will guide and protect you with their lives. They were made specifically for you, you know."

"I can protect myself," I defend.

"Out of all that—that's what you took away from what I said?" Her eyes narrow when I nod. "Of course you can, but it never hurts to have more people in your corner. You—of all people—should know that."

Her words strike a chord within me. What I wouldn't give to have met the guys when I was younger and have someone to protect me from the shadows back then. Skylar was my only cheerleader, but he was going through as much as I was, if not more, than me.

"I'll send word for you when it's safe to do so. We have much to discuss," she says, backing toward the door.

"Wait! How will I know it's you?"

"You'll know. Trust your instincts. They haven't steered you wrong yet, have they?" Then she's gone. Disappeared into thin air. Poof.

"Yeah, like that's helpful!" I shout into the now empty room.

I suppose that answers my question about whether Bedi is a human or not, but it does make me wonder, what is she?

A sense of urgency snaps me back to reality and I hastily snatch my backpack out from under my nightstand. Somehow they didn't overturn it and my backpack is still there. As I'm walking out, I eye my stash of vibrators spread across the room longingly. Even they were not spared from the wrath of whoever trashed my room. *Maybe the guys will buy me more...*

Checking the time reveals it's been nine minutes since I left Ash. Knowing her, she's probably going out of her mind with worry. When I'm sure that I have everything, I take off running and don't stop until I'm standing next to my car.

Bright headlights assault my vision, making me flinch from the intensity. The sports car glides into the parking space next to us. When the rumbling engine shuts off, the night becomes quiet once more. No one in this neighborhood drives anything that fancy and it's too late to run.

"Who is that?" Ash asks, having hopped out of the car to join me.

I huff, irked she didn't stay in the car as I told her. She's stubborn as a mule sometimes, but I know if there's a fight, she'll back me up no matter what.

"I have no idea. Do you still carry mace?"

"Yep, I've got it right here," she says, pulling the small canister out of her pocket. I don't take my eyes off the blacked-out windows of the fancy sports car.

My entire body tenses when I hear the click of the door opening, and I ready myself for the inevitable. I really should've stretched tonight. Not to mention the adrenaline is slowly wearing off and all my injuries are starting to make themselves known again.

To my utter surprise, Kaos hops out looking like a freaking mess. His eyes are panicked, and his clothes are slightly torn. Those stormy eyes meet mine as he rounds the front of the car.

"There was a bit of a scuffle," he says. "Elian and I handled it."

In two long strides, he reaches me and wraps me in his protective embrace. A feeling of rightness resonates within me as I inhale his tangy masculine scent. I sigh, snuggling into his arms, and resting my head on his hard chest. Every single thread in my entire body vibrates like I'm a damn magic bullet. The vibrator kind, not the Weaver kind. Kaos is alluring, like a magnet and I'm the piece of metal that's attracted to him.

Fate draws us together, him and I.

"Tell me what happened," he demands, holding my face in his large, weathered hands, likely worn from handling weapons his entire life. The thought sends a thrill through me. I'm sure he has much he can teach me.

"I went in to grab our go-bags and I found our neighbor tied up in my room. Speaking of which, I think she might be someone or *something* else entirely." I pause taking a breath. "Before she poofed into thin air, she told me that she'll send for me when it's safe and she told me to stay with my men because they would protect me. Oh, and she gave me this. It was her gag."

I hand him the handkerchief, watching as he runs his hand over the symbol and his eyes crinkle in confusion.

"Do you know what it is?" I ask.

"No, I don't," he responds. "What else happened?"

I bite my lip, debating on telling him about the noise. I decide it's better not to leave anything out. "There was something else. It was strange, but there was no sound in our duplex until I took this out of her mouth then it all came rushing back."

Kaos curses, running a hand over his chin. "It's worse than I thought."

"What is?"

"The Light Weavers can manipulate sound. This was likely the handiwork of their Elites."

"They have Elites too?"

He nods. Perfect.

"Wait," Ash says. "How did you find us? Dante was the only one around when she told him our address. How do we know you didn't have anything to do with this?" She accuses, waving her pepper spray in his face.

Solid accusation. I take a step back, waiting for his answer.

Kaos winces, looking a tiny bit sheepish. "It's the bond. I'm sorry I didn't tell you sooner, Little Flame. I forget how little you know about who you are."

"The bond comes with a built-in tracking device, or what?" I ask, patting my body down like there's going to be a physical tracker on me.

He chuckles. "I'll show you. Close your eyes and focus on your chest."

I do as he says.

"Good, do you feel that?"

I nod, feeling energy swirling inside my chest. The longer I focus on it the more it starts to reveal itself. There in the center is a bright ball of energy and there are little threads of silver trailing off in different directions.

"I see a ball of light," I tell him.

"Now picture where I am and let the threads guide you."

When I do, there's a tug in his direction, like an invisible wire attached from his body to mine. After I reopen my eyes, the silver wire is still there, running from my heart to his.

"I'm totally going to get spoiled with all this fancy Weaver magic." I chuckle. "Speaking of Weavers, where is Dante?"

"Huh? I thought he was here. He didn't go inside with you?" Kaos asks, looking around like he's suddenly seeing the area for the first time.

I smirk. I've managed to distract him. I didn't think that was possible.

"No, I waited twenty minutes, even circled the block three times," I say with a shrug. "Eventually I decided I couldn't wait on him any longer. Something was urging me to go inside."

Kaos growls and the sound sends a zing straight to my lady bits. "That was extremely reckless, Sadie. What the hell were you thinking?"

"I'm not totally defenseless, Kaos. May I remind you that you've seen me in action."

"That may be true, but you don't know how to defend yourself against our kind! What if there had been an ambush inside waiting to take you? Most of them have magic and you don't even have your powers yet."

As much as I hate to admit it, he's right.

"Fine, but I'm no weakling. You'll see that one day."

Dante pops out of the shadows next to us making me jump back, and reach for my switchblade. "For the love of fuck, you guys have got to stop doing that! I'm going to have to put bells on you or else you might actually get stabbed!"

"Feeling stabby, are we, Angel?" He chuckles, nodding his head toward my switchblade. When I roll my eyes, he apologizes. Although, he doesn't look sorry in the slightest.

"Come on, let's head out." I nod and Kaos starts leading me over to his sports car. His eyes flicker over to Ash and he opens his mouth again, stopping us in our tracks. "The human needs to stay here. She'll be safer away from our people."

"Hell no. I'm not going anywhere without 'the human.'" I air quote, jerking my hand out of his.

Ash smirks, giving Kaos a look like *what can you do?*

Kaos runs his fingers through the black tuft of hair on the top of his head. "I'm sorry, Sadie, but we can't allow her to come with us. Our community is very secretive. The fact that she knows what she does now is not going to go over well."

"Respectfully, fuck your community. I'm not going to leave her here to deal with the aftermath that your world has caused by herself." I turn on my heel and stalk toward my car, forgetting the handle is broken until I reach down, yanking on it only to fly back when the handle snaps.

Damn door ruining my dramatic exit.

"You couldn't work for me this one time?" I whisper-scold my car and shake my index finger at it, probably looking like a crazy person.

When I slowly turn back around, I find Dante smirking at me. Amusement dances in his hellfire eyes. Kaos also looks quite entertained with one corner of his lips turned up and an eyebrow quirked. Hmph. Assholes.

"That pesky door gets you every time doesn't it, babe?" Ash jokes.

So much for friend solidarity or whatever. I shrug, leaning against the car like I meant to do that. Fake it til you make it, right?

"What I said stands. Either Ashley comes with us or I leave. We're a package deal. There's no negotiating."

Dante and Kaos stare at each other for a few seconds before Dante shakes his head. "I'll take the fall for it," he offers, making my heart swell with pride.

Reluctantly, Kaos agrees with a sigh. "For my mate, I'd do anything. Even break every damn rule that's in place."

Ash grabs me and throws me into a hug. "Thanks, babe. Love you."

"You don't have to thank me. You already know where I go, you go. That's how it's always been. I'd never leave you, although I feel like we need to chat about our conversation before the concert and your go-bag." I squeeze her tightly before backing away to give her a look.

She nods, her eyes downcast. "Not here, though," she says, looking over at Dante and Kaos. My curiosity piques. What the hell is my best friend hiding?

Kaos opens the passenger side door of the—holy fuck, it's a Maserati.

Did I have a cargasm? I think I had a cargasm.

"How will all of us fit in this tiny thing?" I ask. Considering the fact, it doesn't seem to have much—if any—of a backseat. It's going to be cramped as hell. That's the crappy thing about luxury vehicles. They're not built with practicality in mind.

"Elian is almost here with the Wrangler," Kaos responds.

Ahh, I was wondering what happened to their fancy Jeep.

"Speak of the devil," Dante mutters as someone comes barreling down the residential street on two wheels and maneuvers into the space on the other side of us.

Elian rolls down the window. "Move your asses. They're hot on our trail." He motions for us to climb in the back and I shake my head. Nope, there is no way I am getting in the Jeep with him. I'd rather saw my arm off.

Well, maybe not, but you get the idea.

"Hey Ash, would you be a doll and take one for the team?" I snatch Kaos' hand and drag him over to the Maserati without waiting for her answer. Dante barks out a laugh before sliding into the front seat of the Jeep.

Ash fake gasps, but climbs in anyway. "I can't believe you'd do me that way, Sadie!" she calls out before shutting her door.

Elian peels out of the parking lot seconds later and my hands clench into fists at my side as I resist the urge to yell at him. He can't hear me anyway.

A low whistle leaves my lips as I sink into the leather seat and admire the inside of Kaos' Maserati. She's a beauty, that's for damn sure. The seats are all black with genuine leather, giving them the manly leather scent Kaos faintly smells like. Guess I know where it comes from now.

The engine roars to life with a vicious rumble. Yep, there's that cargasm.

"Nice car you've got, Steel." I quip, using his nickname.

He glances over at me and his grin lights up his whole face. He palms the shifter in his hand. "Hang on. This is going to be a wild ride." His husky chuckle sends a thrill right through me.

My stomach lurches as we fishtail out of the parking lot, tires squealing and kicking up dust in our wake. One of my neighbors runs outside to check on the commotion, clutching their metaphorical pearls as we zoom past. I laugh a genuine laugh. It's a freeing sound that I haven't heard from myself since Skylar died.

Kaos King is right. This is going to be one hell of a wild ride.

If only I had known exactly how wild.

22

SADIE

Kaos takes us down so many back roads that all the twists and turns start to blur together after an hour or so. It's pitch black outside with the only light coming from the small crescent moon and our headlights. We wind through trees and more trees as I trace the hand embroidered trident on the armrest for the millionth time, lost in thought. The ride has been relatively silent thus far. Mainly because I think Kaos is trying to give me space to sort through the storm of emotions swirling inside of me. He's extremely intuitive.

I don't know how I feel about this whole fated mate idea. Yeah, Kaos and Dante and even Elian, are three of the best-looking men I've ever seen, but I don't know anything about them.

Do you have to? The less rational side of my brain pipes up. Actions speak louder than words after all and they have saved my ass more times than I can count tonight. Other than Elian's abrasiveness, they've been extremely kind.

Food for thought, I guess.

The familiar sight of the Jeep a couple of paces behind us

in the side mirror gives me a small sense of relief. When we hit the four-lane, Kaos signaled for a race and surprisingly Elian obliged. It was one hell of an adrenaline rush, but a Jeep is no match for a Maserati, and Kaos won.

Now we're literally in the middle of nowhere and it would be extremely easy to do whatever they wanted with us. For all I know, they could be taking Ash and I out to dispose of our bodies, but I highly doubt that. Especially after everything they've done to keep me safe thus far. Don't get me wrong, I'd put up a hell of a fight but three well-trained magic users against one human and one magic user that had no clue she had magic until a few hours ago?

Yeah, not much of a fight.

Enough with the morbid crap, Sadie. Enjoy the scenery.

Kaos lifts his hand from my leg to adjust the radio volume, humming along to a song that I know every lyric by heart. During my teenage angst phase, I used to listen to it on repeat. I smirk, turning the volume up a few more notches to belt my favorite line.

He chuckles at my antics. "I'll give you fifty bucks right now if you can name the artist and song on this one."

I scoff. "Get ready to lose fifty bucks, sucker. *If It Means a Lot to You* by A Day to Remember." His mouth pops open. "And I'll do you one better. It's off their *Homesick* album."

He gives me an appreciative once over before digging his wallet out of his back pocket and tossing me my winnings. "What do you say if we make a game of this?" he asks, his dark blue eyes flashing challengingly.

Color me intrigued.

"All right, I'll bite, but what happens if I don't know one?"

He taps his chin in thought. "How about—"

"You know what," I interrupt, letting some cockiness seep into my tone. "It doesn't matter, because I don't plan on losing."

"You're on, Little Flame." He shoots me a devious grin. "Here, connect my phone to Bluetooth." When I get it connected, he hits shuffle on his playlist labeled *Favorites*. The first song blasts through the speakers.

I smirk. "That one is too easy. *Situations* by Escape the Fate."

Kaos nods, tossing me another fifty which I stuff into my bra with my other money. I'm not sure why he seems to be so rich, but honestly, I don't care. Even without the money, getting to know Kaos through music like this makes me extremely happy because the fact he likes the same music as me? Swoon.

Fucking swoon.

"Next, please."

He hits the skip button on his phone and groans as soon as the next track starts playing, instantly recognizing the tune. "This one's too easy too."

"It's your playlist, but yeah, you're totally going to run out of fifties at this rate," I say. "*Antisocialist* by Asking Alexandria."

He eyes me appreciatively and my skin tingles under his stare. "You know, you're pretty good at this." His voice is huskier than usual.

"Pfft," I scoff. "Did you think I wouldn't be?" Okay, I'm a little cocky, but music is one aspect you don't want to bet against me on.

He shrugs, before changing the song again. "I've never met a woman who's into all of the same music as me."

"Yeah. My brother and I were really close, and he got me into all these bands. Skylar and I shared almost everything, especially our taste in music. There were many nights when we'd sneak out and go see a local show in places a thirteen and seventeen-year-old never should have been, but Skylar always protected me."

My heart pangs with sorrow every single time I think about him. It's a bone-deep kind of sorrow that I doubt will ever go away. Thankfully, Kaos doesn't push the issue or try to make me talk about him. Instead, he reaches over and rubs small circles against my knee to comfort me.

I get another six correct before one comes on that stumps me. I tap my foot along to the beat, silently sweating it. Crap. What will Kaos expect of me if I don't get this right?

"Have I finally stumped you?" he asks, his dark blue eyes dancing with mirth.

I wave my hand at him. "Give me a second. I'm still thinking," I snap, closing my eyes like that will help.

The title comes to me right before the chorus. My eyes snap open and I shoot him a smug grin. "*I Get Off* by Halestorm."

"Dammit, and here I thought I'd finally got you on one." His tone is low and slightly strained. I look over at him in confusion, then the lyrics of the song sink into my brain.

Yeah, maybe listening to a song about getting off with your new mate isn't the brightest idea, although, there could be some merit to it. Wonder how mad Elian would be if we pulled this car over…

Our eyes lock across the car. His stormy eyes are hooded, hungry, and dripping with desire. I notice his knuckles are white from gripping the steering wheel as if he's been holding himself back. My musical knowledge has totally been turning him on.

Fucking hell, my kind of man. Gimme.

A zing shoots straight between my thighs. Actually, now that I'm paying attention my panties are already drenched. Looks like Kaos isn't the only one aroused.

There's a silent plea in his eye as he glances over at me. "May I touch you?" he asks gently, politely, holding himself back even though it's clear he wants to touch me, but my permission is important to him.

I'm nodding before he can even finish his sentence. "Please," I practically whimper, my tone breathy and low.

Kaos' fingertips find my knee as he trails a finger up the sensitive skin along the inside of my thigh, sensually slow. My breath hitches when he gets close to my lady bits. I widen my legs for him, but he doesn't touch me where I want. Instead, his fingers dip back down to my knee and he repeats the motion. This time I do groan, but in frustration, which seems to amuse him. "Do you like my touch, Sadie?"

Kaos taunts me, circling up and down several times before whisking his knuckles across my sensitive nub. The seam of my shorts only heightens the playful touch, sending a jolt straight through me.

"Shit, yes," I breathe, my head falling back as he circles me once more.

Kaos' touch is practiced and honed and somehow he manages to ignite every single live wire in my body. He keeps his other hand on the wheel, flying around the S curves with grace. The car takes them with ease despite his obvious split focus.

The tension in the car is becoming almost unbearable. I need something. Hell, I don't even know what I need, but I need it. I crave it. At this point, the pressure in my lower region is skyrocketing with that delicious tingling signaling my orgasm is imminent and he hasn't even been inside my shorts yet.

There's no denying that Kaos King knows what he's doing.

Everything is perfect until the sight of a giant brown blob in the middle of the road startles me out of my pre-orgasm bliss. Oh Gods. Is that a bear? I didn't think we even had bears in this area!

"Kaos!"

"Yes, my Little Flame. Say my fucking name. Scream it," he purrs. He's still too busy focusing on playing my body like it's a damn fiddle to notice the fucking animal in front of us.

My eyes clamp closed. "KAOS! STOP THE CAAAAR!" I scream, bracing myself by grabbing onto the *oh shit* handle for dear life.

Kaos jolts, finally catching a glimpse of what's in the road. His hand flies back to the steering wheel as he slams on the breaks. Our bodies continue forward as the car screeches to a halt and the seatbelt painfully digs into my already bruised neck and shoulders. Newton's law of motion is a bitch.

When I'm finally able to relax my muscles and peel my eyes open, I notice the headlights illuminating a large brown blob mere feet from our bumper, although I still can't tell exactly what it is, but it's large and furry.

Unfortunately, the danger isn't over. As the Jeep rounds the curve, their tires screech as Elian slams on his brakes to avoid crashing into us from behind. Somehow he manages to stop in the nick of time.

Kaos unclips his seatbelt, snapping me back to the moment as he checks me over. "Are you okay? I'm so sorry." His hands skim my neck making me wince involuntarily. His gaze narrows in on my pained face.

"I'm fine," I reply, but my lies fall on deaf ears. He's seen my neck, and it's bad. I've caught brief glimpses of it in the side mirror.

"I'm going to fucking murder him," he mutters, nostrils flaring. He's shaking with rage as he lightly wraps his hands around my throat, the bruises likely prominent. His hands glow black, and the pain begins to recede. "This should help."

"It did," I confirm. "But what did you do?"

"I healed you," he responds, placing a light kiss on my cheek. "Which is something I should've done earlier, but everything has been happening so fast." He glances away, jaw clenched like he's upset with himself.

"You healed me?" I quietly ask again. "Thank you."

He nods. "Anything for my mate."

I can tell he's taking Tyler and Ben's attack personally, but it's not his fault. It's theirs. No one could've predicted the lengths they would go through to get to me.

"Kaos, it's not your fault," I tell him lightly.

With a slight head nod, he jerks his door open and walks away to scope out the scene. He needs to come to terms with what happened like I do and I'll give him the space to do so. I toss my seat belt off and hop out after him, noting how much better I feel now that my neck, ribs, and shoulder are no longer throbbing.

As we round the front of the Maserati, I find the giant brown blob isn't a bear, but other than a giant ball of fur, I can't tell exactly what is it, until it lifts its head. I gasp. "It's a dog."

And a massive one at that.

My head whips in Kaos' direction when he makes a weird noise to find him holding his crotch knife in his hand like the cute pup is going to be rabid and attack me or something. I shake my head, signaling him to put his knife away.

"This could be one of the Elites pets sent to kill us or he may have rabies. You never know, Sadie."

I snort. "It's a fucking Golden Retriever, Kaos. Not an attack dog." His statement does make me question if the Elite do have attack dogs though...

The pup closes the distance between us with its tongue lolling out of its mouth and tail wagging a mile a minute. Its fur is light brown with streaks of red woven in and its eyes are a deep chocolate brown. They're the most intelligent dog eyes I've ever seen. Seriously.

One of our other neighbors a few duplexes down has a

little yappy chihuahua that peed on our lawn occasionally and you could tell nothing was going on behind the scenes if you know what I mean. With this pup sitting before me, he looks like he's plotting.

So, I better pet him and make friends, right? Dogs fucking love scratches. I bend down, sticking my hand out in greeting. It sniffs it carefully a few times before bopping my hand with his wet nose as if to say *yeah, you're cool.*

When he lowers his head, I start scratching as I coo unintelligible things that probably only make sense to a dog. Eventually, I work my way down its back and find its puppy spot. It rolls over, flashing me his belly as I go to town on the spot and its back-left leg starts moving involuntarily.

"Oh yes. Vicious attack dog," I quip, making Kaos grunt.

"Okay, I'll admit, you were right," he says and finally puts his crotch knife away, staring at the pup. He's already a goner like me.

I shoot Kaos a wink. "I usually am right, and don't you forget it." He chuckles and shakes his head at me while I continue giving the pup belly scratches. Eventually, he turns over and licks me on the cheek. "I think he likes me."

"Who wouldn't?" Dante says from somewhere behind me. I didn't even know he had gotten out of the Jeep. I've been so focused on the pup.

I catch sight of a baby blue collar around his neck and my heart sinks. Did someone bring him out here only to dump him? Ugh. I hate the human race.

"Did you belong to somebody, buddy?"

When he turns his head, a slip of paper wedged in his collar catches my attention. "Huh, what's this?" I unwrap the card stock carefully, reading the words several times over in disbelief.

Sadie, change of plans. Find me at the X. Enjoy your gift. He's yours. -Bedi

I flip it over, looking for more instructions, details, *something*, but there isn't anything but a map with a red 'X' like a freaking treasure map.

"What is that?" Kaos asks, zeroing in the slip of paper in my hand.

I shrug. "Apparently, the dog is mine."

He looks it over with scrutiny before passing it to Dante, who also searches for more answers that don't appear.

"What does it mean?"

"My neighbor, the one I found tied to a chair in my room, told me she would send for me when it was safe. I'm assuming this is her way of sending for me."

"We're not taking the mutt. End of story." Elian's dark voice skates over my skin like a violent caress and it makes me shiver.

I count to five in my head so I don't say something I regret. "Fuck off, Elian." Well, so much for that. "He's mine and he's coming with whether you like it or not."

He eyes the dog, and I swear for a brief moment, his gaze softens but it's gone before I can be sure. "We don't have time for this," he says impatiently, his hard emerald eyes snagging on mine and staying there. His nostrils flare when my eyes don't leave his, but I'm not about to let him win a silent power grab. Or anything for that matter. Especially not my heart. Nope. Off-limits to him. I'm firmly on a bad boy ban.

Kaos steps between us, cutting off our battle of wills. "This is something Sadie cares about, Elian." Ever the placating one it seems. "Not to mention there's a note stating the dog belongs to her."

My eyes bounce between the two as they argue back and forth, completely ignoring my presence. Screw it. I'm not standing around while they fight like I'm not here. I ignore the rest of their conversation and head back to the car to rummage around. Honestly, I don't even think they realize I left, judging by their harsh tones and all the chest-puffing going on.

After digging around in my backpack, I find the blanket stashed for emergencies. Now, I just need to convince Kaos to let me transport the pup in his vehicle that probably costs more than every single thing I've ever owned in my entire life combined. No pressure.

Waltzing back over to them, I clear my throat, interrupting their argument. Kaos' eyes swing to mine. I gesture toward the dog and the blanket in my arms. Kaos quirks an eyebrow. He totally knows what I'm going to ask, but he wants to watch me squirm. Fucker. "Can he... you know, rideinthemaseratiwithus?" I say hastily and it comes out sounding more like one word.

"Sorry, what was that?" Kaos teases.

"Please?" I add for good measure. I feel an instant connection with this dog, and I'm not letting him slip through my fingers. I'm not completely heartless.

His eyes soften, and he sighs, running a hand through his hair. "Yeah. Go put the blanket across the back and I'll help him get inside."

I throw my arms around his neck and kiss him, showing him my gratitude with my mouth instead of with words. His lips meld against mine like we were made for each other. Maybe we were. I haven't made up my mind about this whole 'fated mate' thing yet. Perhaps when I have a moment to myself to think through everything that's been thrown my way, I'll be able to do so.

Dante coughs behind us, breaking the moment. Kaos smiles against my lips, lingering for a moment longer, then he says, "We can rescue animals all the time if this is the reaction I get."

"I'm holding you to that," I respond cryptically, making his brow dip in confusion. Boy, did he just open a can of worms and he doesn't even know it. Never tell a woman who loves animals she can rescue them. She'll be dragging in strays all the time. Although, that's how I like most things. A little scruffy, but still beautiful. Like Elian in a way, I guess. But I'm not focusing on that.

"If you say so," he murmurs as I walk to the car.

"By the way, I want a raincheck on earlier," I call over my shoulder as I sashay away, exaggerating the sway of my hips.

He chuckles. "You've got a deal, my Little Flame. Raincheck it is."

He knows exactly what I'm referring to.

23

SADIE

Somehow, we manage to maneuver the Golden Retriever into the tiny backseat of the crazy expensive Maserati, but the pup is so big his head almost touches the roof. It reminds me of a show I used to watch as a kid, *Clifford the Big Red Dog*. Fitting too, considering the reddish brown coloring of the pup.

"Ugh, guess I'm still on asshole duty?" Ash whines when we're getting ready to load up and leave. I nod my head vigorously making her roll her eyes and exaggeratedly hop back into the Jeep with Dante and Asshole—I mean Elian.

As Kaos is shutting his door, Elian swerves around the Maserati. The only warning we get is the rumble of the engine as it passes us nearly swiping the door off.

"What the hell is his problem?"

Kaos sighs, watching Elian drive off. "He doesn't like when things don't go his way. You've thrown a wrench into his very existence and he hasn't come to terms with it yet. He'll come around eventually."

I take a few deep breaths to calm my anger as I gaze outside, watching the trees flicker by. "Uh, I may not be the best with maps, but shouldn't we be following Bedi's instructions? We're getting further away instead of closer." Being terrible with maps is an understatement. Something I should probably correct.

Kaos shoots me an incredulous look. "Hell no, she could be one of the enemies for all we know, Little Flame."

Before the concert I would've laughed him off and told him there's no reason to worry. Now I'm not so sure. Even still, there's a gnawing feeling in my gut telling me to follow her directions and I can't seem to shake it. "Bedi has never done anything to hurt me, Kaos."

"That may be, but the answer is still no, Sadie. I'm not risking your life for some vague instructions from a crazed woman we've never met."

To keep myself from showing him exactly what the word *no* does to me, I rip open my backpack, find one of the small bags of jerky I have stashed in case of emergency, and give some to the dog. He lets out a little yip, wagging his tail excitedly. I laugh as I help him finish the rest and it helps my foul mood a tiny bit.

Hangry Sadie is not a good Sadie. Not to mention the word *no* and I don't exactly get along. It only makes me want to do it harder to spite people. Apparently, spite is not the correct answer to what motivates me. Ask my high school life coach. Poor guy.

Not satisfied with Kaos' earlier answer, I speak my mind, "Shouldn't it be my decision, though? I've never felt anything off about her. She's been my neighbor since Ash and I moved into the duplex. She's kind of strange, but she's never done anything malicious. I don't get those vibes from her."

The first waves of dawn floating through the trees highlight the lighter tones in Kaos' irises. "I'm not comfortable with it, Little Flame. None of us are. You're my mate. Our

Link, and we won't needlessly put you in harm's way on someone else's whim."

"Yeah, but being my mate doesn't give you a free pass to make decisions for me. That is not how this relationship is going to go down and if you think it is, we need to reevaluate."

"When it comes to your safety, we will do anything we can to protect you." His hand crosses the center console to hold my mine, caressing me with those calloused fingers. There's something so calming about his skin on mine and it makes my anger dissolve a tiny bit. He had to go and be all sweet about it. How do I freaking argue with that?

"Fine. I get it, but I don't think it's going to fly with her. Something tells me Bedi is not someone who likes being ignored or someone we want on our bad side."

I settle back into the comfy seat, listening to the soft music with a sigh until an unknown voice startles me. "She's right, you know."

I bolt straight up. "What the fuck?"

The brakes squeal and we roll to a dead stop. Again. He's going to need new brakes at this point. Kaos whips out his crotch knife and the sight distracts me for a moment because I still haven't been able to work out the logistics of where it comes from. Maybe he has a secret crotch pocket.

His attention turns to the backseat like someone could be hiding back there in plain sight. Now that I think about it, maybe there could be. Who knows? I know next to nothing about this world of Weavers they've dropped me into.

Maybe they have invisibility powers. It would be cool as shit if they do. Spy on conversations, scare the fuck out of your friends, rearrange someone's house… It would be quite the power.

"Who said that?" Kaos demands, searching the air.

Okay, he's as clueless as I am.

The gift from Bedi's staring at us with a smile. Well, as much of a smile as a dog can give, anyway. It's kind of cute honestly. "I did," the dog quips. "There's no one else in here."

I scoff. "Yeah, right. Dogs can't talk," I say, which makes Kaos give me a strained look. My head whips back and forth between him and said dog.

"Of course, we can. Or I can anyway," the dog says, sounding somewhat offended.

My mouth pops open in shock. "Did you see that? His lips moved."

Kaos gives me another small strained head nod. Gods, this day keeps getting better and better. Or stranger and stranger, depending on how you look at it, I guess.

"Is nothing sacred? Even dogs can talk now?" I demand.

Although, in my defense, it's been one hell of a day. Not to mention revelation after revelation about things I've only ever read about in books being *real*. One hundred percent legit. Not make-believe.

Magic exists, and apparently, I have it, and now dogs can talk? I've stumbled down the fucking rabbit hole. Damn those chili cheese fries from the festival. Cheese always gives me gas, maybe that gas is turning into hallucinations.

"How?" Kaos inquires, lowering his knife a fraction. "I thought…"

"That I was a mere dog?" he scoffs. "No. I'm a familiar. Sadie's to be exact." The dog shakes his little butt like he's trying to prove a point, and I suppress a smile.

"Now, you need to turn this fancy-schmancy contraption around and head to Bedi's or she's going to be furious, and that never ends well. Believe me." He shakes his head, eyes wide like he's reliving an experience.

As if to stress his point, little scraps of paper start to fall from the sky all around us, littering the ground. A few more seconds and there's so many, it looks like it's snowing. With paper. Ah, hell. What now?

One of the pieces of parchment lands on the windshield with an audible smack. I squint, realizing they're all guides to wherever Bedi wants us to go.

There's a knock on my window and Dante's concerned face moves into my line of sight. I guess Elian stopped the Jeep when he realized we weren't following him anymore.

The sheets of paper float all around him and he has to wave his arms to keep from getting hit with them. "What is going on?" he asks, but I have no earthly idea either.

Dante snatches a piece out of the air, crumples it in his fist, and chucks it off the side of the road with a smug expression on his face. Until it springs back to life and flies toward him with vengeance, smacking him in the face. The force knocks him backward as he struggles trying to pry it off.

Rabbit. Hole.

"Moons above! We don't have the time for this," Elian snaps as he slams the door to the Jeep and storms over with his pocket watch in hand. He flicks it closed and watches the scene unravel with narrowed eyes.

"As you've already said," I call back. I can't resist the urge to taunt him. The look on his face is too good.

Meanwhile, Dante is still wrestling with the parchment. When his hands light up in their blue-orange glow, I start to protest, but it's too late. He lifts them to his face, igniting the paper. I open my mouth to protest, knowing he's going to burn his eyebrows off or worse, but to my surprise, the fire doesn't harm him. Not a single hair on his head is even singed. He huffs and blows a piece of hair out of his face.

"More maps?" Elian asks, snatching one out of the air since they're still steadily falling from the sky. That cheeky old bat. "What's this all about?"

I give him a noncommittal shrug. "Ask the dog."

Yeah, if looks alone could kill, I'd be dead from Elian's gaze.

A vein in his temple throbs as he swings his glare over to me. "Are you that dense?" he asks, voice dripping with acid. There's something else behind his expression as well—something guarded.

"She isn't, you asshole," Goldie pipes up from the backseat, slightly saving me from his ire. Elian's eyes widen comically before he realizes his persona slipped and shuts down with a lip curl and a snarl.

"What sort of trickery is this?" One second, he's a few feet from the car, and the next he's right beside it, wrenching my door open, crotch knife in hand.

Oh, great he has crotch knives too.

Fuck. Me.

"Don't you dare!" I hop out of my seat push against his chest, but he doesn't even stumble and now we're standing impossibly close. Every single hard plane of his body rests against mine in the most delicious way.

"He's my familiar," I finally grind out through clenched teeth. Elian's proximity is enough to have my heart rate accelerating despite his abrasiveness.

"And you believe this *creature*? He could be a spy for all we know." Something dark flashes in his eyes but it happens so quickly that I can't be certain.

"Sheesh, I could almost choke from all the testosterone floating around," Goldie quips.

"Same here," Ash agrees, appearing out of nowhere. "Glad it's not just me."

I laugh making Elian's eyes snap to mine. He spears me with his intense emerald stare and the loathing in his gaze makes my smile drop. What have I ever done to him to deserve this level of hatred?

Maybe he can't take a joke...

The guys burst into an argument about my familiar and what to do with the situation. I'm not their damn babysitter, so I don't intervene, although I do feel guilty for causing strife among their Circle. That was never my intention, but Elian is so fucking hot and annoying—

A rumble underneath my feet distracts me from my thoughts. The trees all around us begin to rustle and crack, growing louder and louder with each passing breath, but Dante, Elian, and Kaos are too busy trying to talk over one another to hear anything out of the ordinary.

"The amount of power needed for this shitshow is astounding! We don't know what we're dealing with or what we'd be walking into. She could've been the one to send those golems," Elian shouts, none the wiser to the tingling in the air, and the faint buzzing of magic.

"Shhh! Do you feel that?" I demand, interrupting their bickering.

Their mouths snap shut and their eyes widen when they feel the ground shake beneath us.

"We need to move. Now!" Kaos says, barely getting the words out as a boulder pops into sight, barreling down the mountainous incline full force. The three of them spring into action like the well-oiled machine they are together. Kaos hauls me out of the way, shielding my body with his. Elian rushes over, tugging Ash out of the way for me.

Dante shoots flames out of his palms at the rock, seemingly trying to break it apart but nothing happens, and it continues its downward trajectory. His face scrunches in concentration as he throws up a bright blue wall of flames that it passes right through, squashing Elian's super expensive Jeep before rolling to a stop in the middle of the road.

Considering it's now on fire and didn't roll off the cliff, I'm going to take a wild guess and say it's a magical rock.

"Huh. Well, now we know that rock doesn't beat fire. Take that, Susie Sullivan," Ash snarks, putting a hand on her hip like we didn't witness a freak of nature destroy a special edition eighty-thousand-dollar Willys Jeep Wrangler. Those babies are not cheap.

I groan. "Why'd you have to bring that up? I'd forgotten about her."

"You know how badly I hold grudges." Ash shrugs as she whips out her phone, snapping a picture of the boulder on fire that's currently resting on top of the flattened Jeep.

True. Ash is someone you definitely do not want to get on the bad side of. I once watched her swap a chick's shampoo for Nair in high school. It burned the girl's scalp so badly that it gave her permanent hair loss. She still wears a wig to this day.

Elian very slowly and very meticulously turns, and when he levels his gaze on us... the look in his eye makes me cringe. He looks slightly stabby and *a lot* murderous.

"My favorite vehicle was smashed and you're both making jokes right now?"

Ash barrels on, none the wiser to the ice in his tone. It makes me want to smack my forehead.

"Um, yeah. Susie Sullivan always thought it was rock, paper, scissors, fire. That bitch would throw out a sign for fire to beat my rock, declaring herself as the winner every single time. Like what even is that? I can't tell you how many matches I lost to her, and now I have photographic evidence she was wrong."

The vein in Elian's temple throbs before he turns away without a word, stalking over to the pancaked Wrangler. His face scrunches and he punches the rock with his hand. When he wrenches his fist back there are angry red gashes across his knuckles and the blood steadily drips onto the pavement. He stares at it for a moment, seemingly lost in thought before he wipes it on his pants and stalks away. Kaos takes off after him, giving me a placating look.

"That was real smooth!" I call out and then turn my attention to the matter at hand. Gods, he works me up like no one else.

"I hate to do this, but you can't send that picture out, Ash," Dante says, plucking the pink phone out of her hand. He promptly deletes the photo before she can hit send and stuffs it into his back pocket.

"Aww, come on, Dante. You were my favorite until now," she whines, playfully jabbing him in the side. She reaches around him and tries to snatch the phone from his back pocket, but he's too fast and dodges out the way.

The jealous monster inside me pokes her head up, making my eye twitch at their banter, and for a moment I have to resist the urge to stab her with my switchblade.

Gods, Sadie. This is your best friend you're thinking about. Ash may be a little promiscuous, but she'd never go for someone you're interested in. You're not even sure if this whole mate bond is real yet. Calm your tits.

They go back and forth a few times before Ash finally relents and promises not to give away the whole magical community.

"Sorry, not sorry," he says to her while handing her the device back. "We can't let the humans get wind of the Weavers and what better way to draw attention to magic than a giant flaming rock?"

"He's got a point, babe. A flaming boulder isn't realistically possible. At least I don't think it is. Somebody google it. My phone is dead and now I'm curious."

Dante whips out his own phone, typing away at the search engine. "Huh. What do you know? Technically rocks can catch fire but not like this." He waves in its direction. "More in the lava sense."

"Wow, they weren't lying when they said you learn something new every day."

Kaos and Elian return a moment later and my eyes dip to Elian's unblemished hand. There are no gashes or scrapes anymore which leads me to believe Kaos healed his hand for him. Ah, well, I was hoping the bastard would have to deal with the consequences.

"I hate to be the bearer of bad news here, but I've sensed twelve Elites heading this way," Goldie says, watching our spectacle with interest.

Yeah, I've got to give him a name besides Goldie. It doesn't suit him at all.

"Dammit," Kaos curses, taking the lead on the situation. "Okay, Dog, scoot over. Elian and Ashley pile in the back. Sadie, you can ride in Dante's lap up front where I can keep an eye on you."

The smirk Dante shoots me is downright scandalous and I'd be lying if I said it didn't send a thrill straight down to my lady bits. "I like this plan," he says with that devilish smirk.

Elian looks like he wants to protest, but he doesn't push it, despite the vein that's still throbbing in his temple. He gets in and Ash files in behind him. After they're settled Dante scoots the seat into place and tugs me into his lap. I'm not expecting the sudden motion and barely avoid smacking my head against the side. I swear I have better reflexes but being around these men seems to make me extremely off-balanced.

As soon as everyone is inside, Kaos shifts into reverse, doing the quickest—and probably most dangerous—U-turn ever.

"Incoming!" Goldie calls out seconds before we come face to face with a sleek black car in our lane. Kaos swerves, narrowly missing the bull bar that would've likely done a lot of damage as we fly past each other in the wrong lanes. He flexes his fingers on the steering wheel, throwing the shifter into sport mode as he guns the gas.

"Wonderful," I mutter. This car is not meant to hold this many people. A crash would likely be the death of me.

Dante buckles both of us into the seat. "Don't worry, Angel. I've got you," he whispers in my ear, his hands tightening on me as Kaos takes another curve at lightning speed.

"Evasive maneuvers, Kaos. You know what to do," Elian barks, leaning forward to watch the scene. And he's a backseat driver too? Gods grant me strength.

Kaos nods, changing his grip on the steering wheel. He takes his buddy's commands in stride as we race down another hill, coming into a straightaway that dips into a valley.

Two more black cars crest the hill opposite of us and a man pops out of the passenger window of the one in front, aiming his pistol directly at our front windshield. Thankfully, the bullets don't penetrate, but they do leave little cracks.

The hair on the back of my neck rises when both cars in front of us come to a screeching halt in the dip of the valley. The one in the back slips over into our lane, turning sideways and the other one does the same in the opposite lane, blocking our path forward completely. Four men in black jumpsuits armed to the teeth step out of each of the cars in unison.

"Gods, they're trying to capture us," Dante murmurs, watching the scene with wide eyes.

"Elian, can you use the shadows to get us out of here?" Kaos asks, watching the scene unfold. From what I know about him he's probably calculating the odds of each scenario.

"No," he responds with a twinge of regret coloring his tone. "It barely works for two people, let alone a car full."

Which is not a good answer because in a few seconds, Kaos will have to stop, and we'll either be forced to fight twelve armed men, or he'll have to plow through them, risking a crash with most of us not properly belted into a seat. Indecision mars his features, as he taps the brakes, slowing our momentum.

I refuse to go down like this. I'm no one's prisoner. A fire surges to life in my belly and I feel the overwhelming urge to protect them. Even if it's irrational and crazy to already be this attached. Deep down my soul recognizes them as my own, even if my brain hasn't caught up yet.

My pulse thunders in my ears, drowning out everything else. I take a deep breath, wasting precious seconds to clear my mind as we sail straight toward the Elites. They're close enough now that I can see the smirks on their faces, thinking they've won, and it infuriates me.

Something inside of me snaps and it's like a levy breaking. Black pulsing wavelengths shoot out from our car in my furious rage. I may not have fully accepted these guys yet, but nobody messes with what's mine.

The pulsing black smoke reaches the Elites' vehicles and each windshield shatters. The waves toss the cars from the roadway, clearing us a path as they land upside down on either side of the valley.

"Holy fucking shit!" I whoop and cheer as Kaos accelerates and we go sailing past the Elites who are forced to jump out of the way or be flattened like pancakes.

Dante makes a weird noise and I find his eyes scanning me like I somehow hold all the secrets to the universe. That's comical because as much as I wish I could give him any information, I'm as clueless as he is. As they all are, judging by their astonished facial expressions.

The sun crests the hill on the horizon, illuminating the field behind us and a glint catches my attention in the rearview mirror. I watch as the car that was tailing us screeches to a halt to avoid the black shockwave still wreaking havoc on the Elites.

A mountain of a man steps out and his cold bottomless eyes lock on mine through the mirror. My breath hitches. The man is terrifying. Lethal. *Dangerous*.

But that's not the worst part. His eyes are completely dead. It's as if there's no emotion or life left whatsoever.

A lead weight settles in my gut. Men like him, like my uncle, are worse than a bloodhound when they get on the trail of something. They don't stop until they're forced to, or they find their target. And something tells me that this man right here, this dead-eyed man will continue to chase after us until one of those two options happens.

Shivers of dread trail down my spine but I don't let any of my unease show on my face. Instead, I give him a small wink and flip him the bird, like I meant to do all of that. Those dead eyes shine, and he smiles but it's all teeth as he draws an 'X' in the air before raising his pointer finger out toward me.

A haze starts to descend on my mind and I don't have much time to think about it because my vision starts to falter, fading in and out.

Eventually, everything goes black, but not before I hear Dante whisper, "Don't worry. I've got you, Angel. I've got you."

24

KAOS

"What happened? Why did she pass out?" I demand, running my hands down her arm, pushing my magic into her to heal, but nothing happens. Or nothing that I can fix anyway. Especially not while I'm driving.

"She'll be fine in a few hours. She used too much energy taking out the Elites. From now on we'll have to watch her, make sure she doesn't expend her magic beyond her limits, or she'll burn herself out." The talking mutt supplies from the backseat.

"How do you know?" Elian questions before I can get the words out myself. Hmm, does the surly asshole care after all? He's always been prickly, but with her it's on a whole new level. If I had to guess… he's purposely pushing her away. I just can't figure out why.

"I'm her familiar," the dog responds, like that explains everything.

"That's impossible. Familiars are a fucking myth," Elian replies coldly, but he's not wrong. We've heard of them, sure, but seen one? Never. Not until now.

"Ah, that's what the Elders want you to think. We're out there, hiding, waiting. Bedi found me while I was in a tough spot, kept me safe until Sadie met her mates, and was ready for me. Meeting you three is what activated her powers."

But she already had a tiny sliver of power before meeting us...

I keep those thoughts to myself for now, instead opting to change the topic and ask the dog, "Who exactly is Bedi?" Elian could argue with a brick wall and that conversation is going nowhere fast.

"Bedi is complicated, and extremely powerful, in case you hadn't noticed, but no one knows exactly what she is. She's taken an interest in your mate, which is odd. Normally she's a recluse, content to live alone in the mountains."

Ash leans forward. "Bedi was our neighbor at the duplex. She moved in next to us right after we did. Honestly, she's like an overprotective grandma to us. Although, she never had a dog..." She trails off, looking to him expectantly.

"Ah, that would be because she kept an Illusion on me. I was there, you just couldn't see me."

"This is truly insane," she whispers and I watch as she leans back against the seat through the rearview mirror, rubbing her temples.

"With all that aside, the real question is; what does Bedi want with Sadie?" Elian inquires, spearing the dog with a deadly look, but if the mutt is concerned, he doesn't show it. Since no one knows much about familiars, considering no one has had one in our lifetime, he could be extremely useful for all we know.

"I can't say for sure. He doesn't tell me much. What I do know is that she has a soft spot for Sadie and thinks she's important." The dog shrugs like a human. It's disconcerting, to say the least.

"I could've told you she's important," I snap. "She's the

first true Link in years and that makes her a giant fucking target."

"That it does," he agrees.

"Do you have a name besides mutt or dog?" Dante asks, being way more diplomatic than me for once.

"Nope, not yet anyway. Sadie gets to decide."

"This is so weird," I mutter, refocusing on the road. I pluck the original map from the cup holder and tell Dante to read me off the directions to distract myself from the shit show.

It takes several hours to reach our destination, and I can tell by the sharp clench of his jaw that Elian is furious by the time we get close. He hates when his plans don't go the way he expects. Or really, he hates anything that he can't control. And this is a massive fucking curveball.

Sadie still hasn't woken up and I'm starting to worry slightly—despite the mutt's reassurances she'll be okay. I'm not ready to take his word at face value yet. Especially where my mate is involved.

My mate. It's such a simple phrase but it holds so much meaning and fills me with inconceivable joy. I never thought this day would come. None of us did. We'd all pretty much given up hope. It begs the question, why us?

And why Sadie?

I watch in the rearview as Elian shoves his phone back into his pocket in frustration. *I haven't been able to get ahold of the Light Weaver's heir,* he projects into my mind.

We've been friends with the heir—despite our parents' wishes—since we were very young. The Night Weavers have always held a grudge for our lighter counterparts, but it was never anything serious until recently. The Elders declared war on them for our differences and we've been at each other's throats ever since.

Well, I should say they have been at each other's throats ever since. We have a pact with our friend to not engage in fights. There's no way to know for certain if he knows they have broken the treaty until we speak to him, but Elian can't get ahold of him.

A soft cry pulls my attention over to my still sleeping mate. She must be having a bad dream because she cries out again, thrashing in Dante's arms. A stab of pain shoots through my heart.

Dante shushes her until she jerks awake. She throws her hands out in defense, catching Dante in the nose before realizing where she is. Her hands fly to her mouth and she makes a keening noise in the back of her throat.

"I'm so sorry, Dante," she apologizes, rubbing his nose.

"Yeah, heads-up, she's real feisty when she first wakes up. I only tried waking her up once before I decided that it's not worth the black eye," her friend Ashley mumbles with a laugh as she pats Dante lightly on the back.

Dante fake groans, shooting her a mischievous look. "You hit me pretty hard, Angel. I think you're going to have to kiss it and make it better."

I roll my eyes and punch the fucker in the arm. Sadie smirks and kisses his cheek. Or well, would've if Dante didn't turn his head into the kiss, capturing her lips in a bruising blend of passion and haste, like he couldn't take not having his lips on her any longer, and I don't blame him.

Sadie squeaks in protest and it's fucking adorable. Though, she'd probably stab me for thinking that. My feisty little mate. Her spunk is something I greatly admire. She's going to need it in this world.

When they break apart, her guilty eyes fly to mine, and

she starts apologizing to me. My lips twitch. "He's your mate too, Little Flame. It's all right."

Her shoulders sag a fraction, and she settles back into Dante. She has a lot to learn about us and our society. Fortunately, she seems to be taking everything extremely well.

She knows how to roll with the punches, which is a good and bad thing. Good because life likes to throw curveballs. Bad because it means she's been through a lot.

One day I hope to know her full story.

25

SADIE

Warmth surrounds me, capturing me in its clutches. I try to wiggle free, to fight the nightmares around me, but the heat only pulls me in closer to its dark embrace. A strong band of steel wraps around my middle as something rocks me back and forth, murmuring in my ear.

Wait, what?

Consciousness slowly reenters my foggy brain, shattering the tranquility of the moment. I jolt, hand flying out to defend myself from my mind's perceived threat. My fingers crash into a nose and a perfect set of amber eyes before my brain catches up and I realize I'm in Dante's arms.

"I'm so sorry," I groan, trying to wipe his face like that's magically going to erase what happened.

"Yeah, heads-up, she's real feisty when she first wakes up. I only tried waking her up once before I decided that it's not worth the black eye," Ash chimes in, leaning forward to pat Dante on the back.

His mouth tips up into a pouty grin. "You hit me pretty

hard, Angel. I think you're going to have to kiss it and make it better."

I bite my lip, debating for a moment before leaning in and planting a quick peck on his cheek. Or I would've if he hadn't turned his head. Too late to stop now. Not that I really wanted to, anyway.

My lips descend on his, and his soft mouth melds against mine perfectly. I can't stop the groan that slips past my lips as his hand slides through my hair, gripping the back of my head as he takes control, coaxing my mouth open to slide his tongue inside.

Then reality comes crashing down, and I pull away, putting distance between us. I miss the connection instantly. There's something about Dante that makes everything else slip away.

My guilty eyes connect with Kaos'. He reaches over and grabs my hand, rubbing the mate mark on my wrist. The silver flares to life, sending a jolt straight through my body.

"You're his mate too, Little Flame. It's okay."

Okay, I guess they weren't joking about sharing.

Elian snorts, grumbling something under his breath, but I ignore him. Instead, I glance outside to check out my surroundings. The scenery doesn't look much different. We're surrounded by trees, no shocker there, the only discernible difference is the sun being higher in the sky than it was when I passed out. The clock on the dashboard confirms I was out for almost three hours.

Kaos brakes, cursing at the map in his hands as we pull off the civilized road onto a nondescript dirt path, barely large enough for his car.

"Uh, guys? This doesn't seem sketchy or anything," Ash says from the back.

"Maybe it wasn't the brightest idea to follow the talking dog and magical map?" Dante supplies unhelpfully.

I shoot him a glare and he throws his hands up in surrender.

Before long, we approach a clearing and I watch as an immense oak tree appears in our path. There is a two-story cabin built into the base, decked out with windows, and… is that a wrap-around porch?

"How is a freaking treehouse better than our whole duplex?" Ash asks, voicing my thoughts aloud. "Bedi's been holding out on us."

Goldie, the talking familiar, lifts his head from Ash's lap, waking up from his nap. He stretches, accidentally nudging Elian who shifts out of the way like the dog bit him or something.

"We're here," he announces, wagging his butt because he can't move his tail.

Suddenly, a trapdoor on the bottom of the treehouse pops open and out shoots Bedi. A much younger, hotter version of Bedi. Even from here I can tell her skin is flawless and her hair that's always been grey is now red, framing her face like a wild curtain of curls.

Her violet eyes twinkle with mischief as we dutifully file out of the car and approach. "I was getting worried those nasty Elites succeeded in taking you out back there."

Kaos and Dante both stiffen at her response but it's not either one of them that speaks.

"You knew they were after us?" Elian asks, violence threading his words. All the guys are tense, their hands near their crotches. Fucking crotch knives.

"I did," she boldly states.

Elian has his knife pressed against her throat before I can blink, and it confuses me. Why the hell is Elian the one defending my honor? He hates me.

"What are you?" he asks.

"The last seer, of course," she says. There's a glint of

madness dancing in her ancient eyes. She disappears in a cloud of smoke and reappears behind him.

Elian whirls around to face her and does not look impressed in the slightest. "Seers aren't real. I don't know what kind of crack you're smoking, but my Circle and I aren't sticking around to listen to a *psycho* pretend to be a *psychic*."

Bedi tsks, not sounding a bit cowed by Elian's sharp tongue. "We don't have time for the squabbling. Sadie needs to have some vital protections placed on her before it's too late." She trails off at the resounding growls and rolls her eyes. "Either take it or leave it, boys. I've had plenty of opportunities to cause her harm and haven't." Her violet eyes flash challengingly. "What's it going to be?"

The guys exchange a look over my head, but I'm not one to have my choices made for me, so I step forward on my own. "I'll take those protections, Bedi. Thank you."

I don't make it two steps before Elian grabs my arm and halts my movements. I grit my teeth, hating, but secretly enjoying the blaze of fire his touch leaves on me. *Bad Sadie. No assholes, remember?*

Besides, I'm getting really freaking tired of men handling me like this. I spin around, using his hold on my arm as leverage as I catch him in the stomach with my Converse. He grunts but doesn't react otherwise. "What she claims is impossible," he tells me.

"How so?" I don't give him time to respond. "Like I'm not supposed to be possible? Like magic isn't supposed to be possible?" I shrug out of his hold and stalk toward the treehouse.

After a moment's hesitation, they scramble after me. Bedi leads us over to the ladder and Kaos cuts in front of me, gently taking my hand off the rung before I can climb up. I start to object, but then think better of it. It's tough when you're used to being the only one looking out for yourself.

"Wait, why are we using the ladder, anyway? There are steps over there." I gesture toward the spiral staircase leading up to the wrap-around porch.

Bedi stops her ascent, looking down at me with a small smirk. "Sure, but what fun is that dear?"

Touché.

Dante and Ash climb up next, leaving me alone with Elian. He runs a hand through the tuft of hair on top of his head. His part has been shaved out, giving it a distinct line to the side.

We quietly stand there watching each other, not giving the other an inch. The tension in the air cackles between us, almost a palpable substance. He's still wearing his leather jacket, and now that it's light outside, his green eyes shine, until he narrows them.

Thankfully, Kaos saves the day by calling out, "Clear!"

The standoff fizzles, yet my body tingles the entire way up the ladder.

When I reach the top, my jaw drops. The whole vibe feels beyond magical. Not only because it's a two-story house built into a centuries old tree, but the atmosphere itself feels otherworldly.

Wafts of lavender and sage tickle my nostrils. Swirling glass bottles and books of all shapes and sizes line the shelves of her living room walls. There's a kitchenette and a staircase leading up to the upper floor on the left. And to the right there's a small workstation outfitted with a fireplace. An actual fireplace. In a treehouse. Somehow that seems counterproductive but I don't bring it up.

Bedi motions to the circular sunken den in the center of her living room wrapped around the base of the tree. "Make yourselves at home. Would anyone care for some tea while you're waiting?"

"No," Elian snaps before anyone else can speak.

My fists clench. "Speak for yourself." I smile sweetly at his scowling face before turning to Bedi. "I'd love a cup. Thank you."

"Me too!" Ash calls out after her as she turns away. Elian gives her a look and she shrugs. "What? Bedi makes the best tea around. I'm not passing it up because you're an overprotective douche nozzle."

"Douche nozzle?" he asks, fingers curling around his leather jacket as he adjusts it and sits down.

"I think that one's pretty self-explanatory," I respond, plopping down on the settee beside Ash. I let out a long groan as the tension in my body eases. Sitting in one position for so long has done a number on my muscles.

"He is, isn't he?" Bedi comments from the kitchen. "I assure you; I've done nothing to the tea." She eyes Elian as she turns around with a beautiful antique copper kettle.

She pours both of us a cup and one for herself. The steam rises instantly, wafting into the air, mixing with the lavender and sage. I inhale the tangy aroma with a sigh, but before I can take a sip of the delicious liquid, Dante snatches the cup out of my hands, taking a giant gulp. His face scrunches as he downs it, making a panting face afterward.

"That's what you get for stealing my tea." I try to take it back, but he takes another sip, eyeing the cup appreciatively like he didn't expect it to taste so good.

"If you die from the poisoned tea, then so will I."

*Aww. That's kind of—*Wait a second. He's trying to steal my tea. I snatch my cup back from his greedy hands, giving him an elbow for good measure.

"Get your own. Nobody steals my food *or* my tea." Bedi's tinkling laugh reaches my ears. When I glance over, I notice how much younger she looks. "How are you so young now?" I blurt.

Ash chokes, spitting her tea out. "Sadie, that's a little rude, don't you think?" But there's laughter behind her hazel eyes.

Unperturbed, Bedi gives me a warm smile. "Magic, of course. This is my true face. I figured you'd trust an old coot versus a dashing woman."

Eh, not a bad assumption.

There's a ring at the front door and I frown in confusion. Bedi is light as a feather on her feet as she waltzes over to the door. When she opens it there's Goldie with his tail wagging and tongue lolling out of his mouth. He had to take the main stairs instead of the ladder and I feel bad for not remembering to ask.

"Such a good little pup, aren't you?" Bedi coos, bending over to give him ear scratches before returning to the living room. Goldie lays down at my feet, giving my leg a small lick.

Bedi's gaze flickers between each guy before her eyes land on me. "You've got yourself quite the little harem, haven't you?"

"It's looking that way," I respond. "I haven't decided if fate is laughing at me or trying to right some wrongs." My admission makes everyone laugh, dissipating some of the tension.

Glancing around the treehouse, my attention snags on a wall of paper behind Bedi, zeroing in on one scrap in particular. I stand, stalking toward the wall next to a writing desk scattered with pens and bottles of ink. I'm not worried about that.

No, now that I'm closer I can tell that each scrap of paper holds an image of a different, unique moment in my life. There are painful memories like of my uncle, his expression menacing, but there are also recent happier ones, like kissing Kaos at the concert. All of them are extremely detailed and seem hand-drawn.

I take a deep breath and move onto the one that caught my attention from across the room. Tears spring to my eyes and it's as if the wind is knocked out of my lungs as I run my fingers across the page reverently. "What the hell is this?" I demand, breathlessly.

"My visions come to me in the form of drawings," Bedi tells me nonchalantly, like she doesn't have the most perfect picture of my brother I've ever seen on her wall.

Skylar didn't enjoy having his picture taken. In fact, he hated it and I don't have any recent ones of him. This vision must've been from my perspective because he's facing me with a smirk on his face and skateboard in hand.

I remember this night like it was yesterday. In reality, it's probably been every bit of six years. We snuck out of our uncle's trailer so he could go skateboarding with his friends at the park. Even though he was four years older than me, he never minded me tagging along with him. Never told me I cramped his style or anything, like most brothers would. But I guess we were closer than most brother and sister pairs.

Trauma tends to do that to you.

"What are the little bottles?" Dante asks, interrupting my thoughts, blissfully unaware of the gaping hole forming in my chest the longer I stare at Skylar's carefree smile. I'd give anything to see it in person again. I choke back a sob; the grief threatening to pull me down with it.

Kaos squeezes my shoulder, bringing me back to the conversation at hand. "What's the matter, Little Flame?" he asks, attuned to my feelings. Either that or it's the bond between us.

Gah, doesn't he know that asking what's wrong only makes women cry harder?

Skylar wouldn't want me to cry. He'd want me to seek my revenge. He'd tell me to suck it the hell up, to be strong. I discreetly, and very carefully, take the drawing off the wall, before tucking it in my back pocket. If Bedi notices she doesn't comment.

But Kaos notices. He gives me a small frown, but I hold my hand up, cutting him off. "He's my brother." That's all I can manage to say without breaking down in Bedi's exotic living room. I can't rehash the agony of losing him right now. He takes the hint and places his hand on the small of my back, lending me some of his strength.

"Hmph, now where did I put that potion?" Bedi murmurs, rummaging through each bottle on her shelf before heading to the next one. "No, not this one. Not that one. That's a disaster waiting to happen." She laughs softly to herself, flying from shelf to shelf until she finds what she's looking for. "Aha!" she cries in victory, clutching a small round vial.

She pops the cork and waltzes over to a cauldron. A real-life witchy cauldron. She cackles as she tosses the contents of the bottle into the bubbling brew like a madwoman. Hell, maybe she is. The potion pops and crackles like pop rocks as she stirs it with a large wooden spoon.

I raise an eyebrow as she closes her eyes, whispering words that seem like gibberish. She tosses other items into the pot from the table beside her. "What are you—"

Her eyes fly open, and she shushes me harshly before I can utter another syllable. When satisfied I won't interrupt again, she closes her eyes and returns to her work.

"Never interrupt someone casting a spell, Angel," Dante whispers, watching Bedi warily.

"You mean this is normal?"

"Absolutely. Those who have an affinity for potion crafting learn it quite early."

I swear my jaw hits the floor.

After what feels like an eternity, Bedi opens her eyes and dips a dropper into the cauldron. She hurries over to me, cupping her hand under it to catch any excess before she plonks the dropper into my teacup. Dante tries to intercept my cup again, but she stops him with a hand to his chest.

"You can't," she hisses. "These protections are for Sadie alone."

"You can't expect me to believe that shit."

Bedi doesn't back down.

"What's in it?" I inquire, trying to ease the rising tension.

"A bit of Banderberries, Elderroot, and Moon Dust. Plus, one vial of Shadow Essence and…" she hesitates. "a pinch of sugar, but that's mainly for taste."

"Sounds like perfectly normal potion ingredients to me," Dante responds, reaching for my teacup again, but I don't allow him to take it this time.

Ash and I exchange a look like; *this is normal?*

"Because when these ingredients mix, they create a powerful protection spell for a woman. Not for a man."

"Where the hell did you get Shadow Essence, seer?" Elian asks, interrupting the conversation. "That ingredient is practically nonexistent, not to mention outlawed."

Bedi smiles deviously. "Wouldn't you like to know?"

The guys explode into an argument, everyone speaking at once, but I ignore them all. It's my decision, anyway. How many times do I have to tell them that?

With one last look at the brew, I bring the cup to my lips. *Bottoms up, I guess,* I think before downing the surprisingly tasty concoction in one gulp.

"Dammit, Sadie!" Kaos growls then steps toward Bedi menacingly. "If anything happens to her, I'll kill you myself."

"Ditto," Dante agrees.

"Relax, boys. It's nothing more than a stronger version of the potion you—and every other Night Weaver—are given as children. Sadie never received those protections and was more vulnerable to mental attacks, especially now that they know about her existence."

She pauses for a moment, debating with herself before adding, "I also put the Elderroot in for some magical birth control." She winks, looking pointedly at all the guys behind me.

She gave me a... birth control potion? Score.

"I didn't even know that was a thing," I say.

She nods. "Whenever you're ready for it to stop, all you have to do is think about it and the spell will dissipate."

Fat chance in hell, but I keep that thought to myself.

Ash bursts out laughing. "Dang, Bedi's got your back, girl! Think about all of the orgies—"

"Enough of that," Bedi interrupts with a clap of her hands. "Let's get you moon-blessed and then on your way."

There's more? "Moon-blessed?" I parrot with a frown.

"Yes. All Weavers go through the ritual at some point, usually when they're young," she explains indulgently, writing something down on a piece of parchment. "We must ask the Night Goddess for her blessing before you can receive your full powers and reach your maximum potential, so let's get on with it, shall we? Right this way."

Something tells me there's more to this than Bedi's letting on, but I don't question it. My gut says to trust her and I'm trusting it.

Bedi pulls a large glass potion bottle off the shelf next to her fireplace and it swings open, revealing a hidden door behind it. Huh. Never would've expected the fireplace. Although, it's not the strangest thing I've seen today. That award goes to the talking dog.

"Isn't that a fire hazard or something?" Ash asks, eyeing the open flame under the cauldron warily.

Bedi raises her hand making a flame appear at will, wiggling her fingers, and the fire dances across them almost lovingly—if that's even possible. Unlike Dante's orangish-blue flames, hers are bright green. "This is my magic, and it won't harm anything unless I tell it to, would you?" she coos to the flames dancing across her fingers.

Once again, I wonder what the hell I've gotten myself into.

Dante places me behind him with Kaos, Elian, and Ash at my back as we follow her down the steps into what looks like the base of the tree. Bedi flicks her hand and candles flare to life around the room.

When the hall ends, a beautiful night sky appears above us with all three moon phases spread out in a semi-circle above where Bedi stands, casting a glow on the altar next to her. Crescent, Half, and Full.

This must mean something to the Weavers because Elian makes a sound of protest. "Only the Elders may perform the Shadow Sacrament," he states. "Not to mention, it's normally performed on kids and young adults. Sadie's already past that age. Who knows what it'll do to her?"

Does the surly bastard care what happens to me? Gasp.

Bedi sighs, spearing him with a look. "The Night's blessing is not something age can restrict. Your Circle is too young to remember, but back in the days before the Elders *stole* their positions of power, a priestess like myself would perform the Shadow Sacrament."

Bedi doesn't give him a chance to say anything else. "Quickly now. I need you all to stand in a semi-circle around Sadie. You shall be her witnesses. Is everyone here all right with that?"

Ash nods, eyes alight with wonder. Dante and Kaos grunt their affirmation and after a heavy pause, Elian files into the circle. Bedi shuffles me into my position in the center, facing the altar and moon phases.

"Night Goddess, hear my call," she calls out into the false night, picking up a small wooden bowl from the altar. "We stand before you to ask your blessing on the young Weaver,

Sadie." I jolt as Bedi flicks cool water on me; it tingles as it slides down my skin, but I don't dare wipe it off for fear of disrupting the ritual.

"Do not fear change, because it is inevitable. The new moon will guide you to new beginnings. Always heed the call."

She steps toward me, lifting a hand to my forehead, and draws a crescent moon with the strange silver liquid from the wooden bowl. "The crescent moon represents the dark sides of you, while sometimes misconstrued as a bad thing, it doesn't have to be. You can always find light in the darkness."

She continues. "The quarter moon represents growth and healing. Don't be afraid to let go of the negativity bothering you." She paints a quarter moon on my right cheek.

"And finally, the full moon. It represents maturity and strength. It's a cause for celebration. Don't be afraid to dance under the light of the moon." She pushes her thumb onto my left cheek, leaving the imprint of a full moon.

Bedi returns to her pedestal that almost looks as if it's carved from the moon's surface itself. "Night, please bless this child." The weight of her power carries the words clearly across the room, which feels much heavier than it did a moment ago. The air is thick, almost stifling. A breeze kicks up, lifting my hair off my shoulders. The stars and moons grow brighter until it's almost unbearably luminous.

Everything blinks out at once, plunging the room into total darkness. My muscles tense and I shift my weight, ready to spring into action at a moment's notice. With the way these past few days have gone, I'm not taking any chances.

Muscular arms wrap around me protectively, pulling me back from the center of the circle into his embrace. "I've got you, Little Flame," Kaos whispers.

"We have waited for you for so long, child." A phantom hand

caresses my cheek. Every muscle in my body relaxes and I intuitively know this entity means me no harm. Tears spring to my eyes as her loving strength wraps around me.

The cadence of her words can only be described as ethereal. *"Use your powers wisely and beware of the dark forces against you. Know we are always watching, waiting for the day when things are made right. May the Shadow's guide and watch over you on your journey."* With one last gentle caress, the ghostly hand trails her fingers down my cheek in a loving way, and then it's gone.

"Who are you?" I whisper, but the room no longer feels heavy with the weight of her power and I know—whoever the voice belongs to—is no longer with me.

"Well, that's certainly never happened before," Bedi says, relighting the candles with a snap of her fingers, and I finally get a good look at the guy's worried expressions.

Great. Another way I'm different from the others. Is a little normalcy too much to ask for?

Bedi reaches under the altar and hands me a smooth, milky white pebble she calls a *shadestone*. She tells me it was charged during my ritual and I'll need it one day. That it will bring me strength and healing. I'm not sure how a rock is supposed to do that, but I'll keep it on me anyway. It can't hurt, right?

There are so many other things I want to ask, but I can't seem to make my mouth move. Every time a question comes to mind, it suddenly disappears. Since my senses are too overloaded to really do anything else, the guys usher me out of the chamber and Bedi's treehouse.

I can tell the ritual rattled them.

It shook me too if I'm honest.

26

SADIE

After an uneventful ride, we roll off the backroads into a town, passing a weathered welcome sign that states *Welcome to Sevierville. Your Hometown in the Smokies.* It's the first indication of actual civilization we've passed since we left the duplex.

Riding in Dante's lap has been pure hell. Every time I shift, his dick pokes me in the ass. It can't be comfortable for him. Although, he's been super accommodating and hasn't made me feel awkward once. That's the thing about these guys, they make me feel like I belong in a way no one else ever has. Dante's been a perfect gentleman.

Kaos takes an abrupt left down a gravel driveway between a large patch of trees. The sharp turn almost throws me out of Dante's arms, and I'm forced to brace my hands against the roof or end up in Kaos' lap. Which was likely the point, considering he smacks a kiss against my lips before Dante pulls me back across the console. "I can't let Dante have all the fun, now can I?"

Lord, these two are going to be the death of me.

I take a moment to study our surroundings because if

things go sideways, I need to know where to go, determine the best route to leave. On our right side, there's a serious drop off. One wrong move or slight jerk of the wheel and we'll be pancakes in the ravine. When the rickety road finally turns the opposite way, leading us away from the cliff, I let out a relieved breath. "That was a long way down."

Dante shrugs. "It's a decent tourist deterrent."

No shit.

A few minutes later, the gravel roadway turns paved. We pass through row after row of picture-perfect oak trees leading to an equally picturesque mansion. It looks like they plucked it right out of an HGTV magazine and plopped it onto a plot of land in the mountains. Honestly, who needs this much space?

Kaos maneuvers the Maserati around the circular driveway, parking in front of the entrance. There's a short staircase leading up to a giant wrap-around front porch. "Welcome to our humble abode," he announces, reaching over to give my knee a small squeeze.

"Humble?" I scoff. "Our duplex was humble. This is something else." I take in the stone facade and the perfectly manicured lawn. We're in the mountains, yet there's not a fallen leaf in sight.

Dante opens our door, and slips out with me in his arms, setting me down with a kiss on my cheek. I let the seat forward, allowing Goldie and Ash to exit. They do with muttered groans about tiny backseats. I can't blame them.

A butler—or at least I'm assuming he's a butler, judging by the full tuxedo—comes rushing out of the front door, his man bun bouncing with each long stride he takes.

"I'm so sorry I'm late. Please excuse my absence, Kings'," he says, giving a short bow to the guys. He extends a gloved hand to me. "Please allow me to take your bag for you, Miss."

When I don't react, he looks up at me expectantly. My

breath catches in my throat because he has the most exquisite eyes with light golden flecks throughout his iris and they seem like they hold so much pain behind them. He's also sporting a massive black eye, split lip, and bruised cheekbone. He clears his throat and my trance snaps. I frown, looking down at my ratty bag that holds everything I have left to my name. "I'd prefer to keep it with me, but thanks for the offer."

His golden eyes widen. "I insist, Miss. I'll take it straight to your room." He grabs the handle and we have a slight tug-of-war before I finally relent. I don't know their customs and the last thing I want to do is get him in trouble.

"Fine, take it. You better not rifle through my shit though or I'll come after you. Panty sniffing is also off-limits. You're not a panty sniffer, are you?"

His cheeks turn a twinge of pink as he says, "Of course not, Miss. I'll have it waiting for you in the room the Kings' have chosen." He takes the rest of the luggage from the trunk and races up the steps.

"Hey, what happened to your face?" I call after him.

Subtle, I am not.

"I'd like to know as well, Vinson," Elian says, spearing him with those intense green eyes of his. Oops.

The butler shifts from foot to foot before turning around. "Yes sir. Unfortunately, our—" He stops, darting a glance at me. "—package was quite wild and escaped while I was switching vehicles. The other package has been dispose—I mean, taken care of."

One glance in Elian's direction shows he's furious. The tight set to his jaw, the blaze of his emerald eyes, but when he sees me looking, he locks it all down leaving that cold facade in place.

"Find it and bring it back here, *or else.*"

A second butler dressed like the first comes scrambling

down the steps, interrupting the moment. He offers to park Kaos' Maserati in the garage. Which is to the left of the mansion. I count six garage doors before I stop and roll my eyes. This is nuts. I've stepped into an alternate reality somewhere along the way.

"Look at this place," Ash says, echoing my thoughts. "You know, we always wanted to lock down some sugar daddies and you finally did it."

"Sugar daddy, eh?" Dante jokes with that dang smirk fixed in place and his eyes twinkling. "I'll be your sugar daddy, Angel. All you have to do is ask." He leans over and kisses me square on the lips, saving me from having to produce a response.

Kissing him is like standing outside in a thunderstorm. The charge between us is fun and exhilarating but also messy and chaotic. Before long Dante pulls away—much to my disappointment.

"Come on, Angel. I'll show you to my bed—I mean around the mansion." He wiggles his eyebrows making me laugh.

"Sure, whisk her away, we can find our own way around! Can't we pup?" Ash grumbles at our retreating backs.

As soon as we step through the front door and into the foyer, I'm blown away. The ceiling expands the entire three stories and there's a skylight at the top that soft light filters through. The entryway then leads past a formal living room that's exquisitely decorated, dripping with opulence.

The next room we pass is a library that would make Belle jealous and makes my book soul happy. There're row upon row of books and even a ladder to reach the top shelves. I'll have to check it out on my own time, for sure. Dante notices my interest with a knowing smirk and promises to show me around whenever I'd like. Score.

The butler who took our bags pops back into the living

room, drawing my attention. "Welcome to King Estate, Ms. Sinclair. My name is Vinson. If there's anything at all I can help you with, please pull any of the designated ropes and I'll assist you as soon as I'm able."

"Uh, thank you, Vinson. I appreciate that," I respond with a genuine smile.

"Certainly, Ms. Sinclair." He bends over at the waist, crossing a fist over his chest, and bows to me. It's one thing he bows for the guys, but to me?

My nose crinkles. "Please call me Sadie, and actually, if you don't mind, I'd rather you not bow to me. That's not something I'm comfortable with."

"Yes, Ms. Si—" I shoot him a glare and he clears his throat changing directions. "I mean *Sadie*, but we are required to bow to you. Such is our custom here."

I take a moment to study him fully. He doesn't seem to be much older than me and he's extremely handsome. I find myself wanting to know his backstory but shut those feelings down fast. *You're mated for shit's sake, Sadie.*

"Vinson, is it?" I ask. "Would you mind if I call you Vin instead?"

"Sure. Feel free to call me anything you'd like, Miss."

"Do you have a preference between them? Personally, I prefer to give everyone a nickname, if that's all right."

"Erm, I like Vin better, honestly. Thank you for asking." His lips turn up into a small smile that he quickly hides when Dante growls.

So possessive. It's going to be fun riling him up.

The air around us crackles and, for once, I recognize the signature of the brooding bad boy with razor-sharp green eyes and perfectly coiffed hair before he pops into existence next to me.

"Stop treating the help like he actually has feelings," Elian says, looking like he absolutely hates himself when he does.

My eye twitches as the urge to stab him takes over. He's lucky my switchblade is in my bag or it'd be through his eyeball by now. Vin's face shuts down and every trace of his former smile is gone.

"Fuck's sake, you really are an asshole," I snarl. "He's a human being, and deserves some respect, or is that too difficult to compute in that bad boy brain of yours?"

Elian's cold eyes narrow on me, like a blast of frigid air so cold it burns me everywhere his gaze roams. "He isn't a human at all, my dear. He's a shifter, and I'll give you a quick history lesson, for free. Since you know nothing about our kind or our customs. The Alpha of all shifters owed the Night Weavers a favor. They're indebted to us by a life debt."

My mouth pops open, but not from shock. No, from rage.

"Indebted to you by a life debt? You, or your so-called Elders?"

How are these the people who are in charge?

Doesn't anyone see how corrupt they are?

The air crackles as he strides toward me and lifts two of those inked fingers, trailing them across my jaw. Indignation flares through me but is quickly replaced by heat when he trails his fingers down the side of my throat, hovering above my thundering pulse. My traitorous body flushes from the contact, making him smile viciously.

"Them, and by extension, me and this Circle."

My temper spikes again, and I reach up, cracking Elian across the jaw. He opens and closes his mouth a few times, rubbing his chin with the same hand he had on mine seconds earlier before he spears me with a look that's pure malice.

I cut in before he can speak. "How dare you, Elian? How fucking dare you? Your head is so far up your own ass, I'm surprised you can even see two feet in front of you. You may think they are beneath you because they're *indebted* to your kind, but they are not. I've been treated like I was less than dirt for most of my life, and I won't stand for it from anyone. Especially you," I hiss.

His emerald eyes flash with something that almost looks like regret, but it's gone before I can be certain. He doesn't get the chance to respond because Dante snatches me around the waist and tosses me over his shoulder, dragging me away from the scene.

"Put me down, you lithe fuck." He doesn't. "I need to kick Elian's ass. Show him who wears the pants in this situation."

One of these days, that infuriating man and I are going to come to blows and the explosion we'll leave in our wake won't be for the faint of heart.

"Vinson, please show Ashley to her room. She's still outside." Dante calls over his shoulder, ignoring my protests.

From my upside-down position hanging near his ass—which is a very nice, tight ass, by the way—Vinson looks totally impassive. If it weren't for the slight tightness in his jaw, I'd never know he's bothered by Elian's callous words.

My eyes find Elian once more before we round the corner. I make sure to give him my best death glare on the way out, but he's not looking at me. He's looking at the ground with clenched fists and sad eyes, which totally wars with the icy exterior he exudes.

Dante's shoulders shake with laughter as he pats me on the ass. "Ignore him, Angel. He must be on his man-period or something. If he doesn't lighten up soon, Kaos and I will take care of it."

"Sure, Dante. Whatever you say." I can't help replaying Elian's words in my head as we walk away. *They're indebted to us by a life debt.*

"Are they really indebted to the Elders?" I ask quietly.

He nods. "Unfortunately, Elian's an ass but he's not a liar. We take in as many as we can, but the pack house is only so big. It's a long story, Angel, but trust me when I say our

Circle is much friendlier to them than the rest of the Night Weavers." He sighs, sitting me down on the ground. "Try not to worry about it too much. There's nothing you can do for them right now."

I notice he says *right now,* and it gives me the tiniest bit of hope that I can do *something* in the future. Because I won't stand for the mistreatment of anyone. Ever.

27

SADIE

Dante shows me room after elaborate room, but I'm hardly paying attention. There's too much to take in and I'm a little raw after everything that's happened the past three days.

Three freaking days. It's hard to believe it's only been such a short period of time. Hell, look at me now versus a few days ago. Lounging around in a mansion like I'm somebody special. Pfft.

Skylar would die to see this place though. He always loved the finer things in life even if we never got to experience them. When we still lived with our dad, we lived in a one-bedroom trailer. It was nothing compared to this, but that ratty trailer was *ours*. Then he died, and social services dumped us on our only other living relative. Mickey Sinclair.

Curse that man. If he hadn't dropped off the face of the planet after what happened with Skylar, I would've killed him my-fucking-self and he knows it. One of these days he'll reappear though, and I won't stop until I murder him with my bare hands.

Ash's family took me in shortly after the fallout of Skylar dying. Thankfully, or else I don't know where I'd be now if it weren't for them. I was broken, and Ash was there to piece me back together again. I spent many nights bawling in her lap until eventually, she helped me get my spunk and confidence back. Then they also died and I've been mad at the world ever since.

"Uh, earth to Sadie?" Dante interrupts my thoughts, wrinkling his nose at me in confusion.

I force a smile. "I'm sorry. My mind was elsewhere. What were you saying?"

"Yeah, I could tell. Where'd you go in that beautiful head of yours, Angel? You looked like you were a million miles away." He tucks a strand of hair behind my ear, and I look away from his inquisitive stare. Talking about my past is too heavy right now.

"It's been a long couple of days," I respond instead.

"True, but it hasn't been all bad. Has it? I mean other than the people trying to kill us, and the car chase, and the boulder fire…" He trails off. "Well, maybe it has been a little nuts." He starts poking my side, trying to get a reaction out of me.

I can't help but laugh, swatting his hand away when he finds my ticklish spot. "So, what were you trying to tell me?"

"Oh, I was telling you a little bit of the history of the house. It was built in the 1940s by the King family and was passed down to us when we came of age at twenty-one, along with the family business. We had it updated recently to bring it to modern times."

"No doubt," I say, admiring the glamorous cream colored walls and crown molding. "Hey, speaking of the King family, why do you all have the same last name?" My nose crinkles. "Are you actually brothers?" None of them look anything alike, but stranger things have happened.

He chuckles. "No. When we were matched at thirteen, we took Elian's last name because he is kind of like our 'unofficial leader.' Some Circles prefer to have one person in charge, but we never liked that idea. We listen to each other and agree upon a decision from there. If all else fails, we put things to a vote."

I raise an eyebrow. Interesting concept—and if it works for them, who am I to argue?

"When you were matched? What does that mean?"

"Our magic starts seeking our other members around the age of thirteen. When the call to join comes, we're powerless to the pull until we find our other members and bond as a Circle," he tells me. "With that said, Night Weaver communities are quite small, so we grew up together and already knew one another."

"Seems intense."

"It is."

"What happens if you don't like your fellow members?" I ask, thinking about the dickish way Elian has treated me thus far.

Dante frowns. "You know, I'm not sure. I don't think it's ever happened. According to Weaver lore, the Night Goddess has a hand in each pairing, and she's never wrong."

"Hmph. If you say so." I've never been one to blindly put my faith in anything, so getting on board with their customs is going to be a challenge for me. We walk under another arch that leads to an informal den. My eyes light up with excitement upon spying both sets of the newest gaming systems and the giant couch placed in front of the largest TV I've ever seen.

"This is our man cave."

"I can see that. Hopefully, you guys don't mind teaching a girl to play."

He eyes me seductively as he leads me away from the man

cave. "Of course not, Angel. In fact, I'd love teaching you to play. But for now, I want to finish our tour."

"Are you sure that's what you want to do?" I ask, and my voice comes out breathier than I'd intended. Dante picks up on it straight away. He raises one of those blond brows at me as his gaze trails down my body sensually. "Like what you see?" I taunt, trailing my fingers up my side.

"Fuck yes," he breathes. "Seeing you with your hair looking wild and freshly fucked even though I know you're not?" He groans. "Getting my hands on you is all I've been able to think about."

He grabs my wrist and spins me to face him as his lips crash against mine. His tongue dances with my own as his other hand comes up to cup my face. I groan, leaning into his touch, loving the way his hands feel on me. His teeth scrape my earlobe and I shiver as his hot breath skims my neck.

"Shadows take me," he breathes as I flip our positions, shoving him into the wall.

Our kiss doesn't even slow as he lets me take control of the moment, and I kiss the freaking daylights out of him. My fingers trail down the rigid planes of his pecs and abs, enjoying the groan I elicit when I dig my fingers into his waistband. As I try to yank his shirt over his head, he switches our positions again.

Things are really starting to heat up, until something cold and wet brushes against my leg. I jerk, ending up smacking Dante in the face for the second time today. When I glance down, I find Goldie looking up at me with his little doggy smirk, totally cock-blocking me.

"You better be glad you're cute," I snap.

Dante chuckles. "Come on, Angel. Let's get you two settled."

He takes us up the stairs and down a hallway, pointing to

each door to let me know whose room it is. Elian and Kaos are on either side of me with Dante and Ash across from me.

When Dante opens the door to my room my eyes widen. He ushers my stunned ass inside and Goldie trails in behind me. This place is insane. Half of our old duplex could fit inside here. Not to mention there's a stocked bar in the corner next to an expensive-looking writing desk and a settee in front of a large TV.

By the window is a four-poster bed that is large enough to fit six people. We could totally have a giant orgy on it or the threesome that's been stuck in my brain since the festival and still have room. There's a fluffy white duvet with a gunmetal grey blanket adorning the end, which Goldie claims instantly. He jumps onto the bed and curls up in a ball on it.

"This is too much, Dante," I say. He glances over at me curiously. "When you're used to a whole house the size of this room, it's a little much, you know?"

He grips my chin, forcing me to look him in the eye. "Nothing is too much for you, Angel. You have no idea how much you being here means to us. We'd completely lost hope that we'd ever find our Link. You're one of us now, so let us take care of you." He leans in, kissing my forehead.

"Okay, fine." I wiggle my finger at him. "But you're not getting off that easy. I want to learn more about your world sooner rather than later. I don't like being kept in the dark, especially when my life is on the line."

"You got it. We'll take you over to the compound tomorrow and see if we can't establish a baseline on your magic."

With that settled, Dante leaves to get cleaned up with promises that food will come later. I determine a shower is in order for me as well and dash into the ensuite bathroom. I slump down against the door with a heavy sigh. So much has happened in three short days. My head is having a tough time keeping up. But my heart—or should I say *my vagina*—is having no trouble at all.

If only things were that simple.

28

SADIE

Dante isn't back by the time I finish my hot shower, so I decide to find the kitchen on my own. Goldie tags along with me to keep me company and, surprisingly, we don't run into any of the guys or the staff.

The kitchen is a chef's wet dream, fitted with every kind of appliance you can imagine. There's a legit industrial size fridge that reminds me of the ones we had at Harborview. Man, I don't miss that place one bit.

"What can I get for you?" A masculine voice rumbles.

I whirl around, only settling a fraction when a familiar pair of gold eyes meet mine. "My goodness, you almost gave me a heart attack, Vin."

The corner of his lip turns up in a small smile. "I'm so sorry, Miss. I didn't mean to startle you."

I take in the apron wrapped around his waist and the flour on his hands. "Wow, you're a chef too, eh? Man of many talents."

"I'm whatever the Kings need me to be. Now that you're here, what would you like to eat?" He names off several food choices, none of which I understand or can repeat.

"You know what? Just whip me up something you think I'd like." I move to sit at the Carrara marble island the size of Tahiti sitting smack dab in the center of the room. Goldie nips my hand, reminding me he's still with me. Guess he doesn't like to talk around strangers. "And something meaty for my dog, if you don't mind?"

With a nod, Vin starts rifling around the cabinets finding seemingly random ingredients. I pay him no mind while he cooks around the stovetop. When he's finished, he places a plate topped with a big juicy steak on the floor for Goldie, then extends another plate with two perfectly aligned sandwiches cut in half my way.

Picking one slice up, I take a tentative bite. Pleasure explodes across my taste buds like nothing I've ever experienced before. I force myself to hold back a throaty groan, lifting the top of the bread trying to figure out what's inside, but there doesn't seem to be anything extra hiding between the pieces of bread. It looks like a typical BLT.

"My Gods, what is in this sandwich?" I ask. "It's divine."

"A secret ingredient. That's what makes it taste so different," he tells me with a conspiratorial smile.

"What is it? Or is this one of those 'if I tell you, I'll have to kill you moments?'"

This makes him bark out a laugh. "For you, we'll skip the death part." He leans in across the counter to whisper in my ear. His voice is gravelly and low and his gorgeous golden eyes sparkle. "The secret is grape jelly. The sweetness of the jelly plays off the saltiness in the bacon."

"Like a sweet and salty combo? Nice. I knew there was something different about it, but I couldn't put my finger on what exactly it was." His eyes dip to my lips and my breath catches in my throat.

His large hand lifts to my lips, dragging my lip down as he

wipes away some of the jelly I must've missed, then he pops his thumb into his mouth. The sight shouldn't be erotic, but it is. My breathing starts to quicken and I can't seem to bring myself to look away. In the next second, he withdraws, putting space between us, which is probably for the best. He clears his throat, glancing away from me. "The Kings own a grape vineyard, so all of the jellies and jams are locally sourced from their farm."

Huh. Guess that explains where all their money comes from. "Well, I'm impressed, Vin. Great job."

"Thank you. I appreciate your kind words," he says. "Is there anything else I can do for you right now, Sadie?"

The dark circles under his eyes seem to be worse than earlier and the overall tiredness wafting off him is almost palpable, seeping into the air around us. Not to mention his bruises. "Actually, am I allowed to give you a break? You look like you need it."

"I'm afraid that's not possible, Miss—"

"Nope, fuck that. I want you to relax for a moment. If anyone asks you about it, tell them to come to me and I'll set them straight."

Vin looks torn, but eventually, he gives in with a nod, gratitude shining in his eyes as he leans against the counter. "Would you mind?" He motions toward the second sandwich I haven't touched. It hurts my fucking heart to hand it over, but I can be nice. Sometimes.

"What did you mean by 'package' earlier?" I ask. "When you were talking to Elian, I mean."

He coughs, choking on the bite he just took. "I'm sorry, Miss, but that's not something I'm allowed to discuss with you."

"Why on earth not?"

"Elian's orders," he says with a shrug, but I can sense more under the surface he's not saying.

For his sake though, I drop it. I'll take it up with Mr. Brooding Asshole myself.

My stomach rumbles so I sneak back over to the fridge, checking each shelf for something to snack on. So many exotic fruits and vegetables, but no snack foods. I check the pantry and strike out there too.

"Don't these people have any beef jerky or BBQ chips? Hell, at this point, I'd take saltine crackers."

Vin makes a rumbling noise of protest at my list of snacks. "Those are terrible for you, Sadie," he says like I don't already know.

"I don't need a babysitter but thank you for thinking of my health."

He takes a moment to swallow before responding. "I go to the grocery store on Fridays. I can stock up for you then if you'd like?"

"Sure, but I'd like to go with you if that's okay?" As nice as Vin seems I don't trust him to buy the right kind of snacks. It takes finesse. Not all brands taste the same.

He nods, gazing at me like I'm an enigma.

"Great. I'll see you then. For now, I'm going to find out what happened to Dante. Let's go pup." I back out of the kitchen, turning the corner only to come face to face with a chest. A warm bare chest.

"Speak of the fucking devil." I laugh when he spins me around in his arms. "Hello there, Dante."

"Hey, Angel." He sighs heavily. "Unfortunately, I have bad news." The spinning stops as he looks down at me.

"Well, don't keep me waiting. Spit it out."

"We received word that the compound has been attacked and put on lockdown, which means we won't be able to take you there and test out your powers."

Disappointment flutters through me. I was hoping to

figure out more about my magic, but I shove that down. He said they were attacked.

"Is everyone okay?"

He shakes his head. "We're not certain. The Night Weaver who called us was extremely upset, and the line was disconnected before we could get any answers. They're trained for this type of situation, so I wouldn't worry too much though."

"Does this sort of thing happen often?"

"Not with the compounds. Most of the time they try to pick us off while we're alone and vulnerable. Elian's ward should keep us safe though. It hasn't failed us yet."

His assurances do nothing to help settle my concern. My gut says the attack wasn't random and I don't trust Elian enough to have faith in his wards.

"We'll see."

29

SADIE

After my talk with Dante, I went back to my room and fell fast asleep. The bed they gave me literally feels like a freaking marshmallow, and I was out like a light within seconds of my head hitting the pillow.

When I wake, it's because Goldie licks my face, leaving a trail of slobber. He grumbles something about needing food. I groan, pushing my messy morning hair out of my face, wincing when the soft light streaming through the open curtains hits me right in my sensitive eyes.

"Argh. What time is it?" I croak, falling back onto the bed and slamming my pillow over my eyes.

"Breakfast time," Goldie responds, nudging his nose under the pillow to lick my cheek until I finally drag my ass out of bed.

Sometime while I was eating with Vin last night, Dante left satin pajamas on the end of my bed with a note saying to join them for breakfast. The silky top is a little skimpy and more Ash's style than mine, but beggars can't be choosers. I shrug on my Converse and some rumpled jeans from my bag, leaving the burgundy top on for shits and giggles to see how Dante and Kaos react.

Deciding to stop by Ash's room on my way down, I open up her door to find her passed out across the fancy bed, dead asleep. I whisper her name, but she doesn't stir so I gently close the door and back away. She needs to sleep. We've both had it rough lately.

Delicious scents waft toward my nostrils the closer we get to the kitchen. I walk through the doorway, startling Vinson as he furiously works over the gas stovetop. There are pots galore, one on each burner and then some. His messy brown hair is thrown into another man-bun today, keeping it from falling into his face while he cooks.

"Good morning, Sadie. Can I help you with anything?" He looks up between stirs, and his eyes widen when he takes in my appearance, but hastily averts his gaze when he realizes he's staring at my cleavage.

"We're starving for breakfast. Looks like we're in the right place."

"Ah, yes. It'll be ready soon. The Kings should be down any moment if you want to join them in the dining room. It's down the hallway to the left. Same side as the kitchen." He still won't meet my eyes.

Goldie snorts, watching our exchange with interest and I murmur a vague thanks as I leave.

Elian's demanding presence washes over me before I even walk into the room. He looks up from the laptop in front of him as I round the corner and his sharp green eyes meet mine. I ignore him and keep walking.

Goldie follows me as I spot the coffee machine and waltz over to pour myself a cup. Conveniently, there's a large stack of mugs next to it, saving me from having to ask for one. His eyes narrow as he watches me and I can sense the gears turning in his head, judging me as I dump an enormous amount of sugar into the cup before sitting down in the chair furthest from him with Goldie at my feet. I'll take all the space I can get.

The table is gorgeous though. It's one of those fancy banquet style tables that only rich people have. I feel like it's better suited for parties than everyday use, but what the hell do I know? I grew up poor.

Kaos comes striding into the room like a breath of fresh air moments later. He also pours a cup of coffee sans sugar and cream before plonking down in the chair next to mine, squeezing my knee under the table. Thoughts of yesterday pop into my mind as his hand travels up my thigh and I try not to shift.

Elian looks between us, his eyes hard, before returning to whatever he's working on.

Dante glides in next, totally shirtless. All coherent thought leaves me for a few moments as I try not to drool over his lithe body. His abs contract with laughter as he catches me looking, but I don't shy away. Not at all. I eat up his appearance because damn, he's gorgeous. He has one of those delicious V's that lead down to the gold, and I want to lick it.

Kaos produces a shirt out of thin air and tosses it at him. It hits him square in the face, catching him totally off guard. Unlike how Tyler would react, Dante merely chuckles, giving Kaos a good-natured head nod as he tugs it over his head, hiding his abs from my greedy view. I sigh.

It was quite the view while it lasted.

"Good morning, Angel. Did you sleep well?"

"I did. Thanks for asking."

Dante and I exchange a glance and those hellish eyes draw me in. They're so fascinating, the way they dance and crackle, almost like the fire he wields in his hands.

Elian snaps, interrupting our moment. "We have business on the agenda today." He steeples his inked fingers on the table, the epitome of calm. "As of this morning, I still haven't heard back from the Light Weavers. Now, I don't want to assume anything until I hear back from him, but we need to be cautious until we learn more. I don't like unknowns."

I snort. That's an understatement and I barely even know the guy. The amount of restraint he must have. I wonder, does that carry over into the bedroo—*Nope, don't finish that thought, Sadie.*

Before anything else can be said, Vinson and two other shifters I've never seen before file into the room, carrying trays piled high with food. No one speaks while they sit the food down and then leave as soundlessly as they came.

My eyes bounce between each man at the table incredulously. None of them pay any attention to me while they dig in, piling everything onto their plates.

"Agreed," Kaos says after he's finished grabbing his food. He looks over at my empty plate and frowns, exchanging my empty one for his stacked one before starting all over again. When I raise an eyebrow all he says is, "Our mate deserves to eat first."

I'm not going to argue, but I'm not used to men caring for me like this. It's been me and Ash against the world for so long, and before that, it was me and Skylar. I think I've forgotten how nice people can be.

"What's the deal with them?" I ask. "The Light Weavers, I mean."

"As you know, they're the opposite of us. They draw their powers from the sun and daylight while we draw ours from the moon and shadows," Kaos replies.

"I gathered that already," I say around a mouthful of a biscuit—get this—with jelly already on it. Yep, someone already put the jelly on there for me. Speaking of jelly, I need to ask about their business. "Who are they and why do they want me?"

Elian eyes my full mouth in disgust. "We're technically at war with them, but we made a pact with their future leader not to engage in fights. They leave our Circle alone and vice versa. Obviously, something has changed. Perhaps they want you for themselves." He pauses to dab his mouth with a napkin. "But that would be preposterous. Light and Night don't mix. It's forbidden."

"Back up. There's a war?"

Elian exhales heavily, casting a glance in my direction that looks a lot like pity—but that would be ridiculous coming from him. "Yes, our Elders started a war with them a few years ago, although, no one knows exactly why. We've always coexisted, despite our differences until recently."

These Elder folks continue to get better and better. By that, I mean they make me want to whip a switchblade out and slit their throats.

"Let me get this straight. Your people are at war with a similar group of people—who have similar powers, but no one knows why?" He nods, tilting his head to the side in thought. "Why would anyone agree to that? Who goes to war without a known cause?" I direct my question toward Kaos, figuring he'll be the most honest and contemplative.

He shrugs. "We don't know, and we don't agree with hating them over our differences. That's why we have a treaty with their future leader, but we can't get ahold of him, so he's either broken our agreement and he's ignoring us, or something far more sinister is going on."

Wonderful.

Elian turns his attention to Kaos, curling his inked fingers around his coffee mug as he takes a sip. There's a rose on the back of his hand and a knife going through his pointer finger. There are also three lines wrapped around his ring finger. It makes me wonder what they symbolize.

"What's the status on the information you're hunting? Any luck with the archives?" he asks.

"Nothing concrete yet, but I'm still searching."

"What information?" I interject.

Elian sighs. "We're searching for answers about your powers. There's never been anyone in our lifetime that can do what you did to the Elites the other day. Small telekinesis powers like lifting a book, yes. But flipping two vehicles and stopping a third? No."

His statement makes my stomach churn. What the hell makes me so different? I don't like it. Bad guys always hunt the different ones, the powerful ones, because we're their worst nightmares. People like my uncle like to break the strong-willed, like the porcelain plate at Harborview; shatter their souls so they'll never be strong again.

They can try to anyway. I broke after Skylar died, but never again. I fitted those jagged pieces back together, and I'll continue to fight until my last breath.

"Now," he starts. "Next week you're going to start training with Kaos and Dante. You need to hone in your powers and learn to defend yourself so what happened at the concert doesn't happen again."

Outrage flits through me and I choke on a piece of bacon. Did this motherfucker call me weak? I'll fucking show him weak.

I stand, pushing my chair back. "Fuck you, Elian," I spit. "If you didn't notice, I was handling things perfectly fine."

"If by fine you mean letting those weaklings almost bond you to their Circle against your will, then sure," he sneers.

The anger takes hold of me and I snatch my butter knife from the table. Before anyone can even blink, I rear back and throw it in his direction with all the extra strength I can muster.

Unfortunately, the asshole has catlike reflexes and disappears in a cloud of smoke before it can bury itself in his chest. Instead, it embeds itself in his swanky wooden chair exactly where his heart was with a loud *thunk.*

He reappears a few feet from his chair. His face shows nothing, but his eyes show a minuscule amount of respect.

"What in the name of the Night Goddess has gotten into you, bro?" Dante snarls, glaring at his friend like he wants to stab him as badly as I do.

By all means Dante, please do.

Loud voices echo from outside, fluttering into the dining room seconds before there's a crash outside, shattering the intensity of the moment. My muscles tense.

Could the Elites have caught up to us so soon? The way the guys talked, Elian's ward should keep anyone with ill intent out, and something tells me they don't have good intentions.

Kaos stops me in the doorway. "Stay here," he tells me before racing out of the dining room with Dante and Elian hot on his heels.

Stay here, he says. Fuck that. These men will soon learn that I'm not the cower from danger type. Goldie gives me a slight nod and we rush out of the dining room together.

Dante, Kaos, and Elian appear to be talking to someone, but I can't see who because they're too fucking tall. I silently make my way between them and my heart stops.

"Why won't they let me come inside?" The shrill voice demands, sounding like nails on a chalkboard.

Goldie growls, parting the guys like they're nothing. He bares his teeth at the intruder. It makes me want to bare my teeth too, but that would look silly, right?

Too bad I don't care.

I snarl at the she-shark Savannah, which makes her squeal and jump straight into Elian's arms. She wraps herself around him like a boa constrictor squishing the life out of its prey. When she looks over at me, she sniffles and even has some fake ass crocodile tears pooling in those conniving eyes of hers.

Oh no, what ever will I do to combat the crocodile tears? Somebody give me a fucking break. Isn't the mean girl act a little overdone? Like seriously, what did I do to deserve a mean girl in my life?

Elian drops her like a sack of shit, wiping his hands down his fitted white tee, like touching her is repulsive. Much to my disappointment, she doesn't land on her ass and doesn't even seem bothered by his callousness. When she smiles, I remember exactly what she is—a shark. I brace myself for her words, already knowing I'm not going to like what comes next.

"Guys. What is this bitch doing in my mansion? Which one of you brought her back here?"

That's when I notice the bag in her hand and the open trunk of her car filled with luggage. My heart sinks to my stomach and I spin on my heel, glaring at the three assholes who are looking anywhere but me. Dante even has the audacity to stick his hands in his pockets and whistle. I reach up to finger my brothers' necklace, trying to soothe my anger. It doesn't work. *I'm going to murder them, all of them.*

Savannah reaches for Elian again and Goldie snarls at her, looking menacing as fuck. Even his teeth look sharper than they did moments before. At least someone has my fucking back.

"Call off your stupid mutt!" she whines, stomping her foot.

I don't do a thing.

Ash must hear the commotion because she comes

barreling out onto the porch and takes in the scene. "Who the hell is this bitch and why haven't you stabbed her yet?"

Excellent question, Ash.

Dante clears his throat uncomfortably. I narrow my eyes on him, crossing my arms over my chest, waiting to hear his explanation. "Um, well, it's kind of a long story—"

Elian sighs. "For shadow's sake. The Elders announced yesterday that she'd become our Circle's Link—"

"Exactly, and I want this fucking one-night stand out of here right now." She crosses her arms over her chest looking way too smug for someone about to get their bubble popped.

"Aww, you haven't heard the news, have you?" I ask, letting a wicked grin splay across my face. She blanches, looking between the guys for help, but she won't find any. "I'm their true Link. Kaos and I are bonded." I turn my wrist around where she can see my tattoo and her dainty features contort with rage.

Ash cackles, taking pleasure in her anger. "Sorry, love. Guess that means you're no longer needed here. I'd say it was a pleasure to meet you, but we both know it wasn't. Goodbye."

I love my best friend.

Savannah bursts into more tears, reaching out for Dante and I see red. My temper flares and it takes all my self-control not to march over there and break her fingers for touching him. I expect him to pry her hands off and tell her to get lost, but he doesn't move. My chest tightens.

"Kaos is the only one marked so far," Savannah says matter of factly. Goldie nips at her again but instead of squealing, she digs her claws into Dante's chest.

She's not wrong though. None of the other guys are bonded to me. Do I really have any kind of claim on them? No, I guess I don't.

The question is why does their inaction hurt so fucking much?

Because you thought they were yours. A small voice whispers in the back of my mind. And yeah, I guess I was starting to think they were mine. I straighten my spine, locking down every single feeling inside like I always do.

Technically I could stab her, or attack her, but what good would that do when the guys aren't even going to tell her off?

Regret flashes in Dante's amber eyes. Kaos stands there watching everything unfold with hawklike eyes and Elian looks impassive to the whole thing like he always does.

I spin around and march down the porch toward the garage with Ash and Goldie hot on my heels. "Screw this." I have no idea where I'm going to go but I'm not going to stand here and be humiliated like this.

Sadie Sinclair bows for no man.

The timing of this couldn't be worse though. Just when I start to think that men could be different—that these men could be different.

"Sadie!" Dante calls, dashing after me. I don't slow. "Sadie, wait. Don't leave. Please! This is all quite a shock and I'm sorry."

One slip up, and I'm gone is what I told them. Well, this is their one.

"I warned you," is my response.

"Little Flame, you can't leave." Kaos' nickname for me makes my teeth grind together and my feet come to a stop.

I whirl around to cast a withering glare at my so-called mates. "You have no right to call me that, Kaos. I know when I'm not wanted or appreciated and I'm not sticking around to be treated less than I deserve."

"But, Sadie, you don't have a handle on your powers—"

An empty hole forms in my chest and I stop him before he can finish that sentence with a caustic laugh. "I'm perfectly capable of fending for myself. I've done fine on my own so far and I'll continue to do so."

Without waiting for a response, I take off again, heading for the garage. I'll steal one of their fancy cars if that's what it takes. I try to yank the door open but it's locked. Of course. I slam my fists against it in frustration.

Violence never solves anything.

Yeah? That may be true, but it makes life a hell of a lot easier sometimes. I rest my back against the door, looking up to the sky to silently ask what I've done to deserve this life.

When I level my gaze on Dante, he looks like he's having a silent battle with himself. Kaos speaks before he can do anything. His jaw is clenched so tight I'm afraid he might crack a tooth. "An order is an order, Dante."

Order? What order?

"Screw their damn orders!" Dante snarls, stalking my way with his eyes fixated on me and only me. He reaches out, wrapping his fingers around mine. I swear he stares directly into my soul, stripping me raw as his palm hovers above mine. The slight space between them crackles with energy.

How dare he?

"You're not even going to defend me and you think you can bond to me without my consent? Fuck you, Dante. That's not how this works," I say.

"I fucked up and I'll admit that," he says simply. Like this isn't a monumental deal—not to mention something we will have to deal with for *life*. His eyes flick away from me for a half of a second before returning, dancing with those wild flames. "We all fucked up and I'm sorry about that, but I'm not going to let someone who means absolutely nothing to me ruin my chances with you because of some jacked-up orders from those old meddling bastards."

"This is insane! You don't even know me." I take a deep breath, counting to five in my head to calm down.

CHAPTER 29 | 235

"I don't have to know every little detail about you, Angel. From these past few days alone, I've noticed your strength and resilience. You're a fucking fighter and I should've fought for you just now." He runs a hand through his hair, and I look away. The intensity in his eyes is too much for me. "Besides, we'll have plenty of time for me to find out every little aspect of your soul." His calloused fingers caress my face, pulling my eyes back to his. I fight the annoying fluttering in my stomach. "Right now, it's more important to show you that this is *sacred* to us. You are our Link. Our true mate. Not her."

"It's a little late for the pretty words, don't you think? Actions speak louder than anything."

"It's never too late, Angel. And if you'll forgive me, I'll make sure she never steps foot on this land again."

I feel, rather than see, Ash, Kaos, and Goldie backing away to give us space. Still, I don't relent easily.

"With Kaos, it was different. I didn't know what I was getting myself into, but now I do and I'm hurt, Dante."

"Let me make this right. Please," he pleads.

"What if you regret it?" I ask softly. "What if Savannah is the right fit for you as a Circle?"

He cuts me off before I can say anything else. "That's not possible, Angel," he murmurs, "I want this. I want *you*. I barely know you and yet, I know you're so Godsdamned strong. You'd move mountains for the people you love, and I want to be one of those people one day. I want to be worthy of *you*."

My heart swells as a lone tear slides down my cheek. Dante reaches up, brushing the watery liquid off my cheek before he brings it to his lips, kissing it away. His words and actions touch some dark corner of my soul that I'd thought I'd locked up tight.

Our palms connect and a blast of heat surges from our

bodies. Orangish blue flames surround us, flaring into the sky. After a few moments, it dies down, and our muscles tense, locking us in place. At least now I know it's the bond forming.

Power like I've never known before starts rushing into my body, threatening to scald me where I'm standing. If I could move my mouth, I'd probably scream. It's the most excruciating thing I've ever experienced in my entire life and the edges of my vision start to turn black.

Everything hurts.

Before the darkness drags me under, I glance over to find Kaos holding Savannah back by the neck, a vicious snarl on his face. She knows what's happening and she looks devastated. An angry guttural scream breaks free from her throat and it's the last thing I hear before I blackout.

Consciousness slowly returns to me in the form of a headache. I groan. *Why are the sheets so warm and how did I get in bed?* I wiggle, trying to escape the bands wrapped around my middle, but freeze when those bands move, pressing into me tighter as something even harder brushes up against my ass.

My eyes snap open and I jerk upright, wincing from the searing pain in my head as I turn to face him. He's already awake and smiles at me, tucking me into his chest. His smokey scent wraps around me, making me feel safe, even if I'm still mad at him.

"What the hell happened and why are you in my bed?" I ask.

"We bonded," he says, placing his hand over his heart then tugs on the silvery thread connecting us as mates. He chose *me*. Over Savannah the Shark. Fuck yeah.

"You're still in the dog house."

He frowns, rubbing his fingers through my hair. "I know and I'd expect nothing less, Angel."

"Why did I pass out?"

"To be frank, we're not entirely certain. Our best guess is that the power will continue to intensify with each mate because you're channeling all of our powers through your center at one time."

At least there's only one more mate and I'm not sure if that will ever happen, or if I even want it to at this point. Elian needs to do some massive groveling. I won't be satisfied until he's on his knees begging for forgiveness, and something tells me Elian is not that kind of man.

"By the way, what did you mean by orders?"

He groans, scrubbing a hand down his face. "I'd hoped you had forgotten that."

"Not a chance."

"I figured as much. As soon as the Elders received word about your presence, they forbid anyone else from bonding with you until we go before them and settle the dispute with Savannah. She thinks she can override your claim."

Surely he's not serious.

"You're joking, right? I thought your people considered true Links to be sacred and all that shit?"

"We do. As in our Circle, but over the years with the Elders being in power they've twisted the narrative, and power matches are all they care about."

Wonderful. The deeper I get into this society, the more I hate it.

"Hey, Angel," Dante says, garnering my attention. The intensity in his gaze sets me on edge and it's strange to see him look so serious. He's always cloaked in lazy amusement and smirks.

"Yes?"

"Please don't shut me out again," he says softly, gazing at me with such vulnerability my chest tightens. Someone has abandoned Dante in the past. It's in the way he always wants me close and the hurt in his eyes when I tried to leave earlier.

I sigh. "All of you fucked up royally. I told you I'd give you one chance and you blew it. With that said, I'm willing to give you all another chance, but if I'm going to stay, I need to know she's never coming back here. Ever. I won't tolerate it."

He nods his head in affirmation. "I couldn't agree more, Angel. I will handle it."

"Good, because I don't know if I'll be able to resist stabbing her next time." I punctuate my words with a jab to his abs. This makes him laugh and he grabs my hand, turning it over to show my wrist. There's now a half-moon resting right above my pulse with a 'D' intersecting the 'K.' Huh, that's pretty cool.

"You know, I've never met anyone like you, Angel."

"How so?"

He traces the mark, turning it silver. "You have this reserved fire in you. I've never seen it before in anyone and I know one day you'll be a force to be reckoned with, especially when you explode."

"I don't know about *that*."

"I do. I can feel it," he says.

Playfully, I smack his chest. "Why, Blondie, are you trying to butter me up?" I tickle his side, loving the feeling as his abs jerk under my fingers.

"Nope," he says, popping the P. "I'm being honest."

"Sure," I whisper and press my lips to his.

The sweet kiss quickly heats up into something more—something heated and desperate. He kisses back with a fiery passion that could rival the sun, exactly like his personality and his amber eyes.

He groans, shifting so he can lean over me and push me

into the mattress. His length grinds against my thigh as he thrusts slightly, almost like he can't help himself. My core throbs in response, feeling like it's a raging bonfire and Dante is stoking the flames.

Something about Dante tilts my axis back into alignment when it's off-kilter, and shoots my soul into orbit.

Someone clears their throat, snapping us out of our passionate haze. I exhale sharply, tearing my mouth away from Dante's. Kaos appears in my line of sight, looking extremely turned on before he masks it. Oops. I can only imagine what I must look like to him, swollen lips, bed hair, same clothes as yesterday.

"Sorry to interrupt," he says but he doesn't look sorry. Not at all. "I'm glad to see you're okay and awake. I thought we should have a little chat."

I sit up, pushing Dante—who is still draped over my body—away so I can face Kaos fully. "How long was I out?"

"About six hours give or take. I've been busy taking the trash out," he replies, lips quirked to the side. Hopefully by trash, he means a certain hussy after my fucking men. I mean... uh, yeah, my men. Fuck it.

"Really?" I ask, eyeing him suspiciously.

He nods, eyes flicking to the door.

I groan, throwing my pillow over my head. "Is Elian coming to this little pow-wow too?"

"Damn, Angel. Ready for a foursome already?" Dante jokes falling back into the cocksure asshole I'm used to. "We can make that happen, you know..." He leans back to lazily recline on the headboard and crosses his arms behind his head.

I shoot him a glare and smack his stomach but little good that does. Probably hurts my hand more than it does him.

I notice his symbol for the first time and my breath catches in my throat. A half-moon, with my initial in the same spot, and not only did Dante get his symbol—he got Kaos' as well. Interesting. I wonder what the whole design will look like when completed.

Too bad that would require bonding with Elian. Fat freaking chance.

"Will the symbols build each time?" I ask, running my finger over my design so it lights up in those silvery letters.

"We think so, yes. You should get one for each of us and in turn, we get them as well."

A soft smile graces my lips. I love that. I like seeing my mark on them. If their expressions are any indication, they do too.

The room settles in a peaceful calm as we all sit examining our marks, until the air shifts and darkness comes crawling through the open doorway. I know it's *he who shall not be named* before he even walks through the door.

"What'd I miss?" The man himself asks, sauntering in with a cruel smile fixed upon his luscious lips. It's the kind of smile that nightmares are made from and instead of being repulsed as a normal person would be, my heart flutters. His darkness calls to mine in some fucked up way.

He's not yours, I remind myself but the words seem hollow.

Try telling my magic that.

"Savannah is gone," Kaos tells him. "The bad news is Dante broke the Elder's orders not to bond with Sadie until they could convene a meeting. She's convinced her claim overrides yours." Dante scoffs, interrupting Kaos. "I know. As if she could ever compete with our true mate."

"What I don't understand is why the Elders care? What's it to them?" I ask, trying to puzzle it out in my head.

My Sworn share a look.

"They want to control every aspect of our lives because control equals power to them. We live extremely long lives and without true Links to procreate, our race is slowly dying out. They're hoping one day their fake bonds will set and we won't completely die out. With that said, there will be consequences for Dante's actions, I'm sure, but we'll worry about that when the time comes."

"Not if I can fucking help it," I mutter. I'm not even a part of this society yet, not really, and that seems wrong to me.

Something deep in my chest starts to unfurl with the more I uncover about the Night Weavers, and it feels a lot like vengeance.

"What else do I need to know? I've seen Elian pop into existence from the shadows, but is that something all Night Weavers can do?"

Kaos opens his mouth to respond when Elian shoots him a sharp glare, cutting him off. He clears his throat. "Er, it's not my place to say what everyone else has, but you already know I can heal and produce shields, and Dante is a pyro."

I'm like the epitome of *curiosity killed the cat* and, in this case, it might kill me. I want to know so much more about their powers, but I know they're not going to budge with Elian in the room.

Kaos continues, "Now that Dante and I have bonded with you, we might have powers appear over the next few weeks." He seems practically giddy with that statement and it makes me wonder if he doesn't like his healing power. Maybe he wishes he had offensive magic like Dante.

"Do you have any other abilities? Aside from what happened with the Elite?" Elian asks, watching me from the corner of the room where he's reclined against the wall. So he doesn't want to tell me about his magic but wants me to tell him about mine. Seems fair.

I study him for a moment. His arms are crossed over his chest and his head is tilted back like he doesn't have a care in the world. It highlights the chest piece peeking out of his collar. I can't really make out the design, but it makes me want to find out why he's so inked compared to the other two.

I decide not to stoop to his level. "Extra strength, advanced healing. Nothing special until yesterday. Before then, it was mainly vibes from other people. Like if something bad is about to happen, I get these little tingly feelings."

Kaos nods. "Most of us have those abilities as well."

"See? I knew you were weak," Elian says, running his tongue across his lips.

"What is your problem with me, Elian? What have I done to you?" I demand, shoving to my feet.

He throws his hands up and walks right back out of the room like he couldn't care less about me or the whole situation, slamming the door so hard I'm surprised it didn't pop off the hinges. Gods, he's infuriating. It's almost like he's trying to push me away.

When his negative cloud of energy finally fades from the room, I blow out a deep breath. I don't know why I keep expecting him to give me a shot. He's been nothing but rude from the beginning.

Oh, well. I refuse to spare him another thought.

"I'll back you up if you want to kick his ass," Goldie says, lifting his head from the floor. "Believe me when I say you're not weak, and he will soon come to realize that."

"You don't have to assure me, pup. I already know."

30

SADIE

Later that night, I wake in a puddle of sweat, gasping, and clawing at my chest as the monsters from my nightmare take their time leaving my sleep-addled brain. *Deep breaths, Sadie. You're having a panic attack,* I remind myself. But it's no use, I can still see Skylar's face, so perfectly still, yet so angelic, even in death. His blond hair splayed out like the perfect halo until the red tainted everything.

Gods, I miss him so much my grief threatens to consume me. Tossing the covers off me, I stand, startling when I catch something moving in the confines of my bedroom.

Thankfully, my switchblade is within reach and I snatch it from the side table. On silent feet, I creep through the room, opening my senses to the night. Nothing seems off, but there must be something…

Gut-wrenching heartache and pain slam into me as a hand wraps around my throat and I'm thrust into the wall, but it's nothing like what happened with Ben. Actually, it's almost like these feelings aren't even my own. He's careful with me, making sure my head doesn't hit and the hold on my throat is anything but uncomfortable. He knows what he's doing. What I don't know is why it turns me on so much.

"Why are you in my room?" I ask, slipping my switchblade behind my back in case I need it. Elian is a colossal douche, but I don't think he'd ever truly hurt me.

The soft moonlight pouring through my breezy curtains highlights his features and the fact that he's completely shirtless. I'll admit he looks better without one. His tattoos sprawl across his chest and neck, but it's too dim to make the specific designs out. Which is a bummer because I'd love to analyze them further. Something tells me they'd give a glimpse into him as a person and I find myself craving to know more about him—despite his very off-putting demeanor. Either way, he's stunning it takes my breath away momentarily.

Elian looks much more like himself in the dark, because this is where he thrives.

He frowns. "I heard you whimpering in your sleep and came to check on you." His voice is gruff and gravely from sleep. Those emerald eyes of his flash and flick away for a millisecond before returning to hold mine. "You know, you're quite the conundrum, Mercedes Sarina Sinclair," he says calculatingly. Somehow, it doesn't surprise me that he knows my full name, but it also makes me wonder what else he knows that I'm not ready to share with them yet. Especially him.

"I'll take the bait," I say breathily as his inked fingers readjust on my neck. I'm not exactly certain why I'm allowing him to put me in such a compromising position, but I can't deny there's something exhilarating about the push and pull between us. "How so?"

His eyes dip to my exposed cleavage like he can't seem to help himself. "I'll admit, you've surprised me. You're beautiful and capable, but so naive, and so full of rage and hatred.

Yet you don't have an outlet for which to let your troubles explode. Through all of that, there's still a tint of light to you that you try to hide from the world. Your aura is radiant and the most brilliant I've ever seen."

His words strike a chord within me and I glance away because I don't like feeling so uncovered and raw under *his* scrutiny.

"Look at me," he commands and for some reason I do. "This world is going to tear you apart, eat you up, and then spit you out. Can't you see that? You'd run far away from all of us if you were smart."

I can't let him have all the power here, and surprisingly he doesn't stop me as I rake my fingernails down his chest, relishing when his abs contract and he lets out a breath. He'll likely have my marks there tomorrow and the thought makes me smirk.

His dick thumps against my thigh and I'm forced to hold in my groan. I blame it on the dark giving me the courage to be forward with him and my sleep addled brain.

Yep, let's go with that.

I ignore his question, opting to ask one of my own. "Why do you hate me so much, Elian?" A part of me is hoping for an honest answer, but I know better.

He laughs, sending thrills down my spine. "I don't hate you, but you, my dear, have ruined absolutely everything." His hands leave my neck as he tucks a strand of hair behind my ear and leans in. He rests his temple against mine in an oddly intimate gesture. Under his breath he adds, "But I'm coming to realize that maybe that isn't such a bad thing." The words are soft, so soft if it weren't for the fact his lips are a hairsbreadth away, I'd be afraid my brain made the whole thing up.

He shifts so that his lips hover above mine, not quite touching, but close enough I can feel his breath feather across mine while he stares directly into my eyes. My pulse thunders and my mouth turns dry, but there's not a lot of time to think about it, because in the next instant he disappears into a black cloud of smoke.

That fucking bastard.

After his demanding presence fades away, I find myself wondering what the hell is wrong with me. I should've fucking stabbed him while I had the chance, but a part of me didn't want to. A very small part, but one nonetheless. One that feels the undeniable connection flickering between us, simmering beneath the surface, waiting for his waves to crash into my life raft. His current could either safely deposit me on shore… or drag me under. I'm hoping it's the former.

With a heavy sigh, I toss my switchblade back onto the nightstand and cocoon myself under the covers once more. Something tells me I won't be sleeping much more tonight, if the pulsing between my thighs and racing thoughts are any indication.

31

SADIE

Several days pass without further incident, and it's relatively quiet in the King household. Elian avoids me like the plague, and there's been no sight of Savannah since the incident. They've assured me she won't be around to bother me anymore, but I don't believe it. The look on her face when Dante chose me was desperate and more than a little obsessive. It reminded me of Tyler.

People like that can't let things go.

Dante, Kaos, and I fall into an easy rhythm. We eat meals together, and I spend time with Ash in between. She told me she wants to go home to tend to her parents' gravesites soon and I don't blame her, but I can't shake the feeling it's a bad idea. If anyone finds out how much she means to me and touches her; I will maim them.

The depth of our friendship knows no bounds and there aren't any lengths I wouldn't go through for her. She walked through fire for me during one of the lowest times of my life to forge the broken pieces of my soul back together, and I did the same for her when her parents died a few years ago. We tempered our friendship in fire and rose from the ashes with a different kind of unbreakable bond. We pick up the pieces of one another while straightening our crowns.

A bad guy pops around the corner on the TV, startling me out of my thoughts. I train my gun on him and pull the trigger a few times until blood spews from his wound and he collapses in a heap and I run over his body in pursuit of my next enemy.

Kind of fucked up but hey, it's entertainment and bonding time with the guys.

The end game screen pops up a second later displaying my final score as thirty-four kills and two deaths. Smug satisfaction enters me when I see both Kaos and Dante's gamer tags underneath mine. Again.

I drop the controller and do two fist pumps in the air. "Take that bitches!"

Kaos grins, giving me a high five like we're two bros or something. Dante groans, tossing his controller onto the carpet.

"Not again. How did you go from noob to kicking our asses in two hours?" His bottom lip sticks out in a cute pout and there's a gleam in his eye, one that shines brighter than the sunshine flowing through the curtains.

He doesn't look upset in the slightest, despite his sad expression. I don't think Dante is capable of being sad. Not for long anyway. He's one of those assholes that can always find the joy in life.

"Fourth time in a row too." I recline against the couch. For whatever reason, it's easier to play this game on the floor than it is on the couch. Dante and Kaos both followed my lead without questioning it and we've been sitting here playing Call of Duty for ages.

I'll admit I like the high stakes and fast-paced maps, but my favorite one is the shortest one. You can run around killing everyone with one shot from a shotgun. Dante and

Kaos both kept telling me *it's cheating*, but shut up about it when I took the lead for the team.

"Aww, Blondie. Can you not handle getting beat by a girl?"

He rolls his eyes, that signature smirk fixed on his lips. Although, I do think he's a little salty about it because they coddled me while teaching me, only for me to turn around and start annihilating everyone. I'm quite sure they expected me to struggle like well, a girl.

Think again.

"On the contrary, I find it so fucking hot," he says, his voice a husky purr like a smooth exhale of smoke.

A grin overtakes my face when I find his amber eyes fixated on my lips.

Kaos coughs, looking between the two of us with clear interest. "I'm going to go pop some popcorn. Afterward, we can watch a movie and save ourselves the embarrassment of getting our asses handed to us a fifth time." He places his controller on the coffee table and gives me a quick kiss that has my toes curling, before sauntering off.

I watch his backside as he leaves and damn, does he have a nice ass. Especially in those grey sweatpants he's sporting. Hell, I'll bet he even has some of those back dimples too. That's exactly what I need, more dimples in addition to the ones on their faces.

Always tempting me.

Soon the wondrous smell of popcorn popping reaches my nostrils and I take a few deep inhales enjoying the moment. Until something crashes outside, and I curse, scrambling to my feet with a sense of Déjà vu.

I swear to the Night Goddess, if this is Savannah's bullshit again... I don't think I'll be able to hold myself back from gouging her eyes out with a rusty spork.

My fingers itch for my switchblade but, like a half-wit, I

left it on my dresser this morning not expecting any trouble. I can hear Ben's voice in my head scolding me, which sends shivers down my spine. The sooner I forget about him the better.

Dante and Goldie—man, I've got to think of a name for him—are already trailing out of the man cave and into the main house.

Kaos rendezvous with us moments later, knife drawn. I hear muttered curses and more splintering as we approach the front corridor. Kaos peeks out the glass, his eyes scanning both directions before swinging back to us in confusion. His hand rests on the handle and he signals for us to be quiet as he twists it open and steps out onto the porch.

Only there's nothing there.

As we're about to step further onto the porch, another awful creaking noise captures my attention, seconds before someone cries out in pain and the wooden beam collapses. Somehow, the man manages to roll out of the way. Good thing too because he likely would've been crushed.

When his pained eyes open, they capture mine through the dust and the debris flying through the air. My lips part in shock at the mottled bruises all over his face and the blood dripping from his abdomen where he was trapped in the roof.

I'd recognize those sparkling silver eyes anywhere and I feel guilty for not contacting him sooner, but in my defense, it's been a little hectic and my phone is still dead. My stomach churns with worry as I race over to check on him. "Reed!" I cry out. A hand to my chest stops me short of reaching him. "What the fuck?" I snarl, startling Dante with the ferocity of my tone.

"You know him?" he questions, looking between the two of us like he can't quite believe what's happening right now. Me neither asshole.

CHAPTER 31 | 251

"We met at my work a few nights ago before I was fired, and he protected me from a man who tried to lay his hands on me. Not that I needed the extra help, but it was nice."

Dante and Kaos share a loaded look over my head.

"Sadie," Reed whispers, moments before his eyes roll to the back of his head and he passes out. What the hell happened to him? These injuries didn't come from falling through a roof.

I try to escape Dante's hold to make sure he's still breathing, but he doesn't let up. Instead, Kaos grabs me by the forearm and hauls me back inside the mansion. Dante follows closely behind, blocking me in.

My jaw clenches. "What are you doing? We need to help him. We need to figure out why he's here and what happened to him," I say feeling an overwhelming tug in my chest for my starry-eyed stranger.

Kaos' head whips around, his eyes hardening as he closes the gap between us, leaning so close that our breath mingles together. "You realize who that is, who he is, don't you?"

I shrug, trying not to let Kaos' nearness affect me but it's hard. This man is magnetizing. I lean in a little closer until his lips are almost on mine.

"The only thing I know is his name is Reed and he protected me, even when he didn't have to." I pull back slightly to get my bearings again, but Dante doesn't let me get far, pressing his lithe body into my back.

Damn these alphaholes.

"Reed is the future leader of the Light Weavers, Sadie. He's the heir we've been talking about." Kaos drops that fucking bomb into the air and watches it explode. And by that, I mean my head explodes.

Well, not literally, but my mind is blown.

"Say what?" I ask, reaching up to rub the smooth metal of my necklace. I let the feeling of the metal wash over me.

"He's the future leader of the Light Weavers," Kaos repeats, running a hand through those inky black locks of his. "He is who we had our pact with."

That's when clicks in my brain. Reed is who they have their pact with and we're still not sure if he broke it because Elian couldn't get a hold of him. Shit.

But for some reason, I can't shake the feeling that Reed isn't here to hurt us—or me rather. He had plenty of opportunities after we left Harborview, or even at the restaurant. Hell, he could've let the meathead beat me to a pulp, but he didn't. He protected me and gave me a huge tip.

His thoughtfulness must count for something, right?

Then again, he didn't know who I was at the time. No one did.

Elian pops out of the shadows in the entryway, tainting the air with his heavy aura. Luckily, I've learned to recognize his presence, or else he'd be getting an elbow to the face.

His green eyes waver as he takes in the scene on the porch. Though he doesn't show any outward expression, I see it, the moment his eyes harden. He may be a frosty asshole on the outside, but his eyes give him away. Much like my own do.

"Well, well. Look what the Sun God dropped into our laps," he says, stalking toward Reed.

Finally, Dante and Kaos release me and we follow Elian onto the porch as he leans down, checking for a pulse with his long-inked fingers.

"Alive," he states clinically.

My breath escapes me in a rush.

"Looks like he has internal injuries too. Dante, help me take him to the spare bedroom. Kaos, I want you to heal him enough that he lives, but not enough that he can attack us. We need answers," he says, slipping into the leadership role. I can see why, truly, but I don't like it. Every part of me wants to rebel against his orders, more so than the others.

When he picks up Reed, his jaw clenches and with Dante's help they maneuver him inside. Reed doesn't move or even make a peep as they carry him up to the spare bedroom and set him on the small twin-size mattress.

Kaos instantly gets to work, and his brow dips in concentration as he takes note of each injury. His hand stops above Reed's stomach and he winces. "He has severe internal damage." A black glow emanates from his palm as he uses his magic to try and heal him. "He's lucky to be alive."

After what feels like an eternity, the bleeding slowly comes to a stop and I notice a bead of sweat break out across Kaos' forehead. Now that I'm paying attention, I realize that he's looking quite pale. Does healing people drain him?

I walk over and place my hand in his. Right away I feel a tug inside my chest as my magic leaves me and enters Kaos to help replenish him.

"That's enough for now," Elian says, watching the whole situation from the corner in a high back chair that looks way too much like a throne for my liking. His icy energy leaks throughout the room like little ice crystals embedding themselves in my flesh. He smirks, almost as if he can sense my thoughts but it's gone in an instant.

"He needs more," Kaos protests, not moving his hands from Reed, despite Elian's order.

Elian stands, his green eyes narrowing on Kaos. "Not now. You're making yourself too weak. My wards should hold any unwanted stragglers out, but we need you in tip-top shape in case it doesn't." Kaos finally relents and Elian's gaze flickers to Reed. "I'm still not sure how he managed to get through, but I will do a perimeter check shortly and scout for holes."

Dante nods. "I agree. We don't know how many hostiles

are after us, and if Reed can get through then they might be able to get through too."

"I don't think he'd hurt us," I defend, eyeing Reed softly.

All I can think about are those silver eyes holding mine as he fended off that man at Harborview for me. Not to mention the cash he shoved in my hands after hearing about my struggle. Reed is a good guy and I refuse to believe otherwise until I'm proven wrong.

"I'll have one of the shifters watch the door," Elian says, already halfway out it. "Kaos, I want you to come back in a few hours when you've replenished some magic and finish healing the internal injuries. Dante, you're with me."

Guess he thinks that his word is law.

He doesn't know Sadie Sinclair very well then.

I can already tell he and I are going to have to have it out one of these days and it's going to be interesting. Likely will end in an inferno of passion, but I digress. I don't understand what his problem is with me, but I intend to find out.

Call me a cat because curiosity is killing me. Hopefully, I have nine lives like one too because something tells me I'm going to need every single one.

32

SADIE

A little over a day has passed since Reed dropped through the roof of our porch, obliterating it. Since then I've been pacing the halls of the mansion, practically wearing a path in the carpet from my anxiety, despite me telling myself to calm down. We're still not any closer to getting the answers as to why and how he got here, and why he was injured so badly.

Why here?

Why did his people attack and try to kill me at the festival?

How did they find us?

How did Reed slip through Elian's protection ward?

So many questions, so few answers.

Kaos has been in and out of the guest room every few hours to heal Reed's injuries a little more and I've been standing outside it. He opens the door, startling me out of my pacing. His stormy blue eyes lift to meet mine.

"Any news?" I question, biting one of my nails.

He shakes his head. "He needs rest to let his body recuperate." He grabs my hand and walks me down the hall. "He'll wake up in his own time. We can't rush it. Vinson is on guard duty tonight."

I nod, not knowing what else to say. I'm not sure why I'm so worried and why my stomach is in knots over it. I barely know the guy.

You barely know the Kings too, that same inner voice whispers.

Shut the hell up. I tell my consciousness.

Great. Now I'm having conversations with myself.

Kaos chuckles, squeezing my hand reassuringly as he walks me back to my room. "You've been through a lot in a short period. It's normal to feel a little off."

"True, but that switch has been on so long it's hard to turn off."

He pauses in front of my door, glancing away briefly before turning back to capture my eyes. "Look, Sadie, I feel like we should talk about what happened the other day." My eyebrow raises. "With all of the commotion happening, we haven't really had a chance yet."

"Spit it out, Kaos. You're still pretty high on my shit list."

"I'm sorry for not jumping into your defense, I am, but I had my reasons. Seeing Savannah was a shock and she's slightly unstable—"

"That's a fucking understatement," I interject.

His lips twitch. "Yeah, she's psycho and she won't hesitate to retaliate for this. She believes she has some sort of claim on us."

"I can handle myself, Kaos. Let me fight for my own mates." I take his hand, running my fingers over his mate mark. He smiles softly at me. "Next time you better fucking back me up though. If you're not on the sidelines acting like a Godsdamn cheerleader, you might as well forget me because I won't settle for less."

"You got it, Little Flame," he says softly. "Now, I want you to get some rest, some real rest, okay? You've been helping to replenish me—" I shoot him a look and he places his hands up. "—which I appreciate, but that also means you're weakening yourself too."

The problem is, I don't feel drained in the sense that my magic is depleted, especially not like what Kaos experiences healing Reed.

He leans his forearm against the door, smiling softly at me and his blue eyes dip to my lips. I freeze. Crap. Is this the part where I'm supposed to invite him inside? I don't know how these things work. Ask me about music and I can have an answer in a heartbeat, but how to handle a man that wants me?

Nope. Brain empties of all rational thought.

I clear my throat, twirling a curl of hair around my finger that hopefully looks playful and seductive. "Will you come in with me?" I ask, looking up at him through my lashes.

Good, you sounded somewhat normal.

Then, I ruin it of course. "I mean if you want to. If not, it's cool. I thought maybe we'd both sleep better if you were in my bed and…" I trail off when his smile turns into a fullblown grin, those dimples peek out at me.

I'm certain my cheeks are red as hell right now, but I play it cool by leaning against the door, trying to match his pose. Yeah, I fail miserably. Why do I suck at this?

He laughs, leaning down to capture my lips with his, stealing my soul through my mouth. It's almost as if Kaos takes notes while he kisses me, adapting to my sounds and what he knows I like. The man is perceptive as hell and I'm digging it.

He opens the door behind us, somehow managing not to break our kiss. He walks me backward toward the bed until the back of my knees hit the hard frame. Our kiss heats up. A nibble here, some tongue there, before he moves to my neck making a zing shoot straight to my clit. My neck is definitely one of my erogenous zones and now Kaos knows it too. I feel him smirk against the soft flesh. He bites down lightly, pulling a gasp from my lips.

His cock jerks against my leg as he works his way to the top of my breasts. He pulls my legs around his waist and presses me into the mattress. *Is this it? Is this the moment I finally lose my virginity to someone?*

But no, because fate is a cruel bitch.

Someone bursts through the door a second later, startling the shit out of us. We break apart like we're two guilty teenagers about to get scolded and not the twenty-something consenting adults we are.

"Wha—oh, shit. Sorry. You're busy, huh?" Ash cackles before waltzing back out the door. "I wanted to let you know, I'm leaving to go to mom and dad's gravesite tomorrow. Dante assigned one of their staff members to take me down there. So, uh yeah. I'll catch you later, babe!" she calls out before I hear her footsteps fade away.

I let out a deep breath, turning to see where Kaos went after we broke apart. I find him lying on the bed with his eyes closed and a peaceful expression on his face. I wave my hands around trying to see if he's still awake, but he doesn't stir.

Eventually, I hear him snoring lightly and I sigh, climbing into bed next to him without taking my jeans off. It's probably for the best he fell asleep because he's been burning the candle on both ends, but it did give me the clarity to realize that I'm ready. I'm ready to shed that part of myself that I've been hanging onto for so long. It's early, but I think I've finally found the right men.

Men as in plural. Who would've thought that's my new normal?

CHAPTER 32 | 259

My eyes pop open as I wake from the nightmare plaguing my dreams. They're becoming more and more frequent these days. My chest heaves and it takes me a few moments to come back down to earth.

Kaos shoots awake with wide eyes. When they find mine in the darkness, his expression morphs from confusion into concern. He reaches over and runs his glowing black hands over my body, checking for injuries, but there's no injury his healing magic can fix. This is all emotional. Still, he tries, and that means more than I can express.

When he finds me unharmed, he pulls me onto his lap and wraps me in his strong arms that feel much more like home than anywhere I've ever lived. He rocks me softly while running his fingers through my tangled hair. "Are you okay?" he asks, placing his forehead against mine.

"No," I whisper back. "But maybe someday I will be."

We sit like that for a long time. Him, rocking me back and forth, his forehead against mine, and the evil dreams fade back into the dark abyss from which they came. His comforting scent of bergamot and leather is all I focus on. As strange as that combination sounds, he smells comforting, and that's exactly what I need right now.

His calloused fingers tilt my face toward his and that's all the invitation I need. I press my lips against his intending to give him a chaste kiss, but it quickly turns into something more as I feel his hard bulge against the fabric of my jeans. I gasp, and he sweeps his tongue against mine. I turn in his arms, pressing my suddenly aching center closer to his.

"Fuck," he hisses, grasping my hips in a firm hold as I begin to rock against him in slow tantalizing motions. He adjusts, making sure his rock hard member brushes against my clit with every slide. "You have no idea how hard it's been to hide this—" he thrusts upwards, making me moan, "—from you this entire time." One of his hands slips up to cup the back of my neck. "With your perfect ass poised right over my cock."

I start to rock faster as the movement hits my sweet spot with every single motion. "More," I murmur, voice hoarse with desire, not knowing what exactly I'm asking for, but Kaos knows.

Boy, does he know.

He grips my hair, pulling my head to the side to give him better access to my neck. I moan, loving the sharp sting of my hair being pulled. Kaos grins against me, nipping and sucking the soft flesh and each time applying a different pressure to keep me guessing.

My hips start to work faster of their own accord as the pressure continues to build and build. "Oh shit," I say, working my body into the perfect frenzy until the pressure becomes too much and I see stars. Vivid fucking stars. My hands and vibrators have definitely not done me justice over the years.

Kaos grips my hips tighter, taking over control of my motions to heighten my climax. He holds them so tightly that I know that I'll have his fingerprints there tomorrow, but the thought doesn't bother me. I'd be happy to wear his brand on my skin.

A second later he grunts, thrusting his hips into mine. The moonlight shining through the curtains highlights his expression as he comes, bringing an extra level to the feelings running through my chest. I did that, I fucking put that look on his face.

Little aftershocks flit through my body and I shudder. We both sit there for a moment, panting as we try to come back to earth.

"Fuck, that was hot, Little Flame," Kaos murmurs against

my cheek, chuckling as he turns, pressing a kiss to my swollen lips.

"Yes, it was," I say, running a hand through my hair. It's wild and untamable so I decide not to mess with it and throw it up in a loose pony instead. I haven't showered in two days because I've been so anxious, and it slipped my mind, but now all I can imagine is Kaos standing in there with me lathering my back with soap.

Down, vagina. You already had an orgasm for shit's sake.

Kaos isn't done with me though. Not in the slightest. He props himself up, leaning over me to capture my already swollen lips with his own. He pulls my shirt over my head, nimble fingers unclasping my bra as they both land in a heap on the floor. My jeans and panties follow soon after, leaving me bare beneath him.

I give his still clothed body a once-over. "I think this is a little unfair, don't you?" I feel for the hem of his shirt and yank it over his head. It lands in the pile next to mine. Fitting, I think. "Take your pants off too."

Kaos complies and the next thing I know he's completely exposed, his cock dripping with his come, standing at attention for me again. Jesus fucking Christ. He's huge and he's already rock solid again.

Do Night Weavers have a higher libido?

It sure would explain my collection of vibrators.

Snapping back to the moment, I greedily wrap my fingers around him and give him a few pumps. My fingers don't even touch. He groans, wrapping his hand around mine and encouraging me to squeeze a little harder.

"Like this?" I ask, turning my hand while he guides me.

"Yes," he grunts, thrusting into my hand. "I need to be inside you. Now. Are you ready for me, Little Flame?"

"I've never been more ready," I murmur.

He growls, yanking me toward him so he can line up at

my entrance. He runs the tip of his dick through my folds a few times, soaking himself in my juices, before slowly sliding inside. I gasp as a sharp stinging sensation zaps through me, but the pain is quickly replaced with need when he pushes in a little more.

"Are you all right?" he asks, pausing to look into my eyes.

I nod because it's all I can manage with the sensations shooting through me.

He chuckles. "Then breathe because you're strangling my cock."

Oops. I let the tension riding my body drop and he sinks in a little more, pulling a moan from my lips.

"You're doing so good," he murmurs and sinks in the rest of the way, freezing when I tense.

"Keep going. Don't stop, Kaos."

He doesn't need any further encouragement. He pulls back slightly before slowly burying himself inside me once more, letting my body adapt to his length. He teases me like that over and over until I start rocking my hips against his and he picks up the pace.

"Holy shit, Sadie." Kaos sinks all the way in, grinding against my clit.

"Oh my Gods," I say throatily. "Harder, Kaos, please."

"I'll take care of you. Don't worry." And he does. Kaos delivers exactly what my body needs, picking up on all my cues like the attentive man he is and I fucking relish in it. He reaches down, flicking my little bundle of nerves until I'm crying out.

Incoherent words flow from my mouth as my cunt clamps down on his cock, and with another few strokes, he's finishing inside me with a grunt.

"Moons above, my Little Flame, you are something else, you know that?" he says, leaning his forehead against my breasts with his dick still buried inside of me.

"Really? Do you say that to all the girls you fuck?" I snark.

"No. Never," he responds, making my stomach flip flop.

While he's stroking the silky skin of my belly, I ask, "Hey, Kaos? Why do you call me Little Flame?"

He smiles. "I've seen a fire in you since the day we met, and I think it's fitting. Don't you?" Well, he's got me there. My eyelids start to droop and I yawn, startling when a voice speaks up from the floor.

"For the love of the Night Goddess, could you fucking warn a dog next time? I think I'm scarred for life."

No fucking way.

Little peals of laughter burst from my lips as Kaos and I simultaneously lose our shit.

"Yeah, yeah, laugh it up you assholes. I saw way more of both of you than I ever bargained for tonight."

When my laughter finally dies down I say, "I'm so sorry, pup. I didn't know you were in here, though you could have spoken up at any time."

He pouts, jumping onto the bed to curl at our feet. "You seemed like you needed to get laid, human. You're a little wound up."

"Hey, you little shit, you're supposed to be on my side."

He makes a chuffing sound and then promptly falls fast asleep. Who would've thought being a pet owner would be so fun?

Kaos chuckles, planting a kiss against my forehead. "Get some sleep, Sadie. I've got you." He places his palm above my abdomen, which lights in a blackish glow before the discomfort in my lower region disappears completely, before tucking me under the covers and into his arms.

Well and thoroughly satisfied, sleep overtakes me once again. This time the nightmares stay away, and I can enjoy the blissful peace.

When I wake, it's to a commotion in the hallway. I glance

over to the other side of the room to find Kaos dressing in a different outfit than yesterday and on alert. We share a look and I grab my switchblade off the side table. Never know when I'll need it at this rate.

Dante barges into my room, panting, "He's awake… and he's asking for you."

33

SADIE

Rushing through the motions to get ready, I change into a fresh pair of well-worn jeans and a deep red low-cut shirt I found hanging in the closet. Not sure I want to know where it came from, but I'm short on items to wear and I'm not one to look a gift horse in the mouth.

To say Dante was a little shocked to find Kaos and I naked together would be an understatement. I don't think he was angry per se, merely curious, and a little turned on. But there's not time to dwell on it right now.

As I make my way down the hall to Reed's room, I hear low voices murmuring inside, but I can't make out what they're saying. I freeze outside the door, wondering if he even wants me inside. A soft voice says my name, and I tentatively push the door open, gasping when Reed comes into view. Kaos may have healed the worst of his injuries but he's is still worse for wear. Mottled bruises dot his entire face and there looks to be burn marks down his arms and his neck.

"Oh my goodness, what the hell happened, Red?" I ask,

closing the door behind me with a soft click. Kaos frowns at my nickname for him but I ignore it.

Reed's silver eyes snap to mine, the faraway look in his eyes disappearing briefly as he gives me a weak smile.

My eyes flick to Dante who's standing beside the bed for answers. "We don't know what happened yet," Dante replies, moving to put his arm around my shoulder in a protective move that's unnecessary. "He wouldn't talk without you here."

"Me? Why me?" I ask, confusion twinging my words. Does Reed feel the connection between us too?

"I was wondering the same thing," Elian says, unbuttoning the cufflink on his button-down shirt and rolling his sleeve up, showcasing more tattoos. As much as I hate to admit it, he looks hot as fuck like that.

Hubba, Hubba.

"Sadie," Reed whispers hoarsely, running a hand through his reddish hair. I notice for the first time that his glasses aren't on his face. Probably broken if I'm guessing. "I never dreamed I'd find you here." A small smile tugs at the corners of his lips, but he winces and it drops.

My heart twinges painfully. "What's going on, Red?" I ask again, trying to keep a clear head until I learn more, even though my instincts are screaming for me to run to him and throw my arms around him.

The faraway look in his eye returns and he turns his gaze away from me with a sigh. "It's quite a long story." When his eyes meet mine again the depth of the pain in them steals my breath away. He looks like someone who has the weight of the world on their shoulders and failed.

I lick my dry lips, shifting nervously as I await his answer. I don't try to rush him, I simply tell him, "I have time."

Since the bed is pushed against the farthest wall, I slink

down on the corner and scoot back against the wall to wait for him to be ready to talk.

The light spilling in from the curtains highlights the orange tones in his hair. Sometimes it looks darker, almost brown, but in the sunlight, there's no mistaking it as any color other than red.

"Listen, the first thing I need you to know is that I had no idea who you were at the restaurant."

I tilt my head to the side in question. "What does that have to do with anything?"

"Because after that's when everything started going downhill," he whispers and the pain in his gaze is like a thousand sharp knives eating into my flesh. "The second thing you should know is I didn't break our pact." He pauses for a moment, looking over to the Kings before looking back to me. "My father did. He was furious when he found out how your Circle had been evading us, and tortured one of the men loyal to me to find out the specifics."

Elian's eyes narrow to slits. "You know more than what you're saying," he says, stalking toward Reed but he stops when I put a hand up.

"Let him speak, please," I snap. "Red, you're not making any sense to me right now. Let's start with why you're here. Why are you beaten and bruised? How did you fall through our porch? How did you get through the protective ward?" I only meant to ask one question, but my worry for him is bleeding through.

Reed sighs, looking way too weary for someone his age. "The night I met you at Harborview, there was an attack from your Elders…" He pauses, and a single tear falls onto his cheek. It almost looks silver as it rolls down his face, and hits the white bedsheet. His shoulders slump, telling me the display of weakness cost him a chunk of pride.

Personally, I prefer a man that's not afraid to express how they feel, even if it's hard for me to do the same.

"I rushed back to find they decimated my entire home—my people. The entire community is gone. They were still there, and they made me watch while they murdered my father. While we never got along, it was truly awful…" He trails off in a coughing fit.

Kaos rushes over and starts patting him down again, his hands lighting up in that dark glow as he heals more of his injuries.

"Even the women and children?" Dante asks, utterly horrified.

Reed nods.

Thinking about that makes bile rise in the back of my throat. An entire society decimated, and for what cause? Nothing can justify that. I don't even know anything about the Light Weavers, yet I know that what the Elders did is wrong. So fucking vile, and I make up my mind about them. They will get what's coming to them, even if I'm the one that has to bring about their demise.

"I'm so sorry about your people, Red. Words cannot even express the magnitude of my sorrow for you," I whisper, running my fingers through my ponytail. "Did anyone else survive?"

"I'm not sure. I—I'm a fucking coward. I ran. I used the Light to travel. At first, I couldn't leave, but I begged and pleaded with the Sun God to take me to my mate and I ended up here."

An accompaniment of growls echo across the room. Dante reaches over and plucks me off the bed and away from Reed, tucking me into his body protectively. Essentially, he pissed on me, claimed me without actually pissing on me. Kind of like how licking something or someone claims it as yours, but in more of an alphahole way.

I look up at him in confusion. "Did I miss something? Why all the growling and possessive posturing?"

"He said he begged to be taken to his mate, and the Light deposited him here," Dante responds carefully, watching my face for my reaction.

His mate? But Ash is the only other woman here besides me—*oh shit, me.* It clicks in my brain and I gasp, scrambling to face everyone.

Four? I have four freaking mates.

"Ah, hell."

"Ah, hell is right, Little Flame," Kaos echoes, running a hand through his dark hair as he steps away from Reed. He looks way less pissed than Dante does—more contemplative. Elian's mask is firmly in place and I can't get a read on him whatsoever.

"My father figured it out before I did," he continues. "I didn't know until I saw your face after I fell, but he knew. Apparently, after we met, I had a random surge of power, something that only happens with true mates. After he heard that a Circle of Night Weavers had found their Link. He knew then that the prophecy must be true." Reed levels a glare on my other mates.

Prophecy? Yay, more reason for people to try and freaking kill me. Or kidnap me. Reed's lips twitch and he tries not to look at me but fails.

"Oh, did I say that out loud? Crap."

Red opens his mouth to say something when Dante interrupts him. "Stop. Fucking stop, Reed. Stop filling our mate's head with your lies. I won't tolerate it a second longer."

Once again, I'm snatched into a hard chest and his body sways with movement as he carries me out of the room. "Dante King, you better put me down this instant or I'm going to fillet you like a fucking fish."

"No can do, Angel. You've had enough of this shit for one day."

By that he means, he's had enough of this shit for one day. I can't deny my head is also spinning with all the new information.

"Wait, that's not all!" Reed calls out and his voice cracks. Dante stops and his entire body tenses, awaiting his answer. "You have a snitch in your midst playing both sides. We need to find out who before they get us all killed."

Dante snorts. "We already know, but we don't know who it is for sure. Everyone is practically gunning for us at this point."

Dante whisks me from the room and deposits me into my bedroom, holding my hand as all the thoughts and possibilities swirl in my head. There's no way I can possibly sort through them all and I'm actually grateful for his company.

Four mates. Wow, Sadie, you're racking them up.

34

SADIE

It's Friday, which means it's been almost a week since the Kings took me in, and I'm no closer to uncovering any of the mysteries unveiled yesterday.

According to Dante, Night and Light Weavers don't mix, therefore Reed being my mate is impossible. I'm not so sure, but I can tell he's struggling with the idea so I've left it alone. Kaos is still working on his injuries which were way worse than we thought. The Elders did a number on him before he escaped.

Vinson is supposed to take me into town to get normal people food today and I'm excited to get out of the house. I need a sense of normalcy in my life, and by normal, I mean cheap food that's probably chocked full of fillers and crap that is bad for you, but I've been eating it my entire life. It's comfort food at this point.

Not to mention, I hate being cooped up and with the attack at the compound, they don't think it's safe to venture there to test my magic. Although, Dante says we'll have to go soon and find out because we need to know before the Elders do.

I haven't told the guys about the trip to the store yet but surely, they won't be too upset, right? I mean it's only a trip to the grocery store, and they don't own me.

"Can you help me find Vin?" I ask, stroking Goldie's fur.

He bobs his head in a nod. "I keep track of everyone's scents, so I can find them if we need them."

Well, that's nice, if not a tiny bit creepy.

"You know what? Before we go, let's figure out a name for you. I'm tired of calling you Goldie in my head. It doesn't suit you."

If a dog can grimace, Goldie most definitely grimaces. "You've been calling me Goldie? That sounds so un-badass. What the hell, Sadie?"

"I know, I know." I put my hands out in surrender. "That's why we're doing this now. Anything you'd prefer?"

"Something sophisticated will do. I've been called many things in my existence. Bedi mainly called me *dog* while I was with her. Unoriginal if I do say so myself, but only my owner is allowed to give me a name."

"All right, hmm…" I pause, tapping my Converse against the nice hardwoods in my borrowed room. They're nothing like the ones from our old duplex, these are nice and there's not a scuff in sight.

All the names that pop into my head are silly like Baxter and Buddy and Bandit. My familiar is worthy of a strong name.

"Maxwell?" I ask, then shake my head. "No, that's too cliché…"

"Agreed."

A flash on the TV catches my attention. I left it on as background noise last night because I couldn't stand being left alone with my thoughts. Chris Hemsworth glides across the screen, looking totally badass in one of the Avengers movies with his infamous hammer in hand.

I gasp. "Hemsworth!" What better way to honor the God of a man himself?

He looks over to the TV and back to me. "Hmm. I don't hate it." I swear I see amusement dancing in those little dog eyes. "Hemsworth it is."

Did I name my familiar after Chris Hemsworth?

Yes, yes, I did.

Hemsworth stands up on his back legs, giving me a dog version of a people hug. My heart swells.

"Come on, we don't want Vin to leave without us."

When we round the corner, we find Ash talking on her phone. Her mouth is moving a million miles a minute, but when she sees me, she smiles and hangs up instantly.

"Hey, babe!" She saunters toward me, sporting a black tank top and a pair of jeans today, paired with the same boots from the concert.

"Hey," I say, leaning in to give her a quick hug.

When I pull away she gives me a devious smile. "You're glowing, you know."

"I'm what? Shit, is my magic doing funky stuff again?" I ask turning around in confusion like I can actually see myself.

She smacks her forehead. "No, you dunce. You and Kaos totally fucked, didn't you? How was it? Tell me everything!" She squeals at the dreamy look that no doubt comes across my face just thinking about it.

A laugh bursts from my lips. "Okay, I'll admit, it was amazing. Kaos is so attentive and—" I break off when she starts fanning herself with her hand.

"Mhm, and are you happy you waited, or do you wish you'd done it sooner?"

I shrug. "Honestly, I don't see why it's lorded over women's heads their entire life, but with Kaos it was meaningful, so yes. I'm glad and," I lean in to whisper, "I think I'm slightly addicted. I tried to jump his bones in the hallway today, but Elian interrupted us. The fucking prick."

"He's quite the asshole, isn't he? Good thing he's exactly your type."

"Jeez, way to call me out, Ash," I say, smacking her arm. "Enough with my sex life. Today is the day you're heading back home, right?"

"Yeah. I'm waiting on the staff guy who's supposed to drive me." She runs a hand through her brown locks, fixing a flyaway.

I frown. "For the record, I don't like this. I think you need to stay here, where it's safe."

She props a hand on her hip, cocking it to the side. Typical Ash. "You know how much they mean to me. I can't —I haven't missed a month since they died. I need to do this."

"I know I can't stop you and I wouldn't try, but please promise me you'll be careful and stick with your driver, okay? I'm sure he doubles as a guard. Don't talk to anyone you don't know and keep your mace handy."

She nods, shooting me a sneaky smirk. "I'm hoping my chauffeur will be a hot one. Maybe I can seduce him on the way back. Have a quickie in the car."

I stare at my best friend in awe. "You're too fucking much sometimes, Ash."

She laughs and the lines around her eyes crinkle. "True, but you love me too much to ditch me."

"You're right. I do." I tug her into another hug, watching her driver approach. I know it's time to let her go, but a part of me isn't ready. "Be safe, okay? I'll see you when you get back."

"Catch you on the flip side!"

"Later gator," I say, using the goodbyes we came up with when we were little. We haven't used them in so long it makes a pang of nostalgia shoot through me.

CHAPTER 34 | 275

After making sure Ash leaves safely, Hemsworth leads me to Vin. We round the corner and approach the garage. As soon as we step through the door the scent of grease and oil hits my nostrils. It reminds me of what my dad used to smell like, and I stop and let the waves of melancholy and loss pass. My dad was my world and I miss him so much it hurts. His face is slowly fading from my mind and that bothers me more than anything since my uncle never let me keep any pictures of him.

"Hey there, are you all right?" A masculine voice asks startling me out of my thoughts.

"Dang, don't scare me like that, Vin. You might end up with my switchblade through your eyeball."

His lips twitch. Oh, so he doesn't believe me, eh? I might have to show him what I'm made of one of these days.

"What are you doing out here?"

"I thought this is the day you go to the store. Can I still take you up on the offer? This place is in dire need of snack foods."

"Sure thing," he says, wiping his grease covered hands on a shop rag. "Let me wrap up here really quick. Dante had your car towed in and I've been working on fixing it up. It should be almost finished."

"Wait, what? They sent you my car?"

That's oddly sweet of them. I'd never admit it to anyone, but that bucket of rust means a lot to me. I paid for it, and my blood, sweat, and tears went into fixing it up.

Vin nods, leading me down the hallway office to where the actual shop is and where my car is parked. My eyes dip to his firm ass in those tight jeans as we're walking, but I quickly glance back up.

When we step into the main portion of the garage, my jaw drops. He walks over to my car and shuts the hood, wiping it down with a cloth. It looks immaculate. Somehow the little spot of rust that's been slowly overtaking the back fender is gone and the whole thing is shining like a sheet of wet glass.

Vin tosses me the keys and I excitedly pop open the driver's side door and it opens on the first try.

"Oh my gosh, you actually fixed the handle! I could kiss you for that." I freeze at what I said and quickly hide my expression by checking out the rest of the car, cursing my mouth for moving before my brain catches up. "Huh. I'm impressed," I say climbing in behind the wheel.

He beams at me. "I'm assuming you'd like to take this to town then?"

"Uh, yeah! If that's an option."

"Absolutely. Besides, we need to test it out. See how it handles with all the adjustments I made." He opens the backdoor so Hemsworth can get in—like a true gentleman and then sits down in the passenger seat beside me. My piece of shit car turns over on the first crank.

"No way. What sort of witchcraft is this?" I ask, adjusting my seat and the rearview mirror to my liking. "How did you manage to do all of this already?"

He shrugs. "I kind of have a gift with vehicles."

"I'd say so. Actually, I'd say that's an understatement." His grin is a mile wide and it makes me fuzzy inside. "This is amazing! Thank you for fixing him up, Vin. Next time I want to help though."

"It's my pleasure, Miss. There are some other minor revisions that need to be made if you'd like to help then?"

"Definitely."

Vin removes a remote out of his blazer pocket, tapping on the button, and the garage door rolls up without a sound.

Well, isn't that nifty?

I gun the gas, loving the rumbling sound the engine makes as I circle the loop in the driveway and take off.

35

SADIE

After I toss every single comfort food I could ever need into the shopping cart, we head to the checkout lane. I eye the cart warily because it's practically overflowing between the amount of food Vin bought and my items. Bet that's going to be one hefty bill. At least I'm not the one paying.

The old woman at the checkout counter seems way too frail to still be working in a grocery store and her eyes widen when she sees us coming. By the time she's finished, I'm bouncing on my toes to get out because the process is taking forever.

A good forty-five minutes later, Vin is loading the groceries into the back of my car, while I'm checking out the little shopping mall we're in. My gaze snags on a pet shop sitting in the corner. There's a sign in the window with a large bone-shaped dog tag that says, 'Get your engravings here!'

"Hey Vin, would you mind if Hemsworth and I check out the pet store while we're here?"

His head pops out from the back of the trunk and he

looks over at the pet store and shrugs. "I don't mind at all, Miss." Ugh. I need to break him from calling me that. "I'll finish loading these and meet you in there if you'd like?"

"Awesome, thanks, Vin," I call out, my feet already carrying me toward the store. "How do you feel about getting a dog tag, Hems? Make it official."

He smiles, in that weird doggy way of his and looks around, making sure we're alone before he speaks. "Quite mundane, don't you think?"

I sigh. "Yeah, I know, but humor me, would you?"

"I'm kidding! I think it's a great idea." His voice breaks on the last syllable and I look down to see moisture in his eyes.

"Are you crying?"

He scoffs.

Can dogs scoff?

"No," he responds quickly, too quickly. "Of course not. It's my allergies." He puffs his chest out and holds his head a little higher.

"You're so fucking cute, Hems," I say, playfully ruffling his fur.

His nose twitches. "I am not cute. I'm an ancient vessel built to defend my charge."

"Sure, pup. You keep telling yourself that." I cackle evilly, pushing the door open to the pet shop. A little bell tinkles as we walk inside.

The cute little employee behind the counter looks over at us with a bright smile. "Hey there! Welcome to Blue Collar pet shop, where we make all pets' dreams come true."

Blue Collar pet shop. That's quite fitting.

The attendant opens the break in the counter and walks through to greet us. "What can I help you with today?" she asks, tucking her long black hair over her shoulder giving me a glimpse of her name tag. Which is a silver dog tag engraved with *Emma,* and she's wearing a pair of black Converse like me.

"Nice shoes," I comment conversationally. She beams back at me, noticing my footwear. "Actually, I need to get a tag engraved for my fam—" *Crap.* I clear my throat awkwardly. "—I mean my pup here."

Really need to watch what I say around the humans.

That's not a phrase I ever thought I'd use in my life.

How the tables have turned.

She barrels on none the wiser to my almost slip up. "Absolutely! Right this way." The perky woman leads me over to a huge rack of blank tags and tells me to choose one.

Eventually, I settle on a black bone-shaped one, since the writing will be silver, and it reminds me of my marks from the guys. She bends over and gives Hemsworth a few pats on the head, which he eats up like the greedy little bastard he is.

"And what name will I be engraving on the tag?" she asks.

"Hemsworth," I respond.

This earns me an approving glance and a small laugh. "Very nice. Am I right to assume it's after the actor himself?"

I nod, shooting her a smirk.

"Which brother?"

I scoff. "Chris, obviously."

Emma laughs again, setting the tag under the engraver. While it's doing its thing, she turns back toward me, her blue eyes sparkling. "Liam, who?"

"Finally, someone who understands my love for the superior brother," I say, tucking my hands into my pockets. Ash is a huge Liam fan, especially after he and Miley ended. She thinks she has a shot with him now. Yeah right.

Emma gives me a once-over like she's only now seeing me fully. "You know, I don't think I've seen you around town before. Did you move here recently?"

Her question makes me freeze. Thankfully, I'm used to

having to be quick on my feet and recover quickly. Then again, what harm could it do to tell her the truth? I'll probably never see her again anyway.

"Um, yeah. About a week ago."

Her face lights up in excitement. "Nice! I'm always looking for new friends to hang out with. Being this close to Gatlinburg, we get lots of tourists, but we don't get many newcomers who stay around here."

"I'm sorry. I'm sure that makes it tough to make friends."

"Well, it also doesn't help most of the ones who actually live around here are rude and plain awful." She sighs, not seeming so chipper anymore. "But don't let my problems burden you. I'm sure you'll find friends you can click with."

My lips purse and I give her a small head nod. For some reason, this girl tugs on my heartstrings, but I don't know anything about her, so I remain silent while she finishes up Hemsworth's tag.

I know I'm probably being cheesy because he's an ancient being that can talk but putting the little tag on his blue collar is cathartic for me. He's my familiar and now, I have something everyone can read proving it.

Even Hemsworth himself seems excited about it. Ever since I leaned down and attached it to his collar, he's been wagging his tail nonstop with a little more pep in his step.

Emma glances up at me at the cash register as I'm finishing paying. "Excuse me if this is too forward but, I'm wondering if you'd like to grab a coffee with me sometime? As I said, all the girls around here are awful, and I—I could use a friend."

I mean technically the guys never said I couldn't make friends with humans, but do I want to invite her into my life?

With everything going on it's probably a terrible idea and yet, the sad expression on her face paired with those hopeful blue eyes, makes my mouth dry.

Just say no. I clear my throat, open my mouth to do that, and her face falls like she can sense the direction of my thoughts. Dammit all to hell.

"Sure! I'd love to." I cringe as the words come out of my mouth.

Nice going, Sadie. Invite the human into your life. That's smart. You already have Ash to protect and now you're going to drag another into your life? Sure.

Hemsworth makes a chuffing sound that sounds suspiciously like a laugh. I shoot him a glare that shuts him up.

Emma squeals, jumping up and down as she hands me my receipt. Guilt makes my chest tighten. What the hell did I do?

"We're going to have so much fun, I just know it! Here, let me give you my number." She pulls a pen out of her apron, which is also blue, and scribbles on the back of my receipt.

Moments later the doorbell chimes and Vin strolls in, looking around for me. Time seems to slow down as the door closes behind him and he reaches up to tuck a stray piece of hair into his brown man bun.

Our eyes lock across the store and all my thoughts seem to abandon me in favor of checking him out. He's a little more casual today, in a button-up that highlights his toned arms and a pair of low-slung jeans across his hips. He seems as interested in me as I am him as he crosses the store.

Until Emma clears her throat and it snaps us out of our trance. "Damn, girl! Your boyfriend is an inferno on the hotness scale. I'm pretty sure I need to go mop up my drool."

"Oh, he's not—"

"Ready to go, Sadie?" Vin interrupts, looking between us curiously as he practically rushes me out the door.

"Yep," I respond, going with the flow. "Guess I'll see you around." I give Emma a small wave.

She grins at me and she's just too cute and innocent.

"Absolutely, if you need anything, feel free to text me any time!"

"Will do," I call out over my shoulder as we exit the pet shop.

When we're out of sight and earshot I turn to Vin. "What was that all about?"

He shrugs, looking sheepish. "I could smell the pheromones wafting off her and I figured it was better not to give her any ideas since I'm not interested."

Duh. He's a shifter. Wait…

"You can smell pheromones? Like when someone's turned on?" I cringe when my voice rises a few octaves and clear my throat to help mask it.

He nods and I notice a slight blush creeping up his neck. "Yes, I can."

That's… fucking hell, awkward. I'm going to have to learn how to control my urges around him or else he's going to smell my horniness every time my greedy vagina's around him or one of the others.

I don't know what to respond without embarrassing myself, so I don't say anything. Although, I do let Vin drive us back to the mansion, considering he's the mechanic and all. Plus driving up the mountain gives me goosebumps.

We're almost back to the King's estate when my spine explodes in tingles and I intuitively know something is about to go terribly wrong. A dark sense of foreboding and dread settle in my gut cutting me like a sharp rock. Here I was thinking we were going to get off scot-free. Dammit, I didn't even tell the guys I left, and my phone is dead as a doornail.

Real smooth, Sadie.

Hindsight is twenty-twenty, and as someone who lived through the year, I can say that is indeed true.

A bright flash of light whizzes past the car as we turn onto the dirt path leading to the estate. A few men burst out from nowhere and hammer the car with orbs of magic. My poor old car is not bulletproof or magic proof like the guy's vehicles and the window on the driver's side shatters. Glass rains down on us, cutting into our skin. I bring my arms up to cover my eyes and protect them from the debris.

Vin somehow manages to keep driving but he's hurt. Blood drips from the side of his head and down his arms. Thankfully, most of it seems like flesh wounds. He takes off down the gravel path, dust and rocks flying in our wake as the car fishtails, but he manages to right it.

"Isn't it a bad idea to lead them back to the estate?" I ask, glancing behind us as I try to figure out where they're coming from.

Vin shakes his head. "Getting behind the ward is our only shot. They won't be able to cross into our territory with ill intent."

The ward, duh. Get it together.

A line of hummers burst out of the tree line in hot pursuit of us. Vin adjusts the rear-view mirror, watching them and his mouth turns into a grim line of determination. They follow us, but we have bit of a lead on them since my car is smaller and takes the turns much faster.

A black orb of magic hits the side panel near the tire causing the engine to stall, but it doesn't stop. The feeling of dread in my stomach ramps up a notch, sending a jolt of nausea through me. I can't seem to shake the feeling even as we approach the curve that leads to the estate. Vin taps the brakes, trying to slow down to take the sharp curve, but nothing happens. He taps them again, harder this time. Nothing.

He looks over at me, panic swirling in those golden eyes of his. "The brakes aren't working," he admits, confirming what I already know.

Our eye contact doesn't last long, but it's enough for my

heart to stop. Vin starts pumping the brakes, but the hydraulic pressure isn't going to be enough. We're going too fast and we're too close to the curve.

My adrenaline pumps harder. "What are our options?" He doesn't respond. "We're driving too fast to jump out," I say thinking out loud.

Come on, Sadie. Think.

I inhale, trying to slow my racing heart but no solid options that don't result in death are coming to me. To make matters worse, whatever the black orb did is now making the car extremely unstable and we're starting to careen toward the ravine.

"Brace yourself!" I shout, then I do something totally stupid and reckless, especially at the speed we're going, before he can protest. I yank the emergency brake up and pray to their Night Goddess to guide us through this turn. She seems to favor me, so hopefully, she's listening. "Drift!"

Vin reacts to my command instantly, whipping my poor car around the sharp curve like this is fucking NASCAR and we're not going ninety to nothing.

To my complete and utter amazement, we don't flip. Vin handles the car impeccably and we come to a stop in the straightaway. Sideways and facing the wrong way, but we're alive, so I'll take it.

Vin glances over at me in shock, giving me an appreciative head nod. Hemsworth yips excitedly like he's enjoying this shitshow. The crazy dog. Although, I can't say I'm not enjoying the rush either.

Unfortunately, now that the car is stopped, we're slowly being surrounded by Hummers. Terrifying men holding orbs of magic hop out, slamming their doors. It takes everything in me not to flinch with each one that closes and it's all my fault too.

I should know by now danger will find me no matter

what I do. Because I'm Sadie Sinclair, and trouble follows me like smoke follows beauty.

"Shall we make a run for it?" I ask resolved to our fate as I reach for my switchblade in my pocket and flick the blade out. There is no way I'm going down without a fight.

Vin eyes me appreciatively. "Looks like there's no other option." His gaze flicks back to our assailants. "Quickly, they're starting to approach."

"On three?" He gives me a slight head nod. "One. Two. Three!" We whip open our doors at the same time, making a mad dash through the only opening they left for us. For some reason, it seems like a trap in and of itself, but I don't have time to question it.

I feel rather than see Hemsworth leap through the seat and out the open door of my car. He makes it to my side in two large strides and jumps, ripping the throat out of an attacker on my left before I can even blink. The man is definitely not one of those mindless golems from the festival. Blood splatters everywhere, threatening to bring the lunch Vin and I ate up.

I know in my heart Vin could outrun me with his shifter speed and leave me behind, but he doesn't. He stays with me and there's no time to decipher why.

I work my legs harder, pushing my extra strength into them and demanding they work faster. The underbrush crunches under our heavy footfalls, snapping twigs left and right. If they weren't already on our heels, I'd scold myself for being so loud, but they know exactly where we are and we need to lose them.

Decisions, decisions.

"On your left," Vin shouts and I jump to the right, automatically trusting him, and avoid a well-aimed orb of magic.

"Fuck, that was close. How far out are we from the ward?"

"Too fucking far," he grumbles in response. "Watch out!"

We're forced to separate as a tree forms in our path. When we're around the tree Vin's eyes widen and he opens his mouth to yell at me but it's too late and he's already rushing toward me. My heart wrenches painfully as an inky black orb hits him, and he cries out in pain, tucking his arm into his chest. He... took that orb for me.

"Vinson! Are you all right?" He doesn't respond, but moves the arm covering it. I gasp when I catch a glimpse of his injury. The skin is already turning an angry red as blisters pop up and the veins turn black before my eyes. I don't even want to imagine what it would've looked like if they had managed to hit him somewhere vital, or me in the chest where it was aimed.

My intuition warns me seconds before a harsh battle cry sounds off behind us, and the number of orbs being thrown our way triples. Neither of us can focus on anything other than sensing where the orbs are and dodging them.

Somehow, I lose track of Vin and Hemsworth in the commotion, which is not good. Not at all. All my defenses are screaming at me to find them.

A large oak tree appears on my left, and I dart behind it, resting my back against it to catch my breath. I'm also silently hoping Vin or Hemsworth will pass by and I can rejoin them.

The first thing I notice while I'm sitting still is the forest is eerily silent and the orbs are no longer whizzing past me. I'm not stupid enough to think I've lost them because we haven't hit the ward yet, which means they're out there somewhere, waiting.

"Well, well, well. Look what the shifter brought me," a dark voice singsongs, their tone dancing with amusement. Every single muscle in my body tenses when I hear that slimy voice I never wanted to hear again. There's a shift to the right seconds before I'm tackled and we roll. The twigs and vines scrape my skin harshly, cutting me open with each movement. I try to stop my momentum, but it's no use and we eventually crash into a tree.

My switchblade is knocked from my hand from the force of the impact, leaving me without a weapon, and my side twinges with pain.

I'm on my feet in an instant, despite the dizziness overriding my senses as I search the area for him, but I'm alone. Arms band around me from behind and I throw my elbow back into his sternum, making him grunt and let go.

Instead of getting away, like I'd hoped, he grabs a fist full of my hair and yanks me back to him. Unlike with Kaos the sharp sting only pisses me off and rage starts coursing through my veins.

He chuckles and the sound grates on my nerves. "I want you to know, the Elders awarded me this privilege. As soon as I dispatched that shifter a week ago, I went to them and asked if I could be the one to lead the search party for you."

Oh, Gods. Vin's black eye and his use of the term *package* pops into my mind. I'd bet my last dollar Tyler was the package.

"My team has been waiting outside the ward this entire time, and look, you were stupid enough to leave without your mates. Did you think a dog and a lowly shifter would be enough to stop us from taking you?"

"Fuck off, Tyler. Let me go and I'll think about sparing you."

Not really, but he doesn't need to know that.

Another chuckle. "Nah, I don't think I will. You see, you're quite the catch, Mercedes. Everyone is looking for you. Besides, you're useful to the entire Weaver community and I'll enjoy getting to see you passed around."

Acid rises in the back of my throat and I'm forced to swallow it down.

He continues, "Since you know about magic now, I guess there's no harm in telling you the truth. If you can be a true Link to the Kings, theoretically you could be a true Link to anyone, and if you hadn't killed Benjamin that night, you'd already be mine."

"You would truly bond to me against my will, Tyler?" I ask, looking at him. Nothing but madness swirls in his eyes and there's no trace of the boy I used to know—used to love—left in those baby blues. From a distance, they're oh, so deceiving, lulling you into a false sense of security until you get closer and there's nothing but a monster left. I guess even Lucifer was once an Angel.

If the saying is true, anyway.

Tyler smiles and it's all sharp teeth and cruelty. "That soul of yours will belong to me one way or another, Mercedes baby."

A man steps out from behind a tree, watching us. "Get her tied up and let's go. We don't want to be here when her mates show up," he barks.

A broad smile crosses my face because he just reminded me of something super important. Our eyes connect and I catch a flicker of fear cross them. My phone may be dead, but I don't need it. I can talk to my mates in my head.

Man, I've got to start thinking like a Weaver and not a human.

Kaos! Dante! I need help. I'm surrounded and I can't take them all on my own.

Kaos' response is immediate. *What do you mean? Where are you, Little Flame?* There's a pause and he says, *You're not in your room. Did you go for a walk?*

I wince. I really should've told them where I was going. *Outside the ward,* I respond. As soon as the words leave my brain, I can sense his shock, but I stop his reply. *I know, but yell at me later. Tyler is here with other Night Weavers and they attacked Vin, Hemsworth, and I.*

Fuck, Dante curses. *You're going to have to hold them off until we can get there, Angel. Elian isn't here and he's not answering my summons.*

Hang tight, Little Flame. We're coming. He ends the mental connection, but the tug in my chest lets me know they're at least able to locate me.

Not a moment too soon either. Tyler pulls one of those glowing silver ropes out of his back pocket and binds my wrists together. My connection to my mates vanishes, leaving a gaping hole behind. I hadn't realized how much I could feel them until now when the connection is gone. I know they're not truly gone for good, but the loss swirling in my chest threatens to pull me under.

Seconds later, a different man leads Vin through the trees, holding an orb of magic to his back to keep him in line. Fuck, I was hoping he'd gotten away. I notice his wrists are bound similarly to mine and my heart sinks at the sight. When he reaches us, the man knocks him over the head and Vin falls to the ground like a sack of potatoes.

A blur of movement comes barreling through the air toward Tyler and I. I'd recognize that reddish brown fur anywhere. He leaps through the air, aiming for Tyler's throat but he's too fast and dodges. Tyler swings back around and kicks Hemsworth in the stomach. My poor sweet Hems whines as he sails through the air and lands against a tree. He doesn't get up.

Now they've fucking done it.

No one hurts my friends or my familiar.

They will pay.

Rage, unlike anything I've ever known, courses through every ounce of my being as I stand there silently simmering. My vision bleeds to black until it's all I can see, but I don't need my sight anymore. It's like looking through a kaleidoscope and everyone's energies are bared before me. Tyler and the others are a murky black, while Hemsworth and Vin's are a shining white, but they're fading.

The gaping chasm in my chest flares to life and I scream, letting the power flow through me until the ropes around my wrists fall to the ground.

"Oh shit! Get that bitch under control!" One of the lackeys calls out.

I can smell his fear.

Ignoring them, I reach inside my center, grasping the bright ball of energy my magic is made of, and tug on every last drop available before releasing it out of me in a giant, wonky blast. Wave after wave explode from my chest. The lines resemble shock waves—almost like the Elite incident.

Thump. Thump. Thump.

The men around me seize, their faces contorting at odd angles as they cry out in anguish. One by one they drop to the ground like dead flies until their murky energies wink out completely. The wrath coursing through me doesn't care that I just murdered half a dozen men.

Does that make me a bad person?

The only one who isn't affected by my burst of power is Tyler and only because I'm saving him for last. I make out a bit of fear seeping into the madness in his eyes through the black curtain of my vision as he stares at me in utter shock.

"What happened to you, Tyler?" I ask as I circle him, toying with him. "I don't understand why you've chosen to become this—this monster," I spit. Even my voice no longer sounds like my own.

His fear is quickly replaced by anger as he comes at me with my own damn switchblade. I sidestep him easily, predicting his move to come straight for my throat. Right now, he feels like child's play compared to what I know I'm capable of.

"Tsk, tsk, Tyler," I say with a tinkling laugh. "I gave you the opportunity to speak and to explain your actions, yet you try to kill me instead. Such a pity, but I'll enjoy killing you."

I raise my voice, projecting out for all to hear, because I know the Elders are somehow listening in on our battle. "Let this be a lesson tonight. Anyone who fucks with me, comes after me, my family, or my mates, will die."

"You're not capable of that you stupid bitch. I'll never understand why Mick—"

"No more games," I interrupt, sideswiping his feet out from under him in a movement so fast even I can't track it. His back hits the ground and he bounces, grunting from the force, but doesn't cry out. "I wonder, will you beg for your life?" I ask, landing on top of him. My hand snakes out, wrapping around his throat and I squeeze.

With a burst of strength I'm not expecting, Tyler manages to throw me off and I go flying across the clearing. I dig my heels into the dirt and come to a stop right before a tree.

"Impressive, but it won't happen again."

"You like that, did you?" He circles me. I don't take my eyes off him. "The Elders gave me a power boost and all I had to do was come after you. Something I was already planning on. The stupid bastards."

A part of me feels like I should keep him talking, try to get more information out of him, but the raging part of me demands his blood and something tells me it won't go away until I crush him in my palms.

Tyler rushes in to greet me with his fist and I sidestep it, ducking underneath his arm to go in for a throat jab. It connects and he goes waddling back, clutching at his throat as he struggles to breathe. I don't give him any leeway. I slam him against a tree, making sure his head takes the brunt of the force.

Still, he doesn't cry out, but he does manage to throw me off.

I grit my teeth together as we circle each other once more.

"Time to end this," he says.

"I couldn't agree more."

Pushing all of the extra strength into my limbs I rush toward him again. In a sneaky turn of events, he uppercuts me making blood fill my mouth as I bite my tongue, but I barely register the pain. I catch him in the gut with my fist, and he wraps his arms around me, bringing me to the ground. We wrestle for control and for a moment I'm terrified he's going to end up on top, then it'd be over.

Fuck that.

I use the shadows to my advantage, giving me a burst of air that allows me to flip our positions. The first thing I do is knock him square in the nose, breaking it for a second time.

Tyler grips my thighs and rises with me wrapped around his body. He tries to throw my back into a tree, but I climb his ass like a damn jungle gym and end up on his back. I let the rage consume me, to fill my every pore. The shadows follow my emotions like a tidal wave and come surging into me. For some reason, a set of words pop into my mind and I instinctively know I'm supposed to say them.

"Tyler Scott Maynard, tonight you will die. In the name of the Night Goddess, the God of Dawn, the God of Dusk, and the God of Light, I hereby sentence you to death. May you pay for your sins in the afterlife." Again, my words don't sound like my own.

His eyes are wide with fear. "Please. I'm sorry," he begs.

So, he will beg after all. Men, such weak-willed creatures.

"You are not forgiven, and you were never worthy of me.

May the Night Goddess have mercy on your soul, because I will not." The swirling darkness around me snaps his neck, and I feel a tug in my chest as the shadows consume his soul.

I let his lifeless body slump to the ground next to my feet with a thud.

36

SADIE

This night is far from over, even with Tyler lifeless at my feet, the sense of dread and foreboding surround me like a dark cloak of grief. But I shove my feelings down and rush over to Hemsworth. The slight rise and fall of his chest makes my heart soar with joy. I reach out to pet him and as soon as my hand connects with his fur, my magic surges out of me in a rush, healing him. He jolts awake.

"I'm so glad you're okay," I cry, wrapping my arms around his neck.

He whimpers, licking my cheek. "I'm sorry I failed you, Sadie."

"Don't you dare feel bad," I tell him vehemently. "The only thing that matters is you're okay. Thank you, Hems." He nuzzles me and it eases a tiny bit of the ache in my heart. As much as I want to lay here all night and hold my familiar, I know I can't. "I need to go check on Vin. Will you be okay?"

"Yeah, give me a second and I'll join you. Your healing magic is already doing the trick. He needs you."

With a nod, I scramble over to Vin's too still body,

ignoring the twinge of protest my body makes. His arm is getting worse with every passing second. His veins are black and the inky magic is spreading up his chest and crawling up his neck. His shirt is soaked with blood and he's barely breathing. I drop to the ground next to him, placing my palms over his chest, praying to the Night Goddess to heal him like Hemsworth.

As soon as my skin makes contact with his, my magic starts to leave me in waves, making me dizzy from overuse, but I don't care. *Please, heal him.* I repeat over and over again in my mind like a mantra.

After some time, he gasps, and his eyes snap open, finding mine. I hold his gaze for a moment, searching all of the emotions there before I lean back to allow him to sit up, but I don't take my hands off his chest. He needs whatever my magic is doing to him. The corner of his lip turns up as he glances at my hands on his chest. Which only serves to make my heart swell.

"Thank you for healing me," he says softly.

Some of his more prominent wounds are already receding. Although, the blackness crawling up his arm isn't going away yet. Hopefully, Kaos will be able to help him more when we get back, considering I have no idea what I'm doing. I swallow down the lump in my throat, forcing my feelings down and locking them up tight.

"Come on. We need to get out of here."

After the longest—and most painful—walk of my life, the three of us finally pass through the ward into safety. That's when I spot Dante and Kaos pacing inside the ward, their expressions frantic. It's only then I notice our bond snap into place once more.

"Thank the Night Goddess," Dante says, eyes locking on me. "We've been trapped inside. Someone has been messing with the ward and we couldn't leave."

Dante holds dual orbs of his orangey-blue fire magic in both hands, while Kaos holds twin karambits in his. The curved blades glint in the sunlight, making them seem even more deadly. Overall, my mates look dangerous as fuck and I'm digging it. Most women would probably be intimidated, but not me. The sight of them makes my blood sing and I grin at them.

A swirl of black curls up my arm, startling me. Now that I'm no longer in imminent danger and I'm paying attention, I realize the darkness is actually the shadows swirling together as they gather around me.

Dante's eyes dart around me in amazement, taking in the shadows surrounding me protectively. Same with Kaos. He takes in the whole scene with rapt interest. Shaking off his amazement Kaos takes a step toward me. "Are you hurt? What happened?" He wraps me in his arms comfortingly and I let him stroke my hair, drawing on his strength.

After a moment, I pull away so I can explain. "Tyler is what happened," I seethe. "And an ambush." My shadows whip around me harder as they feed off my energy and emotions. Distantly, I know shadows aren't supposed to move like this, as if they're a real being, yet here they are.

"That fucking bastard," Kaos growls. "Is he dead?" I nod. "Dammit, I wish I could bring him back to life and kill him all over again for putting his hands on you."

"Me too," Dante snarls. "I'd cut off his hand and bring it to you." He tugs me in for a quick hug, nuzzling the side of my head and I relish in the comfort, even if I'm not used to it.

"We were going fucking insane with worry, Little Flame. I'm so proud of you for killing him, but he deserved much worse."

"I appreciate the sentiments but something tells me they're going to have fun with him in the afterlife," I respond cryptically.

Taking a few deep breaths, I close my eyes and calm my whirring mind. Eventually, the shadows slink back into the environment around us. When I'm finished and back to normal, Dante and Kaos open their arms, wrapping me in their calming embrace like they can't reassure themselves enough I'm okay.

My side twinges in pain from smacking the tree earlier and I let loose a grunt. Kaos pulls back and runs his glowing black hands down my arm. "It's my side," I tell him. "The fucker tackled me into a tree."

"Why didn't you say something about your pain sooner?" he questions, pushing his healing magic into me until the pain dissipates.

"It hadn't sank in yet. The adrenaline is wearing off," I respond. "So, uh, someone will need to go back to get my car and the groceries." My heart sinks thinking about my precious car, but material things can always be replaced. I'm lucky to be walking away with my life. "And to dispose of the bodies. Tyler and the other Weavers are dead. I killed them. I don't think they were the Elites though. I didn't get the same lethal vibes from these guys."

My Sworn stare at me in wonder, with wide eyes and open mouths. "We'll take care of it. First, we need to get you, Vin, and the dog settled, okay?"

"Okay," I consent and both of them spring into action, helping me toward the house. My exhaustion overrides my independence.

Vin makes a noise and I glance over at him. Sweat rolls down his forehead and he's shaking. Honestly, I'm shocked he's still standing and the sight tugs on my heart.

"Wait, the first thing we need to do is heal Vin. He took a nasty orb to the arm that was aimed at my chest and my magic isn't touching it for some reason."

My statement makes Dante and Kaos look at Vin appreciatively. They give him a slight head nod which is probably the best thing I could ask for them to do. That's their version of a bro hug.

Vin clears his throat, clearly uncomfortable with the attention. "We have a pack doctor at the pack house. Don't worry, as soon as I'm dismissed, I'll head straight there to get looked at. My shifter healing, combined with Sadie's magic will take care of most of the cuts from the broken glass, but the hit from the orb is a different story."

"I'll heal it for you," Kaos states, giving me a small smile. In return, I kiss him on the cheek, glad he offered before I could say anything.

Kaos runs his hands over Vin's chest. His eyes close and his nose scrunches in concentration. He glances back at me and I catch a spark of fear in his eyes. "This is old and very dark magic. He'll need to be closely monitored and healed over the next few days and even then, it's not a guarantee. I'll have to scour the library and see if there's anything we can do to speed the process." He turns his attention to Vin. "I won't lie, you'll likely be scarred in the area."

A lead weight settles to the pit of my stomach. Vin is going to be scarred because of me. Because I wasn't strong or fast enough to protect myself.

"I'll take being scarred over being dead," Vin responds, giving me a comforting glance like he can sense the direction of my thoughts.

I take my guilt and hold it close, using it to harden my resolve. I need to learn about my powers and my magic as soon as possible to make sure I'll never be caught off guard like this again. So others don't get tangled in this and get hurt… or worse because of me.

Fate really likes to test me though, doesn't it?

Dante wraps his arm around me and Hemsworth nudges my leg. Silently lending me their strength. I borrow it because even with Kaos' healing magic, I'm exhausted. Physically and mentally. I need a long bath and a hot minute to process.

"Come on, Angel. Let's get you all back to the estate."

The mansion pops into view a little while later, but that's not what makes my stomach flip with anxiety.

Elian is. He's barreling our way, darkness and maybe a bit of fear glittering in his emerald eyes. "What the hell happened?" he asks as his eyes track Vin's every movement. "Vinson, you're dismissed. The pack doctor can take care of you there."

Hell no. If Elian thinks his word is going to be law around here, he's got another thing coming. The shadows return to me in a flash, bursting to life at my command.

Elian's eyes widen when he sees them before he quickly masks his reaction.

"He's not dismissed. He's coming to the house with us so Kaos can look after him and heal his injuries properly. So, kindly fuck off." My shadows whip around me, punctuating my statement.

Tactful, I am not. To the point, I am.

Dante whistles low, glancing between Kaos, Elian, Vin, and I with clear interest. "Sadie's going to give you a run for your money, huh Eli?"

Elian shoots me a look that could wilt a dozen already dead roses, but I don't cower or shy away from his stare. His nostrils flare as he stalks toward me, stopping inches away from me, threatening to suffocate me with his aura.

Once again, I find myself captivated by those green eyes of his. They should be soft like the moss and the grass they resemble. Instead, they're hard like garnets and emeralds. If I got lost in then, would they protect me or cut me?

"Where were you a few minutes ago?" I ask.

His gaze flickers away and I finally take a breath. "I just

got off the phone with Vald—one of the Elders. He wants to formally extend us an invitation—"

Dante and Kaos start speaking at the same time and I can't understand what they're saying. Elian holds up his hand and they stop.

"We can't refuse their invitation, dammit. I already tried." He sighs, placing his hands behind his back as he delivers the next blow. "Savannah issued a challenge." The words burst from his lips like he's signing my death warrant and maybe he is. I have no clue what a challenge is, but it doesn't sound like a nice little stroll through the park. It sounds like she's trying to get her paws on my men.

"How soon?" Kaos asks breathlessly, laying a comforting hand on my shoulder at the same time Dante asks, "How long do we have?"

Elian rubs his inked fingers across his jaw, those green eyes flicking over to where I know Dante and Kaos are standing. "One month."

"Moons above. We need to start training her, right now," Dante says, trying to usher me onwards, but I'm glued to the spot.

"Wait, what's a challenge? Does it mean what I think it does?"

Elian's stone-cold eyes find mine and don't leave. "This challenge is a fight to the death for the right to claim us." The air shifts when he takes his next breath. "There's more you need to know," he says, gritting his teeth. For one tiny second, I think I see a flash of sadness in his eyes, but it's gone so fast I wonder if I made it up.

The longer the silence drags on the more the little shards of dread claw their way into my gut. I take a deep breath, shoring my defenses against him because if it's coming from Elian King's mouth, it's going to hurt. "Spit it out, Elian. Please."

"Ashley is missing," he confesses, continuing on like he didn't rip my heart out of my chest, stomp it into tiny little pieces, and spit on it, completely unaware of my inner turmoil. "Her guard called for help, but by the time anyone could get there, it was too late. They found his body—"

"And Ash?" I breathe, the silence stretching between us. Sometimes the silence is more deafening than the roar. "Please tell me she's okay."

"She was nowhere to be found."

My heart stutters in my chest as my thoughts start to spiral out of control and I collapse to my knees with a sob, thinking about all the worst case scenarios as the weight of the world comes crashing down around me. I can only be so strong for so long and I've reached my damn quota. Now Ash is missing on top of everything.

This can't be happening.

This can't be fucking happening.

"We will find her, or I swear to the Night Goddess, I will destroy everything until I do." I raise my eyes to Elian's, locking gazes with him. There's a steely confidence there I appreciate.

"We've got your back, Angel," Dante murmurs.

"We'll do whatever it takes, Little Flame," Kaos confirms.

I turn my attention to them, their faces blurry through my watery eyes, and they give me a nod. "I would do *anything* for Ashley. She's my best friend, my ride or die, and I protect those I care about. But those I don't? They'd better watch out."

Flames burst from my palms as I rise from the ground, engulfing me in an inferno built of rage and anguish. I have get to the bottom of this. One way or another. Fate's plan or not. Our lives depend on it. But what if I can't save everyone?

ALSO BY DEMI WARRIK

Yeah, I have to ask; is your kindle okay? Do you hate me now? I know, I know. I'll admit, it was a little evil but it was all Sadie's idea. The good news is books two and three are already **complete! Binge the rest of the series here:**

Bound by Light, Fates Mark Book Two

Called by Fate, Fates Mark Book Three

"My life went to hell in a hand basket faster than you can say, *destiny sucks.*"

Witches, and Shifters, and Vampires, oh my!

Burning Chance, Blood Cursed Book One

Thank you so much for reading!

STAY CONNECTED

Do you want to see exclusive content like cover reveals, teasers, giveaways, and lots more before anyone else? Want to discuss what you're reading? Come on over and join my reader group! We post lots of bookish related things, sexy men, host giveaways, release parties, and have an all around good time. I'd love to have you join me on the dark side.

Demi Warrik's Facebook Reader Group

AFTERWORD

Hey there, my dear reader! Demi here. I know everyone hates cliffy's, so feel free to yell at me in my reader group. But personally? I fucking love them. I love when a book lights a fire in me and makes me *crave* more. I love when it grips me so thoroughly that I'm literally dying for the next book. Hopefully, I've done that for you. It's my goal after all.

With that said, if you enjoyed this book, it would mean the absolute world to me if you left a review on my Amazon page. Reviews are an author's lifeblood and without them, we don't know if we should keep going. Even if it's as short as a few sentences, every single review matters to me. Also, feel free to shout it from the rooftops! I'd love it if you would. Word of mouth gets these stories out there faster than anything.

So, thank you, dear reader. For sticking around and reading this book in its entirety, for committing your time and energy into Sadie's journey.

This tale means more to me than you could ever know… And if I'm honest, it almost didn't happen. This has been a two-plus-year journey in the making and it came to a screeching halt when I had to have brain surgery. Then COVID hit, and I had a bunch of free time, so I picked it back up again. It's absolutely mind-boggling to see it coming to life. Sadie wouldn't leave my thoughts until I finally wrote down her shenanigans and she's quite demanding if you hadn't noticed.

Plus the guys? Swoon.

Fucking swoon.

ACKNOWLEDGMENTS

First off a huge thank you to my husband, who supports me in every single endeavor I make. I can't thank him enough for sticking by my side through all my crazy-ass shenanigans. Trust me there have been a lot over the years. Hell, he didn't even laugh when I told him I wanted to write a smut book. Total keeper, amirite? Love you, boo!

Thank you to my best friend Ashley, who let me borrow her name for this book. Thank you for showing me the wild side of the world when I needed it, girl.

Thank you to my betas Delaney, Lysanne, and Rory. You all freakin' rock and I'm honored you took the time out of your schedules to read my very first book baby for me and give me your feedback. I'm so unbelievably honored. Without you guys, this book would not be the same.

Thank you to my wonderful editor, Raven, for joining Instagram at the same time as me and hyping my posts up even though I had absolutely no idea what the hell I was doing. For believing in Sadie's story enough to want to edit it. Even for just listening to me rant. You are a badass, and I'm glad we found friendship in each other.

And lastly, thank you to my parents for always believing in me. For teaching me to reach for the stars. For raising me to have an open mind and open heart. Even though, I sincerely hope neither of you read this far. Seriously, dad, I don't think I'll ever be able to look you in the eye ever again. There are some things that dads don't need to know their daughters think of. Mom, you've always been the coolest, and I'll probably edit out the sex scenes so you can read without side-eying me. Thanks for taking me to the public library every day, for buying me my favorite books when we could afford them, and encouraging me to get lost in the worlds they held inside. Love y'all.

Man, that was a lot of thank you's! But they needed to be said. I'm eternally grateful to everyone who reads this.

Especially my readers.

Especially you.

ABOUT THE AUTHOR

Demi Warrik is an emerging romance author dedicated to giving you stories you can ditch reality with. She loves animals of all kinds, the smell of books and coffee, which she prefers. In her free time she enjoys writing romantic shenanigans that you'll be laughing about for days. Most of the time you can find her with her nose shoved in a book or plotting someone's demise. In a story, of course! Join Demi on her journey to finally write down the plethora of characters swirling around in her brain demanding to have their stories told. She'd love it if you would.

Join my newsletter:
http://www.demiwarrik.com